PRAISE FOR THE BOOKS
by Robert Rife

"... fun, frightening, and ribald. *It won't be for everybody, but that can be said of all great writing.*"

"... delightfully weird... this story will blow you away!"

"Original, impressive, compulsively entertaining..."

"... scary and frequently hilarious..."

"... blows the genre out of the water..."

"Stephen King meets Terry Pratchett... funny and terrifying..."

"...action-rich... visceral imagery and heart-stopping horror..."

"...irreverent and darkly funny. Injecting brutal scenes with almost lyrical prose lends the novel a definite otherworldly feel."

"Lures the reader in fast... this is a page-turner!"

PROCLAMATIONS

This is a work of fiction. Anyone finding a resemblance to themselves or anyone else... needs a lot of help.

Humans died in the writing of this novel. An author shouldn't be interrupted. No animals were harmed.

Women are fair and wondrous creatures. Men are... well, they're men. Blame God.

To those angelic, exemplary, huge-brained people who love this book: may your life's path be strewn with diamonds. Big fat ones.

EVERYONE: Give to the Humane Society. Often. This author does.

LAB SPILL

A DARK COMEDY. MAYBE.

ROBERT RIFE

FOR MY DAUGHTER

LAB SPILL

Deep Portal Publishing
Member: Polydactyl Productions Group
Seattle, Washington (USA)

ISBN : 979-8-9862806-0-8 (Paperback)
ISBN : 979-8-9862806-1-5 (Hardcover)

Editing: Victoria Edwards
Cover design by Arcane Books
Interior design by Booknookbiz

LAB SPILL

A DARK COMEDY.
MAYBE

PROLOGUE

Hector has been in the old house far too long. Amy waits on the porch as night mutters through an iron fence... where a body had been impaled.

Hector will come out. He won't be the same.

Neither will Amy.

CHAPTER 1

THE WAYDOWNS

A bright yellow growth covers much of the corridor walls, spread out in irregular blotches. Bubbles form beneath the glistening surface, slowly pushing out and then subsiding; occasionally one will burst with a softly spitting sound. It is breathing.

Further down the hall a rat scurries along the floor, keeping very clear of the slowly pulsing mold. Its other head, eyeless, flops from its back. Both mouths continually open and close, teeth clicking. Pausing at a doorway, both mouths tasting the air, it darts across the opening. It's not fast enough. Not fast enough to escape the lightning quick jaws and teeth that snatch, crunch, and swallow. The human had been fast.

Far above, on Ship's Deck 19, Darren watches from his monitor screen, slowly shaking his head. He's been ordered to reclaim that area, to sanitize another part of this long-buried, ancient starship. To retake some more of those decks lost decades ago when an experiment had horrendously corkscrewed. Resulting in the total quarantine of all decks below 19. All decks, complete confinement, no exceptions. Because every living organism beyond 19 had become... different. Had become changed. Altered. Wrong. Including the human staff. Especially the human staff.

After the quarantine came mutiny, followed shortly by anarchy, madness, and rampant cannibalism.

High Command sealed all entrances, welding them shut, painting out all traces. Immediately following this erasure came an incredulous announcement; one that only WW2 military could get away with. Those lower decks didn't exist anymore. They had imploded. They had been vaporized. They were gone. It was Wartime Treason to even speak of them. Knowledge of the lost decks faded into whispered rumors, and through decades became a feared name: The Waydowns.

But despite any official proclamations, all the men, women, plants, and animals sealed below did exist. Those that survived the initial horror, betrayals, and chaos... continued to change. Months became years, years grew into decades, and some of those life forms endured. *So did their spawn.*

The entombed ship continued to function for all decks, Waydowns included. Power units, installed centuries ago, galaxies away, kept on providing. Protein slabs, liquid nutrients continued...and things grew. Many things did.

Whispered tales of the Waydowns weren't just forbidden scuttlebutt to Darren's boss, Dr. Lillith Sally Gaust. She'd been stationed on Deck 19 even before the experiment catastrophe. And she had a way back into those so-called vaporized, nonexistent decks. Knowledge she never shared with High Command. She wanted those lost decks, and all that they held. Or gave birth to. She also began to use the Waydowns as a dumping ground for all her splicing and breeding failures. Dead...or not. They were Lab Spill, no longer human.

Zooming the view back, Darren looks at what will be his entry point. The area is flame blackened for about

30 feet. And a little beyond the charring is the body, lying face down. It's human. Or had been. Viscous fluids drip from too many bulbous arm joints, the neck is odd, the feet... a nightmare. The Spill had run, but not quick enough to escape the firebombing.

A monstrous, once pretty face, abruptly appears on his screen, overriding Darren's channel. Lillith overrides everything. From Deck 19 on down, Dr. Lillith Sally Gaust is GOD. There is no need to tell the staff. They know it.

The few personnel left working on decks above 19 never take the lift down to that dreaded floor. They might never return. Others haven't.

Those missing, became... useful. They became *volunteers* to aid in the advancement of science. Some lasted for years.

"Report," Lillith demands. The voice is old, very old. It's raspy, her face blotchy, scabbed, and the feral eyes boil with fever. She'd been Spill bitten days earlier and the infection is consuming her. Certain areas of Deck 19 had been originally designed for deep space flight, and still sent out time adjustments or time treatments, periodically. It vastly increased longevity, but no one is immortal. Dr. Gaust is finding that out. She wipes at blood beneath her mouth, leaving a glistening smear pebbled with debris. She has been eating.

"The entry point has been fired; we're going in. I'm taking a crew of three," Darren answers quickly.

"I harbor no doubt you're going in. I ordered it. Or have you taken some testicle pills and gotten nerve enough to change a directive of mine? I want you to secure only enough area that can be locked down. Then you will return forthwith; you are going topside on a retrieval mission."

"Yes, Doctor. The crew's ready; I'm going to join them— at once."

"Oh, yes, Mister Gosteen. Indeed you are. And remember, do not kill; I want viable specimens. *Especially* anything that can talk. And stay clear of that mold you call Gunch. I suspect it is the deadliest organism in the Waydowns. DO NOT bring any of that back onto my deck. Immediately kill anyone that comes in contact with it. Mind me, man. MIND ME!" And her image is gone from the screen, but not from Darren's brain. That face is with him always.

Darren Gosteen, head of Deck 19 security, is a heavily burdened man. A doomed man. A man who has seen too much, knows too much... *done too much.* A once good man, now trapped in a job from which he will never be allowed to quit, never be allowed to leave alive. And here, deep beneath the New Mexico scrub and sand, there are fates worse than death. So much worse.

Joining the two women and one man, Darren readies the group for hell. They're all killers, all society discards, and all are expendable, which was exactly why they'd been hired. None of them think they need any preparation. But he knows better. He's seen more of the Waydowns than they have.

"We're under new orders to secure only the immediate area. And remember, do not kill, stun only. We're to bring whatever back *alive*." He's saying this mainly for the women, as they lean more to bloodlust. "*MY* orders to all of you, are the same as always: Defend yourself, and don't get taken... they might not kill you."

"Think we'll be attacked this time?" Patty asks, eagerly. She's psychopathic, psychotic, and other mind aberrations for which there are no labels. Beneath an explosion of short, straw-colored hair, a grinning, skull tattoo leers from her forehead. Army washout, ex–biker, and escaped convict, Patty likes to kill. And she's seen what the Spills are capable of. They are insane with hungers not limited to food, and Patty... is a little like them.

"Maybe— probably," answers Darren. "I've fried the elevator entrance way, and the monitor shows a Spill, laying several yards in. No way to tell if it's one of Dr. Gaust's discards, or a mutation birth descended from in there. It hardly matters, where there's one, there will be more. And the Gunch is growing in spots on the walls, avoid contact at all costs; no one knows what it can do. If any gets on your clothes, shuck them at once."

"All fuckin' right! Ain't this startin' to sound like fun."

"Quiet, Death Head."

The other woman, Elena, stays silently impassive. Brooding, taciturn, unreadable. Barely held eruptions simmer within the shaved head. Big, muscular, and swarthy, she's ex- military, combat veteran, dishonorably discharged. It hadn't been for cowardice.

"Any sign of the Bugs?" asks Huong. Smart, with delicate features, a black belt holder with totally dead eyes. He'd been recruited while out on bail awaiting trial. It seems he'd misplaced his wife and children. The law thought, given the massive insurance policy he'd taken out, that Huong knew where they were at. The cops were right; Huong knew exactly where they were. And they were highly likely to stay there.

"No, no Bug sightings," answers Darren. "The brain above," he says jabbing a thumb upward, "thinks they may no longer exist. The Spills kept eating their larvae, so they tried to nest in an old topside house, but it's doubtful they survived the air. However, if we see one, it'll be wanted."

"Topside?" blurts Patty. "Fuck me! How in hell did they get topside? Ain't *all* the ship buried?"

"Of course it's all buried, everyone has probably figured that out by now," answers Darren. "To clarify it for any piss brains, we're down deep beneath that topside building all of you came through as newbies. When the elevator dropped from there, you entered the ship, and it's entombed by melt-sand radioactive glass. Has been for centuries." He's trying to stop any thoughts of unauthorized leave. *Authorized* leave didn't exist. "But the ship, or how the Bugs got out, is not our business on this picnic. Okay, sweeties, let's go."

The khaki clad group watch the doors slide open, revealing the charred corridor. Blackened walls peeling with strips of dead fungus; and a stench hits them like a giant fist. A tsunami of abandonment and neglect. Of despair, of rot, of death. Of abomination. Ahead, the body lays like their welcome mat. One knobby arm is stretched out ahead of the carcass, as if showing them the way. Enter, enjoy, die.

Patty takes point, voltage prod in one hand, Uzi in the other. Darren follows a few paces back, off to one side. Huong takes the other, Elena walks center. All are outfitted the same, and except for Patty, their Uzis' hang from shoulder straps. Everyone grips a prod, their netguns are holstered, knives sheathed. Beneath their feet, the deck hums from its ancient energy source.

Walking slower as they leave the blackened area,

they pass the dead Lab Spill, ignoring the reek of fried meat. Their destination is the opening where the two-headed rat had gotten unlucky.

Patty halts for a second before showing herself in the doorway. She's feral but not stupid. Taking a deep breath, dropping to a knee, she slides into the opening, Uzi extended.

Behind the group, that dead Spill silently rises. Its jaws unhinge, opening a vast, ulcerated mouth, a gaping maw with jagged teeth.

CHAPTER 2

MANY MILES FROM THE SHIP: ELASTIC ETHICS

While still a child, R.L. had murdered his stepfather. Just a little. The sharp, pecking beaks of the chickens had helped considerably as RL kept on sprinkling out their feed. Tossing the crushed grain generously over those bulging eyes and lolling tongue of that good Christian man... as the cruel bastard convulsed with his heart attack.

Yes, RL and the poultry had sent that bible-thumping, belt wielding nightmare to his *just* reward. Life had gotten a lot better after that. There had never been any remorse. None.

Now, at 43, RL's life is basically good. Well... there were a few problems: Deena Lynn, the street girl he'd been fool enough to *think* he'd fallen in love with, had ran off with some *younger* turd. The fact that she might be pregnant also jabbed a fork into his brain occasionally. About once an hour. And his neighbor, Jay-deray, the woman he's too bacteria-brained to realize he's loved for years, she's steadily riding him about the medieval breastplate. The piece being locked away in his back room safe wasn't good enough; she wanted it GONE. Problems, always problems, always people.

RL no longer thought the breastplate was medieval; it was older than that. Either it was magical, which was bullshit, or it was... not from this planet. Whichever it was didn't matter; it was worth MONEY, a ton of money. But peculiar crap did happen when it was around: wives got happy, things went missing, and there'd been other *occurrences*. Like people vanishing. And monsters.

Yes, he really did need to get rid of the thing. Of course, that didn't mean he shouldn't make an obscene load of folding green out of it. Somehow. There's always a way, and where cash is concerned, any way will do. RL's ethics and morals are... adjustable. Very adjustable, about like Silly Putty. He's an antiques dealer.

Sitting at his home office desk, RL is surrounded by worthless junk; crap that will soon become exceedingly valuable merchandise. As soon as it was at the shop and in the hands of the silly bastard Frankie, whose ethics and morals were even more stretchy than RL's. There wasn't much of anything they couldn't wrap around.

Running fingers through mostly still black hair, RL

can't concentrate because of that damn breastplate. *Quit being an idiot; you can't do anything with it right now. Do something useful...cheat somebody...*

An explosion shakes the house. A blast coming from that back room.

CHAPTER 3

ON SHIP'S DECK 19

On this same morning, above the Waydowns and in Deck 19's laboratory, a *thing* has also been thinking about that breastplate. A thing with an eggplant colored, greasy, duck tailed hairdo... and lavender colored, slightly scaley skin. Or at least it had been thinking about it, until the bomb went off. The bomb it had made. The bomb it had set off.

From mathematically voided miles away, this lavender thing had reached *through* the breastplate and dropped that explosive inside RL's safe. The thing had stood there watching. Standing there had been a slight error in judgement.

The breastplate was actually an Extender, part of a Gather-Suit from this long ago crashed and buried starship. Whenever the piece was activated, it nullified distance, allowing exit or entrance through the ship's portal area; where the duck tailed bomber thing lived and had been... conceived. This thing, Proby, had not grown to plans. No, not exactly.

Proby, flipping the unexpectedly powerful device into RL's safe, had wanted to free the Extender, so he could start back to sneaking out topside. Stealing toys, and maybe find that big woman again. The luscious fat wife that he'd repetitively screwed into a permanent, delighted state of nymphomania. In her dark bedroom, she'd screamingly thought her alcoholic husband had finally risen to the occasion. But that *stud* had been downstairs in drunken oblivion, passed out on his desk. The following day, the old sot had been mystified, not to mention mortified. And afraid... very afraid, for his wife had become happy. And attentive. *Very* attentive.

Proby hadn't known if the grenade would work. It had. He's not thinking about the Extender anymore. Or that big thrashing woman. Or anything else. He lays several feet back from the portal, sprawled face up across an operations console; smoke pouring from his blast seared, gold lamé sportscoat. Buttons from his black satin shirt are scattered about the floor. Steam rises slowly from his pomaded hair, which now sticks out in all directions, like scared spaghetti. He is shoeless, since both blue suede loafers are in front of the portal opening. Where he'd been standing when he released the bomb.

Proby's day isn't going well.

From the lift, in storms one of Proby's very unhappy creators. With his lab coat flying out behind him, Dr. Moto races into the room. *What has the reptile shit done this time? It sounded most destructive.*

"Proby! What have you—! Oh... hmm... have you killed yourself?" *It would be most exceedingly excellent to finally be rid of you.* Slowing to a walk, Moto creeps hopefully toward the blast-barbequed creature. He notices smoke rising from a pair of loafers standing before the portal screen. Steam also drifts slowly out of Proby's ears.

Proby's eyes snap open. His long lashes have been burnt to nubs, and the tip of his nose is black.

"Where... where am I?" he strangles out. Raising his head, looking down the smoking body, he's relieved he's not seeing his own back.

"Oh, here I am."

"So. I see you are alive. How... um, how very fortunate," says Dr. Moto. "What exactly have you done? I thought certainly you were dead." *Why oh, why couldn't you be, you pool of lizard urine.*

However, Proby had been left in Moto's care, so the little bastard surviving wasn't all bad. Displeasing Lillith was definitely something he cared about. She wanted rid of the troublesome turd, but it must be on her terms. As all things must be on her terms.

"I'm... I'm not sure what I did," lies Proby, slowly getting off the console.

Dr. Moto helps him to a stool, glancing over at those shoes sitting below the portal screen.

"And I presume you know nothing of the blast I heard, do you? Never mind." Dr. Moto runs his hand over short, snow-white hair, studying this fried and steaming specimen of a lab experiment. This decades old 1950's teenager; Dr. Lillith Gaust's personal project. Created by her, for her... pleasure. Moto shakes his head in disgust. *This ludicrous mistake... and the creature still believes it's human... and Elvis.*

"Listen to me, Proby, Dr. Gaust has been too sick with that Spill bite to do more than direct the Waydowns reclaim. If she were not ill, I doubt you'd be here. You would be tubed in cold sleep— or dead. Maybe even worse; there's always the pit. You're fortunate I'm the one here, or this latest stunt would probably be your last performance, *Elvis.*"

Proby, his brain still sloshing about from the explosion, is beginning to pat and smooth himself out. His hands reach the top of his head, causing a horrified expression.

"My hair!" Snatching a comb from the black slacks,

he begins frantically raking at the steaming spikes and coils. What had been an artfully coifed, 50's teen-angel do, now looks like something a syphilitic crab would be embarrassed about.

Dr. Moto laughs, patronizing the creature by using the cool cat jive it loves, "You a man without a plan! The King has done been fried, Clyde! You're not looking like Elvis right now, more like a Sad Dad. Go get in your Groomer, and I strongly advise you to not look in the mirror. When you're through, report back. Lillith made me respon—"

Screaming, a Lab Spill vaults into the room, it's rotted teeth dripping as the jaws unhinge.

Dr. Moto swirls about, and the monster is on him, multi-jointed arms wrapping around, cavernous mouth open.

CHAPTER 4

A TERRIFIED TUMBLEWEED

In the house next door to RL, someone else thinks about the breastplate. Not pleasantly, and completely, totally without greed. Jayderay, wrapped in her plush burgundy house robe, paces about the kitchen in matching slippers. She's holding the morning's first mug of coffee and fretting. *Oh, my sweet Lord, I can feel that awful voodoo thing, just sittin' over there at RL's. It don't matter that it's locked up, it can DO things, do the devil's work. I know he don't believe me, and I know he won't get rid of it, not unless I push him. That man and his money, I believe sometimes that's all he thinks about. Why I keep foolin' with him, I just don't know.*

But she did know. Down deep she truly did. She had the same curse many good women do; Jayderay fell hard for bad men. Or where RL is concerned...sort of bad... a little bent... like an auger.

Passing by the invoice strewn kitchen table, she sighs. "Yeah, yeah, I see you all layin' there, waiting on me," she says aloud to the papers. "I know I've got to get the bunch of you all sent out, heaven knows I need the money. 'Cause all my Tidy Tinas do expect to be paid, most particularly the one I just fired. Shanaqueela! Sakes, what a name. It shoulda been *Shana-Squealy*, the way that girl whine and complain about work... and don't do it. How gramma would've laughed at—"

"Well, well," she interrupts herself, "look who just got up! It's my baby girl," she says to the tail wagging dog limping in. She kneels down, hugging and still talking. "I guess RL does have some good in him; he did rescue you, didn't he? We'll go over there later so you can visit with your daddy. How 'bout that? Okay, okay, Princess, don't whine, I know it's your breakfast time." Standing, she starts toward the kitchen counter.

A blast from RL's place rattles the windows. Then a piercing scream.

— • • • —

A bulging eyed RL, now hiding behind his desk, looks fearfully in the direction of the explosion. And a terrified tumbleweed whizzes past him, wearing a tuxedo. It's George, fleeing manically from the blast, his fear-puffed fur trying to run faster than he is.

The phone chirps. Figuring the phone can't hurt him, but whatever caused that boom sure as hell might, he answers. After all, it could be important; it could be about money.

"RL! Are you okay? What's goin' on over there?"

"I don't know, Jayderay, something blew up... somewhere, or... or something," RL answers deceptively, his eyes darting toward the back room.

"What do you mean, you don't know? *You* there! And I know I heard a scream clean on through my closed window. Sounded like you."

"Uh... no, it, um, it wasn't me." It had been. "I think it was George, he just came tearing past me, like there—"

"GEORGE! George my gramma, RL. That wasn't no cat I heard, and that blast was bound to come from that devil's tool you got locked up. And don't start lyin,' I'm in no mood for it." She never was in a mood for his lying, which was a shame. Lying was something RL was really good at. Accomplished, in fact.

"Yeah, okay, you're right, it did come from back there, but I haven't looked yet. Hold on and I'll go—"

"No you don't, RL! I'm coming over so you don't do something crazy. You'll start messin' with that evil thing and get grabbed by some lizard man like I did. You stay put."

"There's no reason for you to—" But she'd gone. RL was actually relieved she was coming; company would be good about now. He bravely decides to wait. *Her and that purple lizard hallucination... said it had grabbed her and it looked like Elvis. God Almighty! AND she thought it had somehow pulled her through the breastplate, like it was a door! That woman, I swear.*

Jayderay arrives, still in her firmly belted robe, but with teeth brushed and some hastily applied makeup. "Sakes RL, it smells like gun smoke in here. What on God's earth have you done? Or more likely, what did *it* do? Did you go back there?"

"I'm innocent, and I did just like you said, I waited for you. I admit, I, uh, I'm a little... reluctant to go look."

"RL, you never been innocent, I doubt you can even spell the word. And the fact you done what I told you to, is a mighty good indication that you scared. My gramma always said, fear was the best minder. But now that I'm here, I'm not in no— I'm not in a real big hurry to go looking myself."

"Well, how about some coffee first?"

"Sakes, no! Not that paint remover you drink. And there's no good in puttin' the bad off. Let's just get it over with. Lord be with us; I sure hope I don't see that Elvis thing again."

Wanting to keep his butt attached, RL doesn't say a word about Jayderay's imagination. Together, they creep down the hall, RL slightly in the lead. Only slightly. Peering into the room is a little anticlimactic;

there's no purple people eater lizards looking like Elvis, or Satan standing there grinning and twirling his tail with long taloned fingers. Just the safe, lying on its side, bulging and open.

Pulling the breastplate out, RL runs his hands over the burnished ancient metal, as Jayderay backs a little further into the hall. The armor's front shines dully, with damascene swirls spreading out from the empty jewelry seats on its chest. The interior looks forge hammered, and dark as... death.

"Look! There's not a scratch on it, yet the safe's dented all to hell, I don't see how—"

"DENTED! RL, that safe look like popcorn. And that awful voodoo thing... *and you,* ain't even— are not even hurt. The devil sure do take care of his own, don't he. You lock it back up. Now!"

"I can't shut the safe, the locking pins are sheared off, and it—"

"I don't care what's broke off from where! Put that awful thing back before it starts doin' more mischief, RL. We— *you* can wire it shut, or wedge something against it. I'll put that Bible I give you on top of it, too. You're takin' that devil tool out of this house, today; clean on out of the neighborhood." She shakes her head, adding, "But, sakes whatever you do, don't take it to your shop! Sweet Jesus help us all if Frankie gets to foolin' with it. That boy sure do get up to enough as it is, without puttin' some black magic in his hands."

"You're right about Frankie," RL chuckles, "he does tend to get up to stuff. Okay, I'll figure something out. And by the way, I keep forgetting to ask; are the police still investigating that body out at the Roaton place? We need to get started on some kind of inventory out there." That handy phrase 'By the way' is often used by oily, devious sorts to change a subject. RL uses it often.

"Yeah, least ways I think they are, but I'll call Preacher Dan. That slick guy can probably get some kind of release for us to work out there. Sakes, I don't want to; I've been afraid of that spooky old house since I was a girl. But first things first, I'm makin' Good- Book sure you get that devilry locked up. If I don't, you'll get to thinkin' about money, and start polishing it up, like some Alladin's Lamp. And what's liable to come popping out won't be no genie. Least ways not one you'd want to see."

"Yes'm, Miz Scarlett."

"Oh, shut up, you," she says, laughing.

Jayderay needs to laugh while she can. She will soon forget about her fear of the of the breastplate. She will soon forget about Elvis lizards and the devil. A very real homespun nightmare is on its way. It arrives this morning.

CHAPTER 5

INVIGORATING ENTERTAINMENT

Not far from RL and Jayderay, out on U.S. 281, an old two-story home rises from the riotous nest of a long untended garden. Hungry vines have swallowed half the structure and covered the surrounding wrought iron fence. It has also covered the dead.

The Roaton Place. A house of local legend. A house of fear. A deserted house. Empty? No, the locals say; it isn't empty. No one lives there anymore, but something moves inside the house. Sometimes rotting velvet curtains part slowly, softly smearing mildew on the window glass. And what moved those curtains, looks out. Those who have seen what looks out, usually do not tell. If they come back.

Inside this diseased Victorian mansion, dark furniture sits on clawed feet, leering with carved faces; dark wood faces that have seen dark things. Things that shouldn't exist. Living things—and things that are not. Dim light from a round, stained-glass skylight, features an oak staircase that curves majestically down to the first floor. Carved barley twist balusters provide looms for the weavings of starved spiders. Fallen sections of railing lie shattered below. And the bleak, lonely dust layers all.

No, the townspeople say, the old Black man died, and nobody lives in the eerie old house anymore. But the townspeople are wrong. There is a body in the Roaton place. And it does live. And it isn't alone.

But the old place hasn't been vacant of humans this morning. Today a couple of cops have been finishing up an investigation. They've been looking into the discovery of a shriveled, sunbaked body found on the rusting iron fence. Spiked on one of the fence's spear-topped posts. Their captain has pretty much decided it was just some burglar who got spooked and jumped through a second story window. A burglar with extremely bad luck. Then the thieving bastard had the temerity to die and stay on his perch, causing all this needless work.

The thief's husk had also provided considerable entertainment for the group of church women who had found it. Several were so infused with excitement they'd trampled their sisters in the retreat. One of them had even pulled ahead of the herd, leaped some bushes in a single bound... and beat the 'Saving Souls' van back to town. Another appreciative viewer was in the hospital. It seems the sight of those remains had cured her constipation... too well.

Walking around outside, the two officers' glance up at the shattered second story window, from which the hapless burglar had plummeted to his rusty spear top perch. Looking down, they scuff about through bits of glittering glass and remnants of rotted velvet.

"Let's get the hell out of here, Johnny; there ain't nothing to find. Our speared stiff was just some dipshit that fell through that window. And that day-basement closet that had the door *nailed* shut? Whoever did that used the biggest damn nails I ever seen; I didn't think we'd ever get the son of a bitch open. That's been bothering all hell out of me; just why was it nailed shut? And something else, that other room, Jesus Christ! With all those swirling scratch marks everywhere, even on the ceiling. Damn!"

"Yeah, all that's been weighing on me too, Duke. You know what's even worse to me? Something clawed its way through the bottom of a solid oak door gettin' out of that closet. A big something. What in hell was it? You remember, not long back we got a report about some farmer finding his prize bull damn near eat up? Everybody blamed it on coyotes, but that's a load of crap. I can't see a pack of 'yotes attacking a full-grown Angus."

"Me neither. Christ, Johnny, don't put anything in our report about that door, or all those weird claw marks in the other room. You and me might end up back out here for another two days lookin' for a boogey man. And that high-toned preacher, the one who inherited this spook joint, has already been raising holy hell about how long it's taking to release this... this morgue."

"Don't worry about the report, Duke. I sure don't want us back out here lookin' for God knows what, either. Hell, we might find it!" Laughing, they walk toward their cruiser.

Crouched in the dense green foliage about the house, something watches them. Dripping mandibles protrude from its twisted lips. It hungers, but not enough to attack the two. It's a something that had once been human. Another failed experiment that had been discarded, tossed into the Waydowns. But it had found others. Others who knew a way out.

Below the creature, back down in that basement with the nailed shut, clawed through, oak door, a closet wall softly glows. The light briefly reveals an elevator. It isn't behind the wall, nor is it on the walls surface— it is molecularly meshed *with* the wall. Transported there mathematically by an experiment gone to hell long years ago. It glimmers occasionally, showing itself with a light provided by a buried starship, hundreds and hundreds of miles away. In another state.

There is something within the old house that can touch this wall, revealing *and* opening the unseen elevator. It's an elevator that doesn't go up, nor down, it's only a door. It's a door opening directly into place inhabited by many. A place none of them wish to be. A place of madness and abomination. The Waydowns.

The two troopers drive away to other duties. Answering calls, protecting the weak, shielding the stupid, sometimes arresting the bad, and generally earning their pay. They talk with one another easily, as long-time partners do. Chuckling and joking about the spooky old mansion.

"Remember that old TV show, The Munsters? Well, it sure as hell could've been filmed back there, like real, real easy."

"Oh, hell yeah it could've! To tell you the truth, I still watch that sometimes on the re-run channel. And you know, I do believe I'd pork Lilly Muster."

"Like shit you would, then you'd have that big Franken-Fuck Herman wantin' to pork *you*! And just think what a schlong that goofy bastard must have; probably with big bolts stickin' out of it."

"Yeah and pissing lightning too!"

So they laugh and joke, these two uniformed men, being blissfully unaware that this is the most fortunate day of their lives.

Behind these two lucky troopers, bushes tremble as leaves are slowly parted by wrongly grown hands. Taloned hands, on arms with too many bulbous joints, pus suppurating elbows that throb and itch. The creature shambles to the vines and begins climbing toward the shattered second story window. Toes like spasming worms, constantly coil and release, wrapping and gripping. It must climb, for the humans had locked the house front door. Humans were always locking things. Always denying. Always cutting. Always hurting. But this creature, this Lab Spill, it likes human. It likes human a lot.

Inside, the creature follows the curving oak stairs down, curling toed feet brushing crumbling plaster bits and wallpaper peelings. It pauses to catch its breath, the topside air is not good, not like in the ship, not like in the Waydowns. Gazing at the oval framed portraits that hang, evenly spaced, following the banister. Its mind seethes with conflicting thoughts... it wonders if they could be memories. It wonders if it could've known any of these people. Could it have touched them. Could it have tasted them.

Reaching the ground floor, gasping, it makes for the

day basement. The toes leave scratching swirls in the dust. And it can't breathe, it can't get its breath, it can't. Falling down the two steps into the basement, it crawls to the closet and through that clawed, and pried-open oak door. The closets back wall begins to glow softly, and the shimmering elevator appears. That elevator that doesn't go up nor down, that elevator that is only a door. A door that leads to many. The entry slides open, the panting Lab Spill is pulled into the Waydowns. Those that pull will not be happy. It was supposed to bring living meat.

And outside, the house towers in the hot morning sun, the clutching green vines slowly eating into it. Glass from the windows glint, reflecting the sun, like living eyes watching from an uncovered grave. The house is patient. It always has been.

CHAPTER 6

A LETHAL MISTAKE

RL takes the care of a gynecologist examining a litigious nun, as he moves about his true love, Elvira. The cloth covered Jag crouching here in the garage. Like most fools with a pet car, he values her more than... well, more than almost anything. Not more than Jayderay, but he'd never tell *her* that— the car or the woman.

He's hunting for wire to hold that safe shut. Hurriedly hunting, as a very serious Jayderay is still in the house keeping a fearful watch on that devil's tool breastplate. Likely clutching a bible and muttering prayers. Not just likely, *is* clutching and praying.

Naturally, the wire is not where it's supposed to be. Inanimate objects are known to gleefully hide whenever a person really needs them. It's a fact of life, being part of God's overall plan... to torment the living shit out of people. Testing them, to be sure they have sufficient strength for the bigger and better delights waiting just around the corner.

RL finds a length of chain, which might satisfy Jayderay better. But the padlock isn't with it. *Well, of course the lock is gone, it's grown little legs and ran off with the wire. Next comes the cow and moon jumping. Problems. Always problems. And I'm about to have a bigger one with Jayderay, she's not gonna stay inside alone much longer... I just really don't need this crap right now.*

Walking through the back door empty handed, he calls out "Listen, Jayderay, I've been thinking—"

"I bet that means you ain— haven't found any wire. RL, that thing is NOT gonna stay anywhere loose, it's got to be locked up." Seeing him coming down the hall, she says, "Just like I thought, you didn't get the wire."

"You know, I left some ammo inside the safe when I locked up the breastplate. Maybe somehow it went off, and—"

"NO, RL! Quit lyin', you didn't leave any bullets in there, and we both know it. The devil is in that armor, it was him that made that noise, him tryin' to get out."

"Look, please just listen to me, Jayderay! Back before that child molester attorney Gunther Fly stole it, I kept the breastplate in just a plain, a normal, an ordinary, everyday black garbage bag, like all us heathens use. And it never *did* anything. It didn't puff out any purple lizards that looked like Elvis, it didn't play spooky music and become a slide into the Twilight Zone, why it didn't even dance a jig with the devil. It did nothing. Nothing, period. So please, just let me sack the thing back up again. I'll even put it in the van and lock the doors. Okay? And when you get permission from that snake oil Preacher Dan to start work at the Roaton place, then I'll take it out there."

"RL! You better not be makin' fun and sayin' you think I 'magined all that!" flares Jayderay, her eyes flashing death. "When I was at that black sinnin' Gunther's house, some lizard DID come out of that thing. It DID grab me, and it DID look like Elvis, and it DID yank me into some kinda awful Star Trek place. I swear it on God's Holy Name. You hear?"

"Yes, ma'am. I do hear you, and I expect that lizard Elvis hears you up on Mars, or wherever he lives. Probably the dead hear you. And every single one of us believes you," fluently lies RL. He believes her about like he believes 'honesty is the best policy' and that 'things always work out for the best.' He's also smart enough to know if she believes it... then he better. Or at least lie about it. Like they were married.

"RL, I am bein' dead serious about this, I'm afraid of that... that can of Satan. If you weren't so greedy, you would be too. And I'm not just real sure how I'd feel workin' around it if you take it to that awful house."

Sensing her resistance weakening, he drops to both knees and clasping his hands together, he says, "Pleeeze, Massa Jayderay! Pleeeze let me take that horrible voodoo doo- doo out to de haunty house. I jus' swears it won't cause you no miseries. And I be there with you mos' of de time."

"Oh, shut up and get up you idiot." Fighting back a laugh, she adds, "All right, RL. I give in, it's sure not okay, but I'll agree to that, at least it'll be away from our homes. And that thing sure oughta fit right nice out there at that scary old place. I'm kinda, but not too, sorry for bein' snappish and ridin' you so hard about that thing, but it's a can of trouble. Anyway, you sack it, and take it out to your van right this minute. I mean *now*. I'll call Preacher Daniel, and make sure it's all legal for us to be out there. And RL—don't you make me regret this. You hear?"

But RL will not be at the Roaton house all the time. Jayderay has just made a mistake. A mistake she will pay dearly for. When the time comes, the word regret won't even come close to what she will feel. While she lives.

CHAPTER 7

THE SHIP- THE WAYDOWNS

Back in Deck 19's lab, Moto whirls to face the charging, screeching Spill; it slams into him, slapping the misshapen arms around his body. Its many elbows spurt and crackle as they wrap about the doctor and rotting breath sprays from the gaping maw.

Throwing a hand up beneath the creatures screaming mouth, he keeps the dripping fangs from sinking into his face. As they fall to the floor, his other hand desperately plunges into a pocket for the prod. Rolling as they fall, the monster continues its slavering, high pitched shriek, even as its head slams into the deck.

Proby, addled by the explosion he'd blown himself up with, looks stupidly about for a weapon. Spotting a round length of wood, he grabs it. Trying to brace himself for a swing, his shoeless feet slip, sending him staggering into the two grappling figures. Falling across them, scrambling to get up, the Spill grabs one of his ankles.

Moto, partly released from the Spill's hold, wrenches completely free, and lurching away, pulls the high voltage weapon from his coat. He can't fire without frying both Proby and the screaming abomination. He's tempted.

Proby, kicking with his free foot, swings the bat, smashing it into the creature's skull. Stunned, its grip loosens, and he snatches his leg away.

The prod spits a blue arc, the current burrowing into and convulsing the Spill. Its limbs spasm epileptically, thrashing about. Moto continues sending the electric bolts into the bucking pitching body, until the prod's charge is spent. Smoke and steam rises from the carcass. And the smell of electricity coupled with cooked rotting meat spread throughout the area.

The doctor is remarkably calm. In his decades with Lillith Gaust, he's been attacked many times. He wastes no pity on Spills. He knows their torment, their hatred, and couldn't care less. Fanning his hand at the smoke, he looks at the charred and smoking body.

"Damn, these foul beasts stink; where did it come from?"

Still holding the piece of wood, Proby answers with a question in much the same, matter of fact tone.

"Gosh, doctor, you mean it's not one of yours?"

"No, it's not branded. It might be chipped, but I'll

not bother to check. Probably found its way into a maintenance tunnel still connected to the Waydowns. We'll dispose of it, but the labbies must not see. Since Tanya went missing, they get upset about the least of things."

Pocketing the prod, he looks at the forever pain-in-the-butt Proby, standing there in his blast blackened, but still sparkling sportscoat. Noticing the stick, he smiles.

"I see my placatory device has once again come to the rescue. I often use that for fidgety volunteers; they can become quite unreasonable. I also do thank you for the help, you may have saved my life. But that will mean little when I tell the Honored Bed Pan of your attempt on the Extender. You've essentially freed it, and it happened on *my* watch. This means I must endure the wrath of—"

"MOTO, REPORT, NOW," interrupts a voice of command that seems to come from everywhere.

"Ah! The Honored Fecal Pile knows already. You and I have not completed this talk." And he was off, not quite running. Even Moto didn't keep Dr. Lillith Sally Gaust waiting. It was not healthy. Not good for the digestion.

Proby sighs. He's in deep shit... like always. This time, it will be deeper than he thinks.

Far beneath Proby, in the endless bowel of the Waydowns, Darren's group advances down the corridor. Elena, in rearguard position, passes the dead Lab Spill. Its eyes open. It silently rises, jaws unhinging.

Up ahead, Patty slides on a knee into a doorway, Uzi extended. Her eyes darting everywhere. A dense, blue tinted fog drifts in slow moving patches, shrouding everything. The debris of chaos litters the floor, power indicators faintly glow red, and control station readouts dimly blink with meaningless gibberish. They have done so through many decades. The only sound is the soft bubbling of the bright yellow mold. Gunch. Advancing a couple steps further, she's constantly sweeping the gun in an arc.

Back in the corridor, the Spill leaps for Elena's back. Sensing movement, she whirls, catching the monster full on. Its mouth covers her entire face, the bottom fangs digging into the soft flesh under her chin.

"REAR!" screams Huong. "REAR ATTACK!"

Darren turns back, unslinging his Uzi, and yells, "Patty, hall!"

Huong, unable to shock or shoot the creature without killing Elena, drops the prod and pulls his knife, lunging into the fight.

Hearing both Huong and Darren, Patty spins back toward the hallway. With teeth bared, eyes bright, her lips red with saliva, she charges back to the opening. And a web draped tentacle drops from above, wrapping around her.

As the Spill sinks its teeth into Elena's face, her training takes over. Falling to her back, she uses the creature's momentum and her knees to sail it overhead. As the creature flips, its imbedded fangs tear at her flesh.

Patty shrieks curses as the web trailing tentacle jerks her upward. Firing wildly into the haze above and screaming, she's relentlessly hauled straight up. Her spraying bullets empty the clip, and dropping the gun, she grabs her knife.

Seeing Huong launch himself into the battle behind them, Darren turns and dives toward Patty's rapidly disappearing legs.

As the Spill's back slams into the deck, Huong immediately drives his blade into its gut, ripping upward. With intestines spurting from the wound, the thing thrusts out an arm, grabbing Huong's throat. It can't bite him; Elena's jawbone is clenched in its mouth.

Darren catches Patty around the knees with one arm, hanging on he's lifted with her. He sprays the Uzi up into the murky heights as she hacks at the rippling scaled muscles of the tentacle.

Unseen, another webbed coil appears out of the haze from across the room. It silently slithers across the deck.

CHAPTER 8

A STUNNING DISPLAY

Calling Preacher Dan, seeking permission to start work at the Roaton house, Jayderay now listens. Conversations with the great man didn't allow for much else.

"Well, sister Janice, I have been informed by our local constabulary that all difficulties out at our departed brother Wus's home, have been, uh... cleared away. They feel that it was just a burglary gone wrong. One of God's lost children must have broken in, and unfortunately fell to his death from that upstairs window. I will pray for his soul, of course, and I know you will too," says Preacher Daniel, into his very latest and awfully expensive smart phone. One must have the best communication available to effectively battle evil.

"Uh, why, uh, sure, yes, I will certainly do that Preacher Daniel... naturally I will," answers Jayderay as she paces about in her kitchen." *I will now that I've said I'm going to. But not a very long prayer, forgive me Lord.*

"So, do I have your permission to go out there, and bring my antiques dealer friend? We need to start getting a handle on the appraisal and do some type of an inventory. Sakes it's gonna be a job. Uncle Wus must have—"

"Yes, sister Janice, you have my blessing, and the Lord's, on the labor you're doing for our church. And you will be rewarded in heaven, rest assured. As your beloved uncle Wus is, right at this very moment, for bequeathing his worldly home and possessions to my— and our, ministry. I will of course be out to check and see how God's work is progressing. Some of the members from our women's auxiliary were going to join you, but... after the... inopportune, uh, *finding* that occurred... well, it might be a day or two before any of them make it out there. I'm sure you understand. God love and keep you, sister Janice and may he bestow his bounty on us all. Goodbye." And a happy and smiling Preacher Dan, puts that new expensive phone into the pocket of his Armani suit. One must look one's best to war with the devil.

"My, oh my, just ain't— just isn't he all silver-tongued and velvety like, Princess," she says to dog, who's still waiting patiently. "I know he a man of God and all that, but I can't help but feel that lying, cheating crook next door is a much better man. Well, some better, anyways.

And I know you sure do think so, baby. Mercy! I haven't fed you yet, and here I am still in this robe, too. I need to get movin' and get dressed, don't I? But first, let's get your breakfast."

In the house across Jayderay's drive, that "lying, cheating, crook" is being watched. He's being watched by George, who also hasn't been fed. And George isn't nearly as patient as Princess is. Or as nice, but then Princess is a dog, while George is a cat. Cats are people and behave accordingly.

Sitting in the doorway, watching RL fooling with the troublesome breastplate, George lashes his tail back and forth. He's no longer the bug-eyed tuxedo wearing tumbleweed that had speed rolled down the hall earlier. His fur has quieted down, and now he's a just a cat. In a tuxedo. One who hasn't been fed. The top-of-the-line dry food, that's out 24/7, doesn't count. And his water hasn't been freshened up either. Life's hard. *You toadstool, I don't know how you did it, but you caused that gun safe to explode while I was sleeping on it. I won't forget this... AND I won't forget there's been no breakfast yet either...*

George's pet toadstool has been fighting the blast-dented safe, gotten it erect and shoved back in its place.

Now, this bipedal fungus is sacking up the piece of armor. And thinking hard.

If this son of a bitch wasn't worth so much, I would pitch it in the river, like SHE wants me to. It's been nothing but trouble... and somehow it cost me Deena Lynn... well, at least that made Jayderay happy... Jayderay!... why'd she have to come over in that short robe, those creamy legs peeking out at me, breasts straining wonderfully against that soft fabric... as if I don't have enough to worry about without... her. Problems, always problems. RL does have problems. One of which is, he's male; he can only think with one of his brains at a time.

"Yes, George, you fat, pink toed bastard, I see you sittin' there watching me, waiting to be fed." He bursts out laughing. "I'd pay a bunch to have a video of you, all puffed up and flying down that hall like the Baskerville Hound was after you!"

...And it can laugh too, how nice. Just you wait you fool; I know where you sleep. You'll think the Baskerville Hound all right... you'll think a whole kennel of them has shit in your bed...Then I'll wish "I" had a video. George sits, nearly motionless, golden eyes balefully glowing, he lays one ear flat and sticking out to one side. A sure sign of extreme disfavor.

After feeding George: The Briefly Contented, RL takes

the garbage-sacked, Pandora's Box of a breastplate out to the van. Shaking his head and muttering about silly women, he locks it up. Fear is indeed the best minder.

Almost back to the house, his phone chirps. It's Frankie. Frankie was invaluable; he could sell hemorrhoids to the elderly. And he was even better at cheating the living shit out of customers than RL was. But the little darling had to be watched over; Frankie tended to get up to things. He certainly needed supervision, or someone very dear to RL might go to jail. Someone like RL.

Answering, RL hears the dreaded words:

"Boss, you, um, (giggle) you probably need to get down here." (giggle-giggle)

Frankie has struck, and the silly bastard has been up to something. Again. It's the giggling that does it. "I'm on my way," says RL. He doesn't bother asking why. The giggling equals disaster, and it's never wise to ignore Frankie. He gets up to things.

———

RL calls Jayderay as he drives to find out what calamity Frankie has manufactured. Letting her know why he'll be late getting to the Roaton place. And he does like hearing her voice.

"Sakes! You mean he didn't say what was wrong?"

"No, he didn't tell me... but he giggled."

"Oh, my sweet Lord! That means you GOT to go see. That boy, that boy. What has Satan put him up to this time?"

"Satan your gramma! Frankie sure doesn't need any help from the devil. He could probably give that red turd some new ideas."

Jayderay laughs. "I 'magine he could at that! And speaking of the devil, have you got that Godless voodoo thing with you? You better have, you promised."

"Yes'm," he answers safely. Not mentioning he hadn't exactly promised but knowing better than to quibble. Women can be difficult. "It's sacked up and on the seat right here beside me," he continues, glancing over at it.

"You oughta at least put it in the back, 'cause something liable to reach out and grab the steering wheel. Mercy, whatever you do, don't take it inside the store. And RL, I've got the keys to the Roaton place, I guess I'll go on out there and make a start. But don't you take too long with Frankie. I'm not real comfortable about bein' out there by myself, and I'm pretty sure none of the other church women will show. Least ways not for a few days. Oh, I gotta go, somebody's at the door, bye."

———••———

Noticing, Frankie's vintage VW bug is the only car parked in the front of NEAT STUFF, RL pulls around to the back of the antiques shop and takes a deep breath. *I shudder to think what he's done.*

As soon as the silly bastard sees him come through the back door, he starts the giggling, and says, "RL, they had it coming, and there are no witnesses."

This is not a good start. "Lay it on me, Frankie. Let's hear it, and I want all of it."

"First off, they're driving some long new lookin' Caddy with New York plates, and the assholes pull in and park long ways, you know, pretty much taking up all the spaces, besides the one I've got. Then they came strutting in, shoving the door hard enough to bang into one of the displays, and then complain about the door bein' too easy."

"After that, the Yankee bitch marches up to me at the checkout counter, looks in at the jewelry and asks me if any of the 'crap' is real. The guy goes straight to the marble statue of David, and says: 'My god, what faggot brought this thing in?"

"Hell, *I* bought that!" says RL with great indignation. He had already disliked the pair from hearing of the door banging entry, and now this! Damn rude Yankees.

'I'm very much aware of that fact," giggles Frankie delightedly. "Then they look at and handle about every damn thing in the place, banging lids, dropping things back down, not setting anything down gently. A couple pieces fell over, and they just walked on. And they laughed, making loud assy comments about our shop and merchandise. I asked, several times, if there was anything I could help them with. The cunt finally answered me, sayin' if she found anything that she wouldn't be ashamed to have in her home, then she'd be sure and let me know. They were real prizes, boss."

"I haven't seen a body, Frankie, and their car's gone, so I guess you didn't kill either one. Why not?" RL had learned the hard way; there are customers that need running off... before something unfortunate happens to them. Like murder. Some people just beg to be killed, and after all, this is Texas.

Frankie giggles some more, and says, "Well, no, I didn't kill anybody this time. In fact, I never touched either one of them."

"I'm beginning to suspect I'll wish you had. Tell me."

"Well... they're coming down the aisle toward me here, at the jewelry display, and they're still spewing out loud insults about the shop. I can tell the bitch is bringing the man to look at the jewelry. And I had absolutely all I could stand of these two. It absolutely was time for... *Showtime!* So, I took the pistol we keep under the counter with that demon mask and tucked it in the small of my back. I slid the back glass of the case open—" Frankie stops, and actually blushes.

RL, seeing the blush, braces himself. What's coming must be a stunner, because the silly bastard is as gay as any dozen trannies, doesn't care who knows, and is never embarrassed about anything. RL is right, it was a *stunner*.

"God damn it, Frankie, tell me, get it out!"

"That's EXACTLY what I did, Boss... I got it out! I unzipped and laid IT out across the jewelry. And here come those two marching up, the twat chattering for him to come see this 'gold plated fake garbage.' And then they did *see*. Indeed they did SEE."

RL stands transfixed by the vision. Unfortunately for his own self- esteem, he's had a glimpse of Frankie's equipment. Hila Monster would be an accurate description. A well fed one. The image forms of that hairy Behemoth laying across the sparkling jewelry... and he explodes with laughter.

Frankie joins in, and RL has to lean on the counter. This is even better than killing. RL ends up dropping to his knees, folding his arms on top of the display case, laying his head down, gasping with hysterics.

"Oh, Christ, Frankie, that is priceless! What did they say? No, no, what did they DO?"

"Like I was sayin' they stamped up to the counter

and she was yammering at him: 'Just wait till you see this garb—' and then she *saw*. Her eyes bugged, and she kept on going 'garb-, garb-, garb-' Then he saw, and made kind of a little strangled sound. By the time they could tear their eyes away from the magnificence of it, and look up at me, I'd pulled out the gun. And I was sorta polishing on it. Casual like and giving them a really big friendly smile—while rubbing on the pistol. Hell, boss, he knocked her down running for the car, and she damn near didn't get out there in time. They fishtailed out onto Speedway with her clawing the door shut. And so then... I called you, end of story."

Now, RL slides down the counter's front glass, laughing and slapping at the floor. What a silly bastard. Another one. Two peas in a pod of a shop.

"God, Frankie, you are just too, too good!" He finally manages to wheeze out the praise.

Frankie, who'd already been quite pleased with himself, now positively beams. "Anyway, Mein Fuhrer, what do you think we should do? Think they'll call the police? I've already hid the gun, I mean *really* hid it."

RL gets under control, and pulling himself erect, gasps, "I doubt they'll call or tell anybody. Even a New York Yankee wouldn't want to tell the law he knocked down his wife running away because he saw a weenie. But just to be on the safe side, I suppose you should disappear till tomorrow. I'll stay and just deny ever seeing those Yankee assholes, and swear I've been here all day, *alone.* Hell, I'm gonna close up early anyway, 'cause Jayderay's going out to the Roaton house, and I worry about her being out there alone."

Looking at Frankie, he grins. "If the cops do show up but miss me, and come tomorrow, you can spin'em a tale. Say you caught them shoplifting; you're as good a liar as I am. Hell, even better than me, with that boy scout face of yours, cowlick, chipped front tooth and all. They'll believe you. And, Frankie... uh, tomorrow, um, how about you give the jewelry a little... cleaning." RL can be a bit prissy about some things.

On the way to answer the door bell, Jayderay heads Princess off, and shuts her in the bedroom. Princess has already gotten a little too protective of her new human.

"You stay in here a little while, baby girl, I won't be long. I 'magine it's somebody who might not be too happy, and I don't want them takin' it out on you." She's expecting the worthless, fired, and bad tempered Shanaqueela wanting her paycheck. It's not.

It's the worthless, never employed, and worse tempered husband; Suga' Boo. A part time drug dealer, wanna be pimp, and full-time prick.

"You the Aunt Jemima that dissed my wife, and I come for her money," says Suga' Boo. "And I ain't takin' no fucking check, you white actin' bitch."

"I know who you are, and what you are," says Jayderay. "You're not taking anything, I'll pay Shanaqueela. Nobody else. And that ends this conversation, now you get off my property."

She's shutting the door when Suga' Boo rams it back open, knocking her down. Taking a look back at the empty street, he steps inside, quietly closing the door. Quickly kneeling besides the dazed woman, he grabs a fistful of hair and slams her head against the floor.

"Oh, I'm gonna get off all right, Mammy," he says to the unconscious Jayderay. "I'm gonna get off real good." Suga' Boo smiles, his lips curl like hungry leeches. Ripping her blouse open with heavily beringed fingers, he says, "They's lots of ways to settle up this account."

CHAPTER 9

MOTO BOWS LOW

In 1956 when the Elvis Presley/rock and roll craze swept America, Lillith Gaust was already a feared doctor, already in control of Deck 19, and already quite clinically bat piss insane. Despite all this, she developed a school-girl crush on the gyrating singer. And a rabid case of the hots for him. Not a problem: she'd grow her own.

Well, sometimes plans work out... sometimes they don't... and sometimes...a Proby pops out. And to make matters worse, she didn't kill him.

Within Deck 19, Proby works feverishly on his eggplant-colored hair, glancing constantly at the Elvis albums tacked up beside the mirror. Light glints off Lavendar skin, as he pats, slicks and the Brylcreem drips. There's enough oil in his hair to compete with Texas. He practices lifting his upper lip into the famous Elvis grin. *...yeah, daddy-o, I got it just right! I'm Elvis: the king, the cat daddy, and man, oh, man, I'm cool as a pool.*

Except Proby knows better. Down deep where he pushes all the constant doubt, confusion, and the eternal loneliness of not knowing what he 'is, he does know better. He's not Elvis, he's not even human. Not entirely. He's only a 1950s' experiment that didn't fail quite badly enough to be terminated. He's a pet; he's Lillith's pet monster. He's a pitiful, lonely, and confused bad joke. And he's screwed up again, trying to get at the Extender. It may well be for the last time.

NO! NO! Push it away. Push it all away. I am human. I am Elvis. I am THE Elvis. I am. I am human. I am... And he drops the comb, leaning his head into the mirror, eyes shut tightly against the stupid looking, lavender faced truth it shows.

A bit later, despite Moto's warning, Proby will not, absolutely cannot, leave the Extender alone. Like any child, teen... or human, that which is forbidden becomes a have to have. Got to have. Got to get. Just got to. Back in the Lab, he gazes sadly at the alcove where the open portal had been. It's closed; now there's only a blank, blue flickering screen. *The Topsiders have covered it, or it's being moved... either way, it can't focus, it can't open the portal, or even produce a view. I'm never going to get ahold of that gorgeous fat woman again...*

Somewhere else on Deck 19, Dr. Moto stands before Lillith, after making a short and quick report. Nervously plucking at his coat buttons, he glances repeatedly over at a figure in one corner. A human figure; he's sure he's seen that face before. Head, and all exposed skin are totally devoid of hair. The person is silent, staring blankly ahead, and wearing some type of floor length surgical smock. Hands are obviously restrained from behind, and this figure appears genderless — except for being quite pregnant. Very pregnant. Ripe.

Dr. Lillith Gaust looks like she's been pulled from the sea... after long immersion. Sparse patches of hair appear pasted to an almost fleshless skull, sunken eyes burn bright with a fever... and her madness. The lips are a liver-colored gash, with a dried smear of blood beneath. A small tuft of white sticks to the red smear. It's fur. Her charnel stench fills the room. She speaks.

"He bombed it... he bombed the Extender?"

"Not exactly. He—"

"Did he bomb it? Or did he not?" interrupts an eerily calm Lillith.

"Yes, Dr. Gaust," Moto answers quickly, now smoothing those buttons, and still taking surreptitious looks at that human in the corner. *I know that face.*

"Proby dropped an explosive into the safe where that

topsider kept it. He could reach in and actually touch the device, but couldn't lift it out due to—"

"Christ shit and fell in it, Moto! I know the fucking math and logistics involved, *Doctor*. Where's the Extender now?"

"Still at that location; but the safe is wrecked, there's no telling where they'll put the thing now," he answers, beginning to button his coat.

"So. The Extender, of utmost importance to us, is now wafting languidly about topside, just waiting for someone with a brain to discover what it can do. Is that right?"

"Yes, Dr. Gaust," he answers, fingers still working on the buttons. And the human in the corner still drawing his attention.

"Did I not put you in charge of Proby and Deck 19?

"Yes, Dr. Gaust." Moto starts unbuttoning the coat.

"That is so good to hear," says Lillith. "I began to fear my memory had gone awry with this infection." *You little slant eyed, Jap prune... if I didn't need you for this Spill bite, I'd have you strapped to a lab gurney... and one of us would surely be ecstatic...* "We will speak no more of this... at this time. Now quit fucking with your damn coat and stop looking over at my new assistant. I need you to examine my wound."

Moto grimaces slightly as he quits fucking with the

coat and steps to her; he doesn't want to touch this horrid, nasty woman.

Far from squeamish, there are few medical horrors that Dr. Moto hasn't seen. And caused. He'd been closely (and quite happily) associated with Japan's appalling Unit 731. Where he had applied himself with great diligence.

Not all WW2 side-swappers were captured Nazis. Others of a different loyalty also got frigid footsies, and some didn't wait for capture. When the Japanese Navy got the Rising Sun stuffed up its ass at Midway, Moto saw the Shodo on the wall. He saw that writing as big glowing radioactive letters; they spelled out: Run you idiot. So, he carefully made contacts and secret travel arrangements. Afterwards, while in his lab, he turned his back to the framed photo of his beloved emperor... and with a smile, bowed low. Then he got the hell out of Dodge.

The American Military shuffled Moto about here and there, with him repeatedly avowing eternal loyalty, (like he had done with his beloved Emperor) he eventually was assigned to Dr. Gaust. She with her orders to combine the frozen aliens with humans, and this posting fit him better than his own yellow hide did. Theirs was a match like no other. Aiding in her drive to create a super soldier, their atrocities beat anything the concentration camps ever produced.

As Dr. Gaust slips the filthy lab coat off her shoulders, Moto looks at the red streaks radiating from beneath the stained, discharge leaking bandage. The area has swelled, and it's visibly pulsing beneath the dressing. He gently peels, and the injury slowly comes into view. A sharp hiss escapes him as he jerks his hands away. As the hiss dies on Dr. Moto's lips, he stands motionless, staring fixedly at Lillith's infected shoulder.

And at the teeth nibbling through the wound. Tiny, sharp, human teeth.

CHAPTER 10

THE SILLY BASTARD GOES CALLING

Leaving RL to face any possible police heat, Frankie backs his VW beetle into the street; and of course giggling about the unique jewelry he'd displayed for the asshole Yankees. *I'll bet that twat had never seen a necklace like that before... a real choker, all right! One big fat diamond... in the rough...* And he giggles again, quite happy about his latest, innovative customer service. *RL sure loved hearing about it... that's a relief, 'cause he can't be counted on to always see things in the proper light. The boss can be a bit prissy.* As usual, Frankie is pretty happy with Frankie. Yes indeed.

With the rest of the day to kill, he drives to Jayderay's home, deciding he'll go with her to the Roaton house. This is one of Frankies better ideas.

Parking in her drive, he strolls to the white front door and finds it ajar, blood smeared on the jamb. Shoving it open, he yells her name, staring in. He needn't have bothered. She was on the way. Gripping a butcher knife.

A bit later, they sit in her kitchen. Frankie listening silently, his jaw muscles clenching. They have often confided in each other. Jayderay always thought of those times as 'girl talk.' Actually, so did Frankie. But those talks had never been anything like this.

"... and when I come awake, that, that... that *nigger* was on me. And Princess was goin' crazy behind the bedroom door. I guess she pawed that levered knob open, 'cause she come flyin' in and latched onto one of his ears. I had heard he deathly 'fraid of dogs. Well, he for sure is now. I grabbed her to me, and he tore loose, then lit out of here hitchin' at his drawers. I don't—"

"Why in hell didn't you let her rip the bastard to shreds? God damn that son of a bitch!" Frankie bolts up from the chair. "I'm going to get RL, and we'll—"

"NO, FRANKIE! You not gonna get or tell RL nothin.' Not a thing, you hear? He a man, and think he have to do something. Either he'd get himself killed or thrown in jail. That... that *nigger* is big, strong, and mean. That's why I grabbed Princess to me. She still crippled, and he'd have killed her for sure."

"Jayderay," says Frankie gently. "We have got to report this; something has got to be done."

"NO! I'm— *we* are not reporting anything to anybody.

I mean it, Frankie. You sit back down and listen to me. If the police know, then RL bound to find out, and off he'd go. And you think of yourself, if something happen to RL, what then? That shop is your home, your life. If RL gets his self jailed, or dead, then you wind up out in the street. That shop *is* you, honey."

Slowly sitting back down, Frankie stares at this amazing woman. "Then I guess you won't go see a doctor either?"

"Honey, I been raped before, back when I was still a kid. I got over it then and I'll get over it this time the same way. I'll stand in the shower and cry and pray. Gramma always said, tears was God doin' soul washin' and today's tears just might make tomorrow's rainbow."

"God damn it, Jayderay, damn it to hell! This isn't right. This just can't be... can't be allowed."

"No, it is not right. And it shouldn't be 'allowed.' But a lot of things that happen sure ain— are not right, and shouldn't be allowed, but they sure do happen," she says, and actually chuckles softly. "They happen 'cause God allows it. If he allows it, then it was meant to be for some reason we can't see yet. It's part of His Plan." Jayderay looks at him closely and continues.

"Honey, the way you been treated all your life 'cause of the way God made you, is not right; the way he lets RL lie and cheat to shame the devil, is not right, but it sure enough do happen all the time. God allows it. And that's what today is, something that God has let happen. It is the way it is. I accept that."

Frankie was about as religious as an empty beer can, probably less. But he knew her beliefs made the statements true for her. It is the way it is. He figures it will have to be the way it is for him too. For now—just for now— *only* for now. He sighs, looking at her.

"Jayderay, neither of those are hardly the same thing, and you know it." Taking a deep breath, he asks, "Okay then, what are you going to do? And, just what should I do?"

"You, Frankie, are going to keep your mouth shut. You hear? I want your promise. And me? I'm going to pray some more, take another shower and probably cry a little more. Then I'm off to the Roaton Place. Why don't you come on out— Wait a minute! Just what are you doin' here, why aren't you at the shop?"

"RL sorta gave me the day off. I, um, I kind of... treated a New York couple to a bit of... uh, a... a kind of surprise. And they were surprised. A whole bunch! What I did—"

"Okay, okay, you stop right there. I can tell I don't want to hear nothing 'bout this; most 'specially since RL sent you off. Well, as you're on the loose, why don't you meet me out at that spooky pile of a house? You likely to beat me out there, but there's a work shed in the back, you can start pokin' around in there. I got the keys, but it's best I don't let you have them. You do tend to get up to things," she smiles a little saying it. "And mind your promise, you don't say a word about none of this to RL. Not a word."

After Frankie leaves, she kneels beside Princess, holds the dog close, and rocks back and forth. The dog whines as she sobs out a prayer. Prays, does this devout woman whose God had allowed her to be raped.

"Thank you, Lord for sendin' me this wonderful dog and helpin' me get through this terrible time."

* * *

Frankie drives and giggles, but there is no humor. He knows Suga' Boo. *I never heard Jayderay use the nigger word before, but she's right, that describes that bastard.*

Frankie has had some dealings with Mr. Suga' Boo. He knows where that piece of shit lives. Frankie giggles some more. These giggles are definitely with humor. Frankie is getting up to something. It is about to be Showtime.

Parking a couple houses down from the address, Frankie makes some preparations. Frankie had been a boy scout, with somewhat less than stellar behavior, but he is always prepared. Then, adjusting the Covid required face mask and gloves, he pulls his 'Make America Great Again' cap from beneath the seat. Tugging the bill down low he saunters up to a house he's been to before. Been to several times. He knocks normally, not with harsh pounding that might sound like police. Standing directly in front of the peephole he holds some folded green beside his chipped tooth smile. He looks like a chipmunk with money.

A full two minutes pass with not a sound from the house. Frankie waits, he knows this type of drill. Abruptly the door is yanked open, revealing the esteemed Suga' Boo. Redolent with weed fumes, he's also towering and glowering. He's not a happy camper and has an obviously self-applied bandage taped over one ear... and a lot of blood stains showing on his shirt.

"What the fuck you want, you flat kneed glitter bug; they ain't no nigga' dicks for sale in here."

"Why, Mr. Suga' Boo," giggles Frankie. "You know you're really not my type, and besides, I'm needing some different kind of groceries," says Frankie, with his smile stretching further. *What an ugly, orangutang fuck this bastard is... and those nostrils... I could flip quarters up either one and never miss.*

The bloodshot eyes take a quick look past Frankie,

up and down the street, the simian brow wrinkling with a Suga' Boo frown.

"You lucky my bitch ain't here; she don't likes me doin' no dealin' from the house. Now, get yo' goofy white ass in here."

As Frankie steps inside, Suga' Boo shuts the door, asking, "And why in fuck you wearin' a raincoat?"

Frankie, with an ever-widening Cheshire Cat grin, just wiggles the money he's still holding up beside his chin. As the 'orangutang fuck' looks at it... Frankie thrusts an ice pick deep up one of those cavernous nostrils.

"And that, Mr. Suga' Boo, is for Jayderay. As she very recently told me: It is the way it is. God meant for this to happen, for reasons you can't see or understand. It's part of God's Plan. You must accept that."

There isn't as much blood as Frankie thought there would be. Nor is there as much *Showtime* reaction from Suga' Boo, either. He just stands there, quivering. And the icepick quivers too, looking quite appropriate imbedded up the man's spacious nostril.

"Nana loo to, to twiga do," Suga' Boo whispers, slowly sinking to his knees; the eyes widening with horror and crossing as they stare down at the ice pick handle. "Bondy, gond, gone, tool," he adds, swaying a bit. Blood trickles down from the other nostril cave, dripping off his lips and chin.

"Why, yes, Mr. Suga' Boo. My thoughts exactly; I couldn't have said it better myself," answers Frankie. "I do see that the sight of that pick is causing you some distress. Let me fix that for you, sir." Yanking the pick out, he quickly jabs about an inch into each eye. Detesting half measures, he then jambs the tool up the other nostril cavern. "There! That's even better, isn't it? Now you don't have to see that nasty ol' ice pick handle."

Suga' Boo sprays out a long bloody breath as he slowly topples backward, his legs folded beneath him.

"Comfy now, big man? Very, very good," says Frankie. He kneels beside Suga' Boo, who is a much better person now. As he checks for a pulse and finding a fairly strong one, Suga' Boo let's out a low, moaning, "Ple... pleas—"

"Why, I'm so happy to find you're still with me, Mr. Suga' Boo," interrupts Frankie. "I do believe you were trying to say 'Please,' is that what you were asking before I so rudely butted in? Well, in that case, I am here to help, yes I am indeed. First, let's determine that you can still feel things." Grabbing a fat thumb, he slowly forces it back until it makes a wet snapping sound. Suga' Boo also makes some wet sounds. Frankie is delighted.

"Very good, sir, you can still feel. I truly, truly do

want you conscious while I administer that help you were trying to politely ask for." While Frankie does his *administering*, paralyzed Suga' Boo— accepts it because... it is what it is. It's part of God's Plan. He does groan considerably at first, and then begins making a gagging sound. All of which Frankie is sure are expressions of gratitude. This time, he causes quite a bit of blood, making up for the disappointing nostril output.

Finishing his work, but still kneeling, Frankie says, "Please do remember, Mr. Suga' Boo, sir, that all this is for Jayderay. And that God intended for all this to happen, he allowed it to happen. It is what it is. And as a reward for you being so good about everything and accepting God's Plan, I will leave the ice pick with you. I do imagine this will certainly be a pleasant surprise for 'yo' bitch,' as you called her. Why, it'll be like she's won the lottery, when she finds your ugly orangutan ass all nice and dead. Which, from the way you bled during the last part of my help, you will be...very soon. Personally, I hope it's not too soon, I do want you to have a little more time to... enjoy."

Before standing, Frankie peels off his now very bloody gloves, tucking them in the raincoat's pocket. He then pulls five quite flashy rings off Suga' Boo's fingers. This is not an afterthought; he's wanted the gaudy things for quite some time. They will sell, and the silly bastard does have a business to think of. Venality is always present in any good business person. And Frankie is very good. Silly, but good.

"These will display ever so nicely in the shop jewelry case, and it so happens that I do know quite a bit about display. (giggle) But you wouldn't know about that, would you? My question is rhetorical, sir, so there's no need to try and answer. I realize, after my last bit of work, talking might be just a trifle difficult for you right now."

Slipping off his raincoat, turning it inside-out, Frankie folds, rolls, and then tucks it away. *Glad I remembered to wear that... it's my boy scout training: Always be prepared. Yes indeedy, and especially for Showtime.*

On the way out, Frankie spots and pockets a hefty baggie of what he knows to be some most excellent marijuana. This is a kindly gesture, which will keep the former owner from having any trouble with the police.

Looking through the door's peephole, he sees no one, exits casually and saunters away. Not that being seen was all that big of a deal; this wasn't exactly the type of neighborhood where people made calls to the police. Strolling gaily, tugging at his cap, Frankie has only one nagging regret. *Damn! I wish I could tell RL about this... but I can't. And besides, he's such a prissy shit sometimes, he'd probably think my last little Suga' Boo touch, was going too far.* Frankie giggles. He's such a gay and silly bastard.

Back inside, Suga' Boo lets out a long choking, gargling moan, and then a brief stream of flatulence. Both sounds are unusually loud in the empty house. These *might* be Suga' Boo's final comments to a very harsh world. Or, if cosmic justice is to be properly served, he will linger on for several more joyful hours... uttering a few more observations concerning God's Plan. It will be what it will be.

Jayderay might say, Mr. Suga' Boo — It is the way it is. Accept it.

CHAPTER 11

MEANWHILE, IN THE WAYDOWNS

Clenching Patty's legs with one arm, Darren feels them both being lifted by the flexing coils wrapped about her. Firing his Uzi up into the haze, he doesn't see the second tentacle, snaking silently across the control room floor. Coming fast.

An ear-splitting screech echoes from the murk obscured heights, and the tentacle gripping Patty goes limp, dropping them both to the floor. From across the room, the other tentacle closes in, trailing glistening webs as it ripples forward.

Out in the hall, with Elena's bone still clenched in its teeth, the Spill digs its twisted fingers into Huong's throat. Gagging, he wrenches the knife from the nearly gutted monster, plunging it deeper in, trying desperately for the heart.

Elena struggles to sit, making choking sounds,

drowning in her own blood as it gushes a red fountain. Hanging obscenely past her neck, the tongue forms a long rope of crimson horror, the upper lip dangles by a shred; the lower one, along with her jaws, have been ripped away. Blood smeared front teeth and gums form a grinning death leer above the gore as it pools out around her.

In the control room, Patty and Darren spot the other fast approaching tentacle, and scuttle back from the wreathing coils. Screaming as he empties the Uzi, they both scramble into the corridor.

"ABORT, GODDAMN IT, ABORT!" he roars, pushing Patty ahead as they run to Huong and Elena.

Huong's thrusting blade finds something vital, and the Spill gasps, spraying Elena's jaw from its mouth. Its hand drops from his throat, taking hold of the Khaki shirt, it jerks him forward, closer to its blood dripping teeth.

"Ton," it gasps out, spraying red, and then again, "Ton." The creature goes limp, collapsing back to the floor as Huong jerks away.

"Jesus fuck!" yells Patty, seeing Elena. Seizing an arm, she drags the woman toward the elevator.

As the dying Spill collapses, Darren pushes Huong away. "Run, go help the other two; I'll finish this," he yells.

"Wait! This creature spoke, should we take it?" Huong asks, his blood splattered face showing no emotion.

"Damn it to hell! Shit— we better. Grab a leg, and we'll drag it with us, but we've got to MOVE, there're things worse than Lab Spills back in that control room. And they're on the way."

As the crowded elevator rises, Elena lies on her side, in a spreading pool of her life. Mercifully unconscious, her eyelids flicker over all- white eyes. The tongue dangles onto the floor, moving with each of the woman's reflex attempts to swallow; her torn upper lip and jawbone are gone, lost in the retreat.

Back in the corridor, a web strewn loop of muscle unfurls from out of the vacated control room, feeling and searching. Part of a bulbous, pulsing green body pushes out some from the doorway, giving the tentacle more reach.

In the lift, Darren kneels beside the mutilated woman. "God damn it, Elena... just... god damn it." Unsheathing his knife, he whispers, "I'm sorry." And he finishes her. Standing slowly, still looking down, he speaks quietly, calmly.

"Listen up, you two. Elena died in the attack. Understand? She would've made too good of an experiment *volunteer*. I'm not going to have any of us disappear from our infirmary into... Gaust's hell."

"Fuck me!" cries Patty, looking down at the Spill. "Are you two blind? I think it's still breathing, and got tits with a split dick-pussy! Son of a bitch, it's a Spill Trannie, wow, fuckin' wow." She kicks the Spill's leg with her boot. "Hey, bitch, you alive?"

"What did it say back there, Huong?" asks Darren.

"It said, Ton."

"Ton? Like with a 'T'?"

"Yes," replies Huong, adding, "Said it twice, and with a woman's voice."

———

Below the rising lift, haze and the smell of discharged weapons drift lazily thru the vacated control room. Both tentacles have vanished. All is quiet, except for an occasional soft, bubble- pop from the yellow glowing mold. A bit of the Gunch pushes up slightly from one of the larger spots, stretches out a few inches, and then settles back onto the wall. It grows.

Patty's still warm Uzi lies where she'd dropped it.

The sound of slapping bare feet come from a connecting area. A figure appears out of the haze, wearing a Lab coat. Only a Lab coat. A definitely human hand picks up the gun.

———

Nearby, and unknown to the person picking up the Uzi, unknown to any other creature in these forsaken, twisted, and merged decks of the Waydowns, something is awakening.

In a large room that has remained shut and locked since the mutiny, it has lain there. Through the long years it lay across a rather odd, very uncomfortable bed. And it never moved— except for the growing. And it has grown; it has grown very slowly. The growth has been painful, always with pain, constant pain. With what mind it had, it dreamed through the decades, strange and ever evolving dreams. Dreams it couldn't understand. Dreams that were always filled with rage... and hate. But it's not dreaming any more. It is awake now. It wants to move. It has a mission. It wants to kill.

CHAPTER 12

BACK IN TOWN

A good bit after Frankie has left the shop, RL leans against the sales counter. He checks his nails, the creases in his jeans, and smoothed the blue chambray shirt. The perpetually worn jeans and work shirt are a front; so he can appear as an employee. Just a 'don't know nuttin' worker, perhaps the store's refinisher. RL does indeed do a bit of furniture refinishing; he sometimes spends as much as an hour adding several decades of age to a piece. And adding great value. Of course, it's all for the happiness of the buyers; they don't want *new,* that's not why they came into an antiques shop. It's just common sense and customer service.

RL disdainfully watches some Farmer John type get out of a worse for wear pickup. The truck is loaded with hay bales, the driver's got on a straw cowboy hat, and one cheek bulges hugely. RL hopes it's a tumor, but knows it isn't.

The man walks to the other side and takes a large

cardboard box off the seat, and RL brightens considerably. Merchandise! Then the yahoo pauses *after* he steps to the NEAT STUFF door, turns his head slightly to one side… and deposits a quart of tobacco juice onto the concrete. It splashes, leaving some lovely spots on the glass.

RL, sighs, it wasn't a tumor. What a pity. He pushes his rolled-up sleeves further toward the elbows, straightens up, and wishes he hadn't sent the silly bastard off.

Frankie handled hayseeds with the greatest of ease. If they were selling, he gave them a deep, but gentle reaming, and sent them happily on their way. If they were buyers, then they too would be destined for happiness… and a diet of Beenee-Weenee with grits till the next payday. All this made two other people happy as well: Frankie and RL.

"Howdy, podner!" booms the seed, coming through the door. "Since you in this here kinda bidness, I was wonderin' if you might be interstid in lookin' at some junk I drubbed outa my daddy's barn. Ain't wantin' much for it, just mainly lookin' to get rid of the crap."

RL decides he could like the man. *He's calling it junk, and it didn't cost him anything. And if I don't buy, he figures to toss it in the next dumpster he sees.*

"Well, sir, I'll be happy to," says RL, actually telling the truth. It didn't hurt this time, and no real dealer ever refuses to look. That's plain stupid, looking is free, and who knows what treasures may lurk with the brain deficient.

The box contains an old brass bladed, tabletop Hunter fan, an open shoe box, and a couple of cream-top milk bottles. The fan wears years of dust and a couple dirt- dobber nests. It's also coin operated with a metal plate next to the slot, reading: 5¢- 30 Minutes. It's an ancient hotel room model. The shoe box is half full of small, flat, round aluminum containers. None of this is junk. Not a bit; not to RL.

As RL looks with exaggerated fear at the fan, but before he can go into his 'I am terribly afraid to plug this old piece in' spiel, the seed speaks.

"I gotta admit, I was plumb too skeered to plug that old thang in."

"That's me too, sir! These old electrical contraptions can be very dangerous," says RL, giving thanks to the God of Yokels. "Of course, I do need to see if it'll even run, but it'll probably blow out all the store fuses." *It'll work just fine... the old Hunters last forever... and if not, I'll cut the cord off, and mark it: 'AS IS-MAY NOT WORK'...* "So, if I get electrocuted, you be sure and call 911, okay sir?"

"Oh, shoot, Podner, there ain't no need for no dangers. Tell you what, you can just have the junk," says the seed, working his cud around to the other cheek. "If you don't want it, I'll find a place and dump it somewheres."

RL decides he just loves this guy.

But then!—the evil, goat breathed reptile, this spawn of a diarrhetic demon, ruins everything. With the wad of tobacco changing cheeks again, he says,

"All this ol' crap come from me clearin' out space in the barn to make a kinda bunch of hidey holes for all them stray cats me and mom feed. You know, fix'em some more boxes up sorta high, so's they can feel safe. Then I stuff'em with old towels so they can keep warm come winter. We even got a propane heater out there for when it drops to freezin'. And any of'em that gets gentle enough, I take'em on down to that low cost spay and neuter clinic, so's to keep'em from havin' any more. 'Course others keep on showin' up," he laughs, "and we just flat ain't got the heart to run'em away."

RL's biggest weakness, besides women of course, is being a sap for animals. Especially homeless ones. He's crawled under houses after injured dogs, climbed rotten trees after terrified kittens, and carried idiot turtles across traffic screaming roads... *for no money.* Miracles do occur.

"I see," mutters RL. "Yes, well, I, uh, yes, I see, sir."... *I hate this bastard...* "Well sir, in that case, I'll give you… I'll give you… I will give you…three hundred bucks for the box full. IF you'll use it to keep caring for those strays." Lazarus rising couldn't compete with this wonder. But, oh, the pain of it, the pain, the soul scouring, bowel wrenching, sphincter shattering pain.

"GOOD LORD, PODNER! You ain't got to do nothin' like that! I really meant what I said, I'm just tryin' to unload this junk for whatever you feel like pay—"

"No," RL interrupts. "I insist, you take the money. You're doing a very good thing, and I want to help you keep it up. I don't… uh… I don't get many chances to… to help others… like I want to." Nausea rips through him, from toenails to hair; all of which may fall out.

Watching the happy seed drive away, RL does not feel the glow of doing a good deed. Not one damn, strangling, bit. He feels sick, gangrenous, and monetarily bereft. And he knows this act practically guarantees that he'll get his weenie fried off when he does try out the fan, because charitable deeds never ever go unpunished. *I better get Frankie to plug the fan in.*

Looking around the empty shop he says to the marble statue of David, "I'm gonna cheat the living shit out of the next fool that comes through the door."

CHAPTER 13

HAPPY WIFE, HAPPY LIFE... UNTO DEATH

The old man has been fucked to death. Well... nearly so.

From the day that evil, damnable, godless, hated breastplate came to Manfred Claude Wetzel's shop, the carnal obscenities had started. Those carnal obscenities that are still possessing his wife... and still consuming *him*. And they never cease. Never ever cease. Even after he'd sold the despised thing to RL, its vile influence had persisted. And the rabid ravishing of Manny had continued. Repeated, constant, never easing, never ceasing, world without end... ravishing.

And the damned thing had taken his teeth! Which Manny has not yet replaced. There has been no time, there has been ravishing. And Viagra.

Piece of armor my ass, it was something the devil squatted and shit out... Please, to fucking God, please let that prissy bastard RL call wanting to sell me his discards from the Roaton house...He's sure as shit sure had time to get that uppity preacher's permission to work out there by now. Please call you arrogant, prissy, rat's ass! And then maybe I can get away before the clutching deadly she-creature gets up.

There was no satisfying the rapacious, the ever grabbing, that ever-needing female maw... the wife. Mildred, aka Millie, aka 'Fluffy.' That doll faced tub full of lust who now lay slumbering ponderously upstairs. All 360, circumferentially challenged, pulsing pounds of her.

Manny had been molested in the kitchen, waylaid in the shop, raped in the bath, clutched, clawed, chewed and dry humped on the stairs. He'd spent more time on his knees than the multitudes of mecca. And in the BEDROOM!!! For the love of all the gods, what he endured in the bedroom defied description. Will this horror ever stop? Will her insatiable, cavernous itching never end? Manny shuddered. Manny shriveled. Manny wept.

The old man slumps in his office chair, resting a sweating brow on the desk's edge, both arms dangle to the floor. A milked cadaver. A *drained* cadaver. Three containers of Viagra lie nearby. Empty. And his booze consumption has been cut in half; he rarely has the strength to lift the bottle. But he must perform. He must. What if she left him? All the money was hers.

Besides, he'd discovered he really loved her. Damn it all to hell. He guessed he always had. Love, it's a hell of a thing. Recently it's been a hell of a fucking thing.

Sparkles pads into the office, tail wagging a bit, looking on in pity.

...the poor old codger, that big she- human seems determined to kill him. Continually taking hold of him, violently jerking him to and fro, ripping his pants down, and when she grabs his ears, forcing him to his knees... then what's done with his face is unbearable to watch. The little dog walks a bit closer, peering intently.

Is he even breathing?

Manny, that living corpse, rolls his head to one side and looks blearily back.

"What the frog fuckin' hell do you want, you little turd? Just give me a couple more minutes, and then I'll feed you— if I got the strength to open a can." He'd started feeding the dog down here in his office every morning, instead of up in the kitchen. Avoiding noise, for any noise might awake that Titanic Terror, and then Sodom and Gomorrah would fire up... for the day. *All* day.

Reaching a trembling hand to the favorite drawer, he pulls a bottle of Jim Beam out, setting it in front of him. *Brother Beam to the rescue, thy liquid is my staff, I shall fear no maw.*

Hearing a noise upstairs, his bowels clench and Manny starts gulping the dark golden elixir of his life, as the other desperate hand delves back into the drawer. And out comes a fresh container of Viagra; the old sot has become one of its most ardent fans. His pharmacist is exceedingly impressed.

A bit later, the stairs worn oak treads groan as the exquisite enchantress descends. Manny also groans, for she will soon *descend* on him. Repeatedly. Rapaciously. Her old boom-box booms, cradled in massive arms that will soon cradle him. And *caress*. Repeatedly caress. Rapaciously caress.

The steps creak dangerously; the boom box booms out Johnny Mathis, with a voice that could make bras unhook themselves and panties melt. Fluffy doesn't need the help. And Fluffy booms out as well.

"Oh, Manny Man, where's my little Studly-Wudly?" Sexual longing drips from every word.

The sultry, wanton voice penetrates the pill bottle little Studly-Wudly has just put down. Its lid pops off; at least something besides Fluffy is eager. Manny sighs, quickly taking two more. With forlorn hope, he looks at the phone, then at the shop keys hanging on the office mirror. Those dusty keys that haven't been used in days, very long days. There's been no opening up... at least not of anything those keys would fit.

How can any woman have so many... so many places? It's not fair... please, RL, please call, you prissy son of a bitch.

From behind, a hand grips his shoulder. A lovely hand with gently tapered fingers. A very needy, lovely hand. It begins kneading him. Tears come to the old man's eyes.

CHAPTER 14

BACK ON DECK 19

Dr. Moto, standing at Lillith's console, studies an x-ray of her growth. He frowns, negatively shaking his head slowly. In a dark corner, her new assistant still stares out at nothing, and is still very pregnant.

"It is definitely part human, but I do not see—"

"Oh, is it? Part human? Why, Dr. Moto, now isn't that absolutely astonishing. Your intelligence is positively breathtaking. This thing is developing in and of me, damn you, so I dare say it is part human. Christ's Shit, man! Can you remove it?"

Moto is silent a couple of seconds. Wondering if he's ready to kill this foul round- eye woman. But knowing the time isn't yet right, he answers her question by asking one.

"I've seen countless Spill bite infections, but nothing like this. How much of the alien blood have you taken?"

"That is not your concern. Perhaps you did not hear me the first time I asked; Can you remove the growth?"

"Yes, that can be done, but with your overall deterioration, if you didn't die, the recovery could be several months."

"I will not die. But I... WE, don't have months. That Extender must be found and brought back into my ship, and only I can orchestrate that. You should be able to inhibit this growth long enough for me to get that idiot Gosteen headed in the right direction. Go, make your preparations and be quick. And send Flail and Fail Gosteen in as you leave."

Minutes later, Darren Gosteen, the sweating and miserable head of Deck 19 Security, stands before Dr. Lillith Sally Gaust. Looking at her, with that bit of bloody fur sticking to her chin, he feels he'd rather be slamming Uranium Isotopes together. Or giving birth to an anvil. A large rusty anvil.

"Mister Gosteen, let me be sure I've heard all this correctly; you didn't secure ANY part of that Waydowns deck? And the Spill you brought back is dead? And Dr. Moto will have to find a replacement for one of your team? So, in short, the mission was what? A total shit spewing cluster fuck?"

"The Spill was waiting for us, Dr. Gaust, and I'm sure the attack was planned. We weren't all even into the first chamber when we were hit simultaneously, front and rear. I don't—"

"An attack on both front and rear? All *one* of them managed this front and rear attack? My, my, they do seem to be developing great capabilities."

"The Spill had help from some— some kind of new creatures. Lillith... Doctor, they were *waiting* for us," says Darren, as sweat blotches begin to show through his khaki shirt.

"Yes, waiting for you, so you have said. What type of 'new creatures'? Not just another insect mutation?"

"No, these weren't any of the Bugs; I believe, as you do, they've all died out. But these new things, all I really saw were their tentacles, and those had what looked like scales with spider webs hanging off them."

"Spiders... with scaled tentacles? Well, now that is good. I wish to hell you had brought me one, instead of that fucking dead Spill."

"I didn't hear it, but Huong claims the Spill did speak, and said the same word twice: Ton."

"Ton? Like the weight measurement? So what? Many can still speak, that means a total nothing. Are you sure it wasn't one of the escaped Almosts? There's no doubt they have fled into the Waydowns."

"Yes, I'm positive it wasn't, it's feet weren't trimmed, and I think it's—"

"Think? Can you think, *Mister* Gosteen? You've not shown me that, lately. But you're what I've got... at the moment," says Lillith, looking at him with boiling eyes. "Why did you even bother to bring me this *allegedly* speaking carcass?"

"Lillith... Dr. Gaust," pleads Darren. "Please listen, the Spill could be important. It may be hermaphroditic. It had breasts, a penis-vagina, and spoke with a woman's voice."

There's a moment of silence as Lillith digests this. She rubs her chin, dislodging the bit of fur. Darren tries not to follow its fall.

"None of that is necessarily indicative that it was a true hermaphrodite. Still, if so, that would be quite a development, and not one of ours. It might actually be descended from a birth the original human staff squirted out. Yes, that would be worth an examination. Well, maybe you are thinking, and there's some intelligence lurking about inside you after all. Somewhere. You were right to bring the body."

Darren is silent, accepting this rare but backhanded compliment, and not daring to jab the hornet's nest by thanking her.

"Disregarding your *current,* and latest, failed expedition, that trip topside you're going on has become more urgent. Thanks to that little shit Proby, the Extender is no longer locked in a safe. You, and at least one of your crew, are going after it. Take a woman, you'll blend in with the populace better. Pick someone who will liquidate without hesitation. I do not want any chatty witnesses left behind. And when you secure the Extender, bring it directly to me and only me. Mind me man, mind me!"

While Darren receives his orders, and gets his butt chewed off by Dr. Gaust, far beneath them in the Waydowns, something continues to struggle.

Behind a door that's been locked for decades, it tries, it fights to rise. The strange bed it's on has no restraining straps, yet seems to hold the creature down, and the effort to get erect is increasing its ever- present pain with a new tearing, pulling, wrenching agony. But it will not quit. It is awake now, and it must move... it *will* move. It must become mobile. What little mind it has left, knows... it has a deep need. A need that will be met.

CHAPTER 15

THE HOUSE AND THE SILLY BASTARD

The structure that would eventually become the Roaton home, had been built of lumber illegally harvested. At that time, such logging thefts weren't all that unusual, and rarely prosecuted. This particular thievery was a little problematic as it occurred on a sacred area belonging to a Native American tribe, known during this period as Injuns. But problems exist to be solved, and this one was.

Some bribes were offered, and naturally accepted. The tribe elders did have to murder a few of the tribe members who felt strongly that sacred areas should remain sacred. They just could not see things in the proper light. In all groups there are always some who insist on being... pains in the ass. The murders eased that pain. Considerably eased it, and the theft was allowed.

So the sacred wood was used, and the Victorian style mansion was psychically permeable from its very beginning. It soaked up the emotions and experiences of its residents. It absorbed love, caring and heartbreak from its original inhabitants, the Clements. And it learned of grief and loss when Mr. Clements died of a mule kick. Mrs. Clements stayed on with the help of her colored handy-man, Boy Wus, and the house learned of true friendship, of forbearance.

But when Widder Clements died, the Roaton family came. Mr. Roaton was strange and different; he was also infected with religion. Rabidly infected. And so the house learned of new things; it came to know cruelty. And horror. It quit fucking around with the learning and absorbing emotions crap after this. It began choosing people. It took people. It took them forever.

The Roaton house has taken many. It has taken them in different ways. It came to know them, know them very, very well. And a few survived; those that did... will stay for all time.

What this house has *never* known, is a Frankie. It has never encountered a silly bastard. The house needs to be careful.

Driving down the weedy, graveled drive, Frankie parks at the back. Having sampled a good amount of the very recently acquired Suga' Boo weed, he's currently a wee bit high... somewhere out past Mars. And he has no thoughts or regrets whatsoever about darling Suga' Boo. That's in the past. It is what it is, and after all, God intended it. It's part of God's Plan. Frankie is grateful he could help.

Walking languidly alongside the overgrown iron spiked fence, patting the dark green vines, he gazes up at the old, storied mansion. He's heard all the local spook tales, and about the body recently found skewered on a fence spike. He's also listened to RL's spit dripping lamentations about all the loot that just has to, *just has to,* be inside. Frankie feels, screw the spooks, it's the loot that matters.

Frankie, much like RL, doesn't care a sheep's shit about ghosts or dead bodies; neither have money or merchandise, therefore they can't be cheated. So they don't count. What does count mightily, is value laden merchandise... like the stuff that's supposed to be in this place. He's eager, he's high, and he's Frankie. What a combination.

Ignoring Jayderay's instructions to explore the outside buildings, Frankie ambles toward the front door. Not having the house keys is of no more concern to him than it would be to RL. The place is vacant and there's no one around. Hell, that's practically an engraved invitation. Actually, it's better, since being invited usually means there's some stuffy butt lurking about, who might think he needs to be paid for what he owns. Or other unreasonable crap like that.

The door stands slightly ajar, and Frankie is almost disappointed at this lost opportunity to practice his skills. Stepping into the gloom, he pauses as his eyes adjust; it takes a bit, as they're like bloodshot cherries in a slot machine. They need a little time for the spinning to stop. And Frankie is seconds away from a payout.

Glancing about, he immediately knows RL is right. ... *this place is absolutely loaded... as loaded as I am...* He giggles. Letting his eyes roam, they follow the sweeping staircase up to the landing. They stop roaming. He does not giggle.

At the railing stands a woman with closed eyes. A woman of shadows, only of greys and moving shadows moving within shadows. There is no color to her, or the lightly glimmering floor length gown clinging to her shoulders. She is all flowing shades of tarnished silvers, gloom, and pewter, like a charcoal sketch. Like storm whipped waves in a harbor. Raising one hand with a badly broken arm, she beckons to him. Her eyes open. Now there is color. Now there is a lot of color.

CHAPTER 16

AMY AND... HECKY

Hector has been in the old Roaton house too long. Way too long. He was supposed to grab something and snap a few pics, to show everyone back at school. To prove he's gotten in, and how tough he is.

"This Chicano ain't scared of no damn house, count on it, baby. Haunted my Meskin ass, if any spooks show up, I'll just unzip this throbbin' tamale of mine and scare'em off. Count on it, baby," he'd said to Amy. "You wait here on the porch; if you go in, you'll just start screaming, crying, and wet your panties." And in he'd swaggered.

Amy still waits, shivering at the front door, clutching her car keys. The night breeze hisses with darkness, muttering at her, whispering of death through the vine covered iron fence nearby. The same fence where an impaled body had recently been found. Very recently.

Hector erupts through the door, knocking Amy flat and stomping on a breast as he rockets to the car. He's screaming, crying and he's wet his panties... down to the knees. Count on it.

———·◆·———

Several days later: Lying on her frilly pink bed, Amy holds the phone with her shoulder. Her hands are busy brushing a dolls hair. Listening to Hector, she rolls her eyes in exasperation. She didn't really like him; he tried too hard to be macho. Unfortunately, for him, the tough guy act was diminished quite a bit by a whistling lisp. This wet noise was due to having two bottom front teeth missing.

"NOT SCARED?! You knocked me down, and then you ran over me getting to my car. AND you wee-wee'd your pants, *Hecky*," she says, knowing he hates the nickname.

"No, no, baby! It was just 'cause I was so 'fraid for you, count on it. I was only tryin' to push you toward the car. To save you, I, uh, I dint know you was still back there, I thought you was runnin' on ahead of me. Count on it," whistles and lisps this tough guy. "If I had remembered my Nunchuks, I wouldn't have come out so fast 'cause I'd have taken care of, that... uh, of what I seen in that house. Count on it." *You little gringa bitch, when I finally get your legs spread, I gonna ram you so hard my tamale gonna pop out your mouth... I'm gonna split you like a banana.*

"Oh, yeah, sure, I can 'count on it,' all right. Like I can count those pics and things you were gonna bring me from out of that house. Sure. I can really count on—"

"Look, Amy, I think I seen something, okay? And I dint have the Nunchuks, and like I says already, I was only 'fraid for you, so I dint take no time for nothing."

"I know you '*dint,*' Hecky. You sure '*dint*' take any time to get ME out of there. And you were so boo-hoo you couldn't even tell me what scared you. My—"

"I WASN'T SCARED! Just only for you, baby. Like I says already, I think I saw some kinda... I don't know... some kinda shadow thing." Hector truly didn't know what he'd seen, his brain refused to wrap around it. He hoped he'd imagined it.

Amy starts laughing, "You mean you ran from a shadow, Hecky? I can't wait to tell everyone at school."

"No, you ain't gonna tell shit, you little— okay, okay, okay. I show you; I show you I wasn't scared. You drive me out there again tomorrow night, and this time I won't forget my Nunchuks. And I bring out all the damn pictures and shit you want. Count on it," says whistle lisping bad boy Hecky.

Hector's beloved Nunchuks are two, foot-long sticks joined together by a short length of chain. They're a favorite of bad asses, and much easier to get than guns or switchblades. They are also a really effective way for those bad boys to knock some of their own teeth out while practicing. Just like Hector has done.

Amy sighs very loudly into the phone. Knowing if she turned him down, he'd start up with the racist bullshit again, which was the only reason for that first date. If anyone could call giving him a ride out to the old Roaton house a date.

"Oh, Hecky... I don't know. Why can't you get some of your gang to give you a ride? Since they're all so rough and tough. Then you can show me everything at school."

"I know what you problem is Amy, you just racist. You prejudiced against brown skin peoples."

Rolling her eyes again, Amy lays the doll between her breasts. ... *I knew he was gonna pull this crap... if he spreads that around to the other spics at school, I'll start gettin' tripped on the stairs, used tampons slipped into my purse... and no telling what they might do to my little car.*

"Oh, now Hecky, you know that's not like me. All right we'll go, maybe tomorrow night. But this time I'm staying in my car."

"Okay! Now you talkin' baby, and I ain't gonna forget

them Nunchuks this time. I'll show that shadow thing. Count on it," lisps tough guy Hecky... with a whistle.

Yes, Hector must remember his precious Nunchuks. They are going to come in really very handy. *For something.*

On their last birthdays, Amy was 15 and Hecky 18. They are unlikely to celebrate another.

CHAPTER 17

PLAYING ON DECK 19

Milk white stanchions rise from the deck floor, supporting another deck far, far above. Like exposed veins, an occasional rivulet of light purple liquid trickles down their sides, forming tiny pools at their base, slowly draining away to depths unknown.

Huge video screens set into curved walls constantly show films and ads from decades long past. A past time, a time of gold, a time when America's military were allowed to fight and win, a time when rock and roll was new, Elvis was king, and Proby had been... hatched. Conceived and born from the girlish crush and hormonal need of a brilliant and feared young doctor.

But sometimes— there are miscalculations, inadequate knowledge, alien equipment, and just plain old bad science... like someone not wishing hard enough— and things don't work out as wanted. And then... a Proby happens.

His gold lamé jacket sparkles as Proby wanders

aimlessly among all the fun machines he's stolen via the Extender. And occasionally he took people to become members of his teenage gang, but the humans never lasted very long. Lillith saw to that. Or like the last two, who had escaped with his help. Proby hasn't paid the price for that yet. But that reckoning is coming. It will be permanent.

Pinball machines blink, juke boxes softly bubble, arcade games chink and ring, and scattered street lamps flicker, creating an empty, deserted carnival effect. Manikins sit on motorcycles in dry fountains, candy and cigarette machines still hold their untried wares, and all the rest of this bewildering array of objects swiped from where ever Proby could find them. Products taken from an opulent, bored populace. Rows of them fill his vast playpen, his nursery, his prison. Filled with nifty keen, cool stuff, because he had just known, if he had them, he would be loved. But it never happened. Love never came. Only all this cold, cold fun. And loneliness, always and forever, aching loneliness.

Mommy and daddy aren't coming to play with you, little lost and lonely boy. They never existed.

He misses his last teenage gang, all two members of it. A too young, but tragically old, father molested, chattery street girl, Deena Lynn. And there'd been a young man, Carl, that Proby had actually become friends with. Proby called him Fabian, and truly liked him. In this cold-sleep area of the ancient ship, time was odd, stretchy, and their days together had seemed like weeks. *But if I hadn't helped them get away, Lillith would have taken them... it would've been awful, they would have died... if they were lucky.*

Proby blows out a disgusted, sad breath, palming back the sides of his pomaded, eggplant hair. Those sides didn't need smoothing, lard usually doesn't. *If only the Extender would open the portal, I could go back out, get some more volunteers, they always calmed down, well... after a little while they did... and maybe I could even find that big woman again... I bet she really would volunteer. Wish I had brought her back that time, instead of those stupid teeth that won't wind up.*

Unconsciously wiping greasy palms on black slacks, he stops at a coke machine, running a lightly scaled hand over its bright red top and rounded shoulders. 'One Dime! 2¢ bottle deposit.' reads the instructions. Tracing the flowing Coca-Cola script on its front with a lavender colored finger, his hand drops to the crank that would deliver a glass bottle out the door below. He wonders what the drink tastes like. *...why does everything I try make me sick? I'm... human... I'm like everyone else... why do I have to be tubed to feed?*

Hissing another sigh, Proby heads back to the twinkling, Christmas lighted arch that leads into the portal area. Beside the opening, a giant, beaming, cardboard Santa silently welcomes all. He wonders idly how many years ago he'd stolen them, and from where. He's going to check the portal screen again, hoping to find that the topside Extender has become stationary and is focusing. Then, out he can go. No, that isn't correct; out he WILL go. Having been told not to, is a guarantee of it... he's a kid.

Some things never change. Proby is, after all, still a teen. Just because he's in his sixties is no reason for him to grow up. He can't anyway.

This forever- teen is unaware he's living on borrowed time. And only because Lillith is too busy to bother with euthanizing her meddlesome failure. But she hasn't forgotten him. Dr. Lillith Sally Gaust never forgets. And this time she has a little hitchhiking Igor, growing on her shoulder, as a constant reminder. She has Proby to thank for the Lab Spill bite that produced little Iggy. No, Lillith won't forget.

And Proby, her once lover, her imitation Elvis cock-up, is minutes away from... screwing up. Again. Permanently.

CHAPTER 18

BACK AT THE ROATON HOUSE

The shadow woman beckons to Frankie from the landing, her charcoal hues rippling shadows into silhouettes. She opens her eyes; they're full of shooting stars, streaking points of white light within violet marbles. The dark full lips form a slight smile, creating gray dimples. The eyes become brighter, as their stars stream faster.

She is beautiful; it is a marred beauty, but beauty still. A scar divides one sable eyebrow, plowing across the nose and furrowing into a cheek. Both arms have been broken. Breaks that were poorly set and had badly, painfully mended.

Frankie walks to the stairs, passing pieces of fallen railing and balusters. He unconsciously kicks a wooden toy duck. It rolls away, trailing string among the debris, but he doesn't notice. Nothing else exists for him at this moment but this woman, her eyes. His shoes crunch on bits of fallen plaster as he climbs the dust swirled steps, but he doesn't hear. His only focus is the woman. This woman of grey fog and mists.

As each step brings him closer, the woman watches, turning slightly to follow his ascent. Her shoulder length hair of midnight ringlets, and the liquid silver gown sway slightly with the movement. She strokes the broken arms, sending shadows chasing shadows across the molten grey gown.

Under the spell of this smoke and shadows woman, Frankie advances as if pulled by ethereal strands. When he stands before her, she speaks. The voice is soft, her breath lightly fogging the air, as if from a deep cold well.

"I am Roaton. I am the house."

Frankie, still higher than up, stares into those entrancing, hypnotic eyes. And then he giggles. What else would a Frankie do. And he speaks.

"O, fairest of specters, I stand immobilized; entranced by your beauty... but you've gotten your timing all screwed up, woman. Listen, you gorgeous, overcast creature, don't you know the sun is blazing away outside?" and he giggles some more. Of course he does, he's sailing among laced marijuana moonbeams.

One hand flies to her grey-white, alabaster face, the fingers covering ebony lips with their matching nails.

Shades achieved without cosmetics. Her eyes widen, the facial scar darkening.

"And besides not being night time with a full moon, or having rain and thunder with lightning," Frankie continues, "I haven't heard a single moan, nary a wail, nor even the clank of a chain. Are you, what... kinda new at this? Or am I too low on your scale to rate a top performance? And, perhaps I should mention, in case you've gotten all dolled up in that sorta see-through gown for me... well, honey... you're scratching at the wrong kind of tree. My branch floats in the other direction. Get my drift?" And with that, Frankie gives her his best, chipped-tooth, boy scout smile.

The shadow woman stands silent for several long moments. And then behind her still raised hand, she laughs softly. Lilting, haunting, echoing laughter. The hand moves to her midnight ringlets of hair, patting it, as stars shoot rapidly within the violet eyes. And the dark mouth speaks.

"Are you sure about that, you pretty, pretty boy? Such a dear, pretty child you are. Do come with me, do come with me, lovely one. Let us try to discover more about which direction it is that you float," she says, softly taking his hand.

Her touch sends an icy thrill up Frankies hand. *His* eyes now widen to the point of dropping out. He doesn't giggle. His mouth is too dry, dry like the inside of an unopened pyramid. And possibly for the first time ever, Frankie is a little afraid. He should be. But he follows.

Hand in hand they go down the long, debris laden hall. Past the dusty, oval framed portraits of the long dead. She seems to drift along, leading him gently, while Frankie steps on dust that lays in odd, swirling patterns. His shoes cause crackling, warning sounds as they step on bits of old plaster and peelings from ancient wallpaper. But he does not hear the warnings. Frankie follows.

She smiles at him, a smile that doesn't quite reach those eyes of shooting stars, those eyes that have seen what eternity looks like. Her hand is soft, so very soft, so cool and dry, as if dusted with powder from unknown, faraway places. The faint smell of roses drift about her. Rose petals long pressed between the pages of a book filled with heartache; filled with memories never to be told. Frankie follows.

This woman of swirling mist and charcoal leads him toward the shattered window at the halls ending, the broken glass framed by long ago rotted drapes. And Frankie follows.

It is the window with the rusting iron fence below. That fence with the impaling spikes. A fence of death.

—————··•··—————

RL piddles and moons about his store, wishing hard. Wishing somebody with a low IQ and overburdened wallet would come in. He's also wishing he hadn't given Frankie the day off. Suga' Boo would echo this sentiment. Most heartily.

Finally giving up on any customers coming in, fleeceable or otherwise, RL locks the shop doors, and heads for the Roaton house. He is still aching from his largess with the hayseed. ... *no good deed ever goes unpunished; the seed was undoubtedly casing the joint for future burglary... caring for homeless cats, is he?... probably just till they're fat enough to eat. Such a lying bastard, and I just hate liars... I'm such a sap.* And so his thoughts go, never far from money. RL knows there are things in life worth more than just money. It would be best not to ask what they are.

RL grew up hard and poor, the two usually go hand in hand. And in some part of him, the lower intestine likely, he did know that money was not everything. *No, money isn't everything, but that's damn sure what it can buy.*

As RL pulls down the weed growing drive, he's a bit surprised to see Frankie's car, but he's glad. Frankie is good at spotting value in things that even the master overlooks. Besides, the boy is fun. He chuckles as an image of that innovative jewelry display pops into his mind. Such a silly bastard and always good for a mood lift. Almost as good as getting money. And he also wonders why Jayderay hasn't arrived.

...I hope that mouthy, snake-oil preacher hasn't cornered her. ... that slick, money grubbing, bible beater... Man of God, my butt... money is all he thinks about... he's a greedy asshole is what he is.

Knowing that not having a key wouldn't stop Frankie from going in, RL heads to the front door. And sure enough, it's slightly open. Calling out to the fellow crook as he pushes in, he stops before getting out the second yell.

Running fingers through his hair with both hands, RL stands looking, hands resting on his head, time passes. The house is totally silent, not that he could hear anything. He's counting money. Everywhere he looks, there's stuff worth money. Lots and lots of money. While he's lost in monetary reverence, his greed is having multiple orgasms, spurting gold into his bank account.

...I just knew this place was a gold mine, I just knew it... I can get—

A hand descends on his shoulder, and he squawks like a skewered buzzard.

"Sweet Jesus, RL! Didn't you hear me drive up?" asks Jayderay. "You 'bout left your skin behind, and your hair's stickin' out like a porky-pine. I'd blame it on a guilty conscience, but you most likely don't have such a thing."

"Damn it, woman don't do that! I was way deep in thought."

"What you was doin' was blocking the door like some model posing for shampoo. And I can just 'magine what you were thinking about," she says, glancing around. "I always remembered this awful place was packed. My gramma dragged me out here a lot checking on Uncle Wus when I was little. And dragged is sure enough the right word. My good Lord, ain— just isn't this plenty spooky. What's Frankie have to say about it?"

"Oh, yeah... Frankie. I think I yelled for him, but I never got an answer," says RL, finger combing his mop, improving not a strand.

"Well I doubt you would've heard the Holy Master's Call, deep as you were into bein' greedy. And I'm not gonna ask how you two got in; I don't want to hear the lies."

"I'll have you know the door was open already, Missy Holy Woman. Or at least when I got here it was."

"As if that would've mattered to you," she chuckles, and then calls out to Frankie, but gets only silence back. "Sakes, he can't be in the house, or he bound to have heard that he-man squall you let out. I guess he must be pokin' around in them sheds out back." She shakes her head, eyeballing the huge room. "As Gramma always said, the first step's the hardest, but *might* get the job done. Okay, I'm gonna get started workin' on some kind of inventory. So don't you just stand around droolin' in your wallet."

"Yes'm, Miz Scarlett, I done hears and obeys. But first I've got to get that breastplate out of the van," he says, grinning. "And then I want to give this place a quick walk through before I start."

"Well, mind that none of this belongs to you, till you pay the church, and just keep that Can of Evil away from me! Set it over yonder in that old recliner where Wus pretty much lived while he drank his self to death. It'll be awhile before we get that far, and I'm not even going to bother listing the nasty thing anyway. In fact," she says eyeing the lopsided, balding velour chair, "I doubt even Manny will take that."

Coming back in carrying that 'can of evil,' RL places it where ordered. And then smirking, he slips the garbage sack off. *...when she sees it's not covered she'll bust the snap off those tight jeans ... and it'll be good payback for scaring the bejeezus out of me... and for those jeans. Damn it, why does she wear them so tight, they make it hard for me to think... about business.*

Taking a garbage sack off of something. Such a

simple act. Such a small thing to do. But it is often on small things, that the fates of many are decided.

Climbing the stairs, RL marvels at the web coated oval picture frames, still aligned perfectly with the rising banister, cobwebs stringing from each bubble glass to the next. Dust and detritus of years lay in odd swirling patterns on steps, landing and floor. Downstairs, he'd been too overcome with loot euphoria to notice those same swirls.

Lusting with greed, RL oozes into the first room he comes to. And at once tries to open a child's camel backed trunk. It's locked of course, more of God's work for sure. But a locked anything is never a problem for him, or Frankie, or any true, bona fide, reptilian antiques dealer.

Looking for something to open the trunk, even a key, RL nearly trips over a drawer from a nearby chest. He figures it's evidence of the pilfering by the poor devil that had been found imitating a sausage on that rusty fence spear. *Serves the thieving asshole right… this is all mine to steal.* Of course, RL's stealing is usually done with money, by paying pennies on the dollar. The difference is only in the legality of the theft.

The room's closet door is open and from this angle he spots the top of a paper sack, far back on a high shelf. Scooting greedily forward, he stretches up on his toes, reaching and carefully lifting the brittle, ancient bag. It's heavy, it was hidden, it's valuable. And looking up hungrily, he gets it directly overhead. Over his head. Of course the bottom bursts open. It was full of coal. Aged, crumbled to powder, coal. Inanimate objects of all kinds are always waiting eagerly to shit on the living.

Coughing, spitting, blinded, and cursing, RL stumbles backward... and trips over the inorganic, lifeless drawer that had slithered up behind his feet. The bastard hadn't managed to trip him a couple minutes ago and it had been seething about it. These things never rest and are ever vigilant to maim a two-legger. Landing hard on his rear, jarring his fillings and vertebrae into giblets, RL decides to sit quietly. To sit and take the time to contemplate the goodness of life, and perhaps offer up thanks for it. *What kind of hog screwin' idiot puts coal in a bedroom closet? ... The kind that probably prays and obeys his mother, and other deviant crap as well... Well, isn't Jayderay gonna have fun with this... but... that's okay, she does kinda seem down... this sure ought to give her a laugh... Damn, I have to get to some water.*

As she looks through cabinets in the kitchen, Jayderay truly is offering up thanks. *...I should've looked out before I opened the door... I know better... but I do thank you Lord, I thank you for Princess, if* *not for her, I'd most likely be dead... and thank you for keepin' her from hurt... and I surely thank you for helping me keep all that terribleness from RL... 'cause if he was to get the story out of me...*

"Jayderay, is the water still on in the bathr—"

"LAND OF GOSHEN, RL! What happened?! Why, you, you—you a Black man! And it's a mighty big improvement, too," she says, howling with laughter. "Well, *now* you sure do fit that name of yours you always keep hid," says this kind, compassionate friend of his, laughing even harder.

Throughout his life, RL has had deep regret and sorrow over not having killed his real father. That drunken, beer barrel who had named his baby son: Rastus (no middle name) Leroy. What a good and clever joke. Understandably, the young *Rastus* had started hiding behind his initials.

RL catches his reflection from the window pane, and then he too start's laughing.

"Damn! Ol' Step N' Fetchit done ride again!" Dropping to one knee before her and grabbing her leg with both hands, he says, "Dis heah field hand is sho' nuff ready for yo' orders, Miz Scarlet."

Shrieking gleefully, she slaps him on the shoulder. "Oh, shut up, you, and rise Sir Rastus Leroy, grab your hoe and get on with—"

"AHEM!" politely coughs Preacher Dan, hovering at the kitchen entrance. "Perhaps this isn't a good time."

"Indeed, it certainly must not be," says a bacon lipped, scowling Mrs. Mable Keenly, who stands massively beside him.

CHAPTER 19

THE SECOND COMING

Inside Deck 19, Proby continues on his way to check the portal screen. Nearing the Christmas arch he notices a foul, rotting smell. Following his nose to an Archery game, he peers behind the canvas backdrop. And finds a dead Lab Spill with an arrow sticking out of one eye. *Huh! Deena Lynn must've missed the target and got herself a Spills-eye instead of a Bullseye... I better get this thing down a chute or Dr. Moto will blame me... or Lillith will... they do for everything else.*

After ridding himself of the inconvenient Spill's body, Proby stands gleefully staring through the portal screen. Which is now showing the Roaton house staircase. The Extender has been unmasked! All he has to do to activate it and open the portal is simply touch the screen. This is way too easy for any teen to resist. Especially a purple one, several decades old. He fidgets, smoothing his duck tailed hair, patting the artfully casual forelock, buffing both shoes on pant legs, and repeatedly looking in the direction of the elevator doors.

With a finger almost touching the screen, Proby stops, and stuffs both hands into his black slacks. ... *She'll know, she always knows... but I if I just do it long enough to find out where it's located... that's what I can tell Lillith, I did it for her, so I could come tell her, like I know she'd want... Sure, I'll be doing good... and I won't really be going out topside, not really, I'll just be taking a quick look around... I'll be helping... I won't really be going out.*

Even for a genetically spliced purple lizard, good intentions are an overpowering justification for doing a great many things. Proby can be so human. So, he activates the Extender. Of course he does, and the portal opens... and out he goes. So human.

Proby has just entered his very own Twilight Zone. He will find torment... and his dreams.

—••—

In the Roaton house, Preacher Dan and Bacon Lips Mable stand at the kitchen doorway, looking hard at RL and Jayderay with a disgust they'd use for a pair of drunken, fornicating lepers.

RL has just spoken in a deep south, Negro dialect. He's in black face, kneeling before Jayderay. *AND* he's clutching her leg. *AND* both of them were cackling with fiendish joy. They're silent now, transfixed in horror under the penetrating gaze of the two church poohbahs.

Bacon lipped Mrs. Keenly, dragon treasurer of Preacher Dan's church, was a black woman with exceedingly unfortunate skin pigmentation. An almost white coloring came out in streaks... on her lips, which were very full and mostly very dark. With the pigment they looked like strips of fat bacon. And at this moment, the bacon is frying. Bubbling, even.

"Brother Daniel, are these the two with whom you have seen fit to delegate the property Brother Wus bequeathed to our church?" Mrs. Keenly spoke with precise, correct diction; a Vassar graduate couldn't have said this any better.

"Yes, Sister Mable. But let me assure you; I've never seen a display such as this."

Behind this group, in the huge living area, a haze is developing around the breastplate. Spider webs of blue lightening flash and crawl across the metal. The haze forms into a cloud, growing bigger. The Extender is opening.

Mrs. Keenly is pushing out her pork fat lips to deliver a scathing indictment of the two sinners. Before she can start spitting grease, RL, an accomplished, impromptu liar since the cradle, or inception, cranks up:

"Well, *Sister Janice*," he says, "I'm afraid this will ruin our surprise for the ministry," he says, looking up at Jaderay with his eyebrows doing a Watusi dance.

Letting go of her leg as he rises, RL turns to the two shocked and righteously indignant church stalwarts. "We've been working on a play that we hope to put on for the benefit of the church, and of course to the glory of Jesus. It's about a poor ignorant, sinful wretch, who, after he finds GOD, pulls himself up out of poverty, and climbs the ladder to success. And he never once forgets that he could never have managed this spectacular feat without Jesus being by his side, guiding and leading him by the hand."

As he delivers this blinding fusillade of blather, back in the other room the breastplate fog has completely enveloped the velour chair, steadily pulsing bigger.

RL's lying also pulses bigger and better, being something he excels in, and the horrendously holy play is rapidly becoming a full-blown Pearly Gates Production. Every tiny bit of it all is to the glory of God. Of course. So much so, that any television evangelist would covetously lay claim to having written it. Lay claim with a lawsuit, a heavy, serious, lawsuit. It would be the Christian thing to do.

Jayderay, weakly but bravely smiling, has kept nodding during this tidal wave of deceit. *I'm so sorry, Lord... please forgive him. He just can't help the way he is.*

Preacher Dan is looking quite pleased, but Miz Bacon Mouth isn't swallowing any of this crap. Her huge breasts, looking like twin mortars, are pointed directly at RL, ready to fire.

But RL isn't through; he's seen the look on Preacher Dan's face and knows a sucker when he sees one. It's a gift.

"And so WE have decided, that with your good looks, you Preacher Daniel, are perfect for the starring role." Behind him, Jayderay makes a small, strangled sound, her knees about to buckle, but she keeps nodding and sickly smiling as RL continues. Her jaws ache.

"In fact, WE don't think even Denzel Washington could play the part any better than you will, Preacher Daniel. Especially the part when this poor man piously climbs to the very pinnacle of GOD- fearing success and achievement."

Bacon Lips is cooked, and she knows it. She glances over at Daniel, who is absolutely beaming. One look at that glowing countenance and even her two mortars droop.

"Well, I'm always willing to do anything I can

to further my— I mean, further our ministry," says Preacher Dan. "From the sound of this, I'm sure it will help our parishioners greatly, so of course you two will have the church's full support."

Sister Mable, silent, but swelling larger and larger beside the eager Dan, is unwilling to give up without at least firing a shot, says, "If I might inject some words of wisdom, I would like to point out tha—"

Jayderay shrieks, pointing toward the living room, yelling, "IT'S HIM!"

Preacher Dan and Bacon Lips whirl about, perhaps expecting to witness The Second Coming. But no, not exactly... it's Proby. And the sight doesn't agree with them.

Preacher Dan screams.

The always painfully proper spoken Mable, quietly says, "Mother Fucker." And bolts for the kitchen door that leads outside. A door located *behind* RL and Jayderay.

Proby, immediately recognizing Jayderay, squeals in terror remembering their last horrific encounter. Turning to run back into the open portal, he trips, smacking into the floor.

Preacher Daniel sees Mable flatten RL getting to the outside kitchen door. She can't get it open. Having tripped, the lamé coated lizard thing lays on the floor like a sparkly rug between the preacher and the front entrance. Daniel leaps the dazed Proby, and with celestial speed reaches the front door, snatches it open, and is gone. Born on the wings of an angel, no doubt. The door bangs into the wall and bounces shut.

As both RL and Proby try to rise, Mable gives up on the kitchen exit, spins about and surges back. She flattens RL again, steps on Proby's back, and runs to the first opening she sees... the portal. In she goes— and comes face to face with Dr. Moto. Calm, inscrutable, and wearing a blood smeared lab coat.

Mashed, addled and still prone, Proby looks over his shoulder and sees Jaderay again. Squealing once more, he scuttles into the living room, frantically aiming toward the portal.

Out of the portal barrels Mable. All of her. Lips and mortars leading the way.

Proby sees a pair of huge bacon lips zooming from the portal, directly toward him. Now, steadily wailing and totally disorientated, he takes to the stairs running on all fours. He should have a tail... like a lizard.

Mable, silent and sizzling, exits the front door with the grace of a locomotive.

Behind her in the lab, Dr. Moto, enigmatic as ever, calmy reaches over and terminates the portal opening.

It becomes a mere viewing screen showing a bit of the Roaton living area.

In the house, the deactivated Extender appears as nothing more than an ancient piece of armor, sitting innocently on the dilapidated recliner. But still uncovered, it provides a limited view from back in the ship. And Dr. Moto watches.

RL, still on the kitchen floor, looks dazedly at nothing. Jayderay, standing beside him silently gazing at that same thing.

"You know," he says tonelessly, "that thing sort of looked like Elvis."

"WHAT!?" barks Jayderay. "So you think it looked kinda like Elvis, do you? RL, how many times have I been tellin' you that these past weeks? Gramma always said men were born without ears, and I sure do believe it. Now get up off the floor, you look like a black—"

"Okay, okay," interrupts RL, figuring he'd rather not hear what she thinks he looks like. "Where did it go?" he asks, scrambling up.

"I 'magine it went back to fiery hell where it came from! And that's where you'll be goin' if you don't get rid of that breastplate. And *I'm* gonna see to that. I've had enough!"

"Jayderay, there's no way it came out of that piece of armor; that's just not pos—"

"FRANKIE!" yells Jayderay as the silly bastard steps dreamily into the kitchen. "Where have you been?"

Frankie stares blankly at them for a moment smiling. His shirt tails are hanging out, and the normally erect cowlick seems ironed to his head.

"Hi, guys," he giggles. And for the first time ever, Frankie notices how wonderfully tight Jayderay's jeans fit and how hard her blouse strains to reign in the two promises of heaven.

"I'm, not, hmmm, I'm not real sure where I've been; I think I kinda had a daydream. You know," he continues, "I was already having a... a really, a really interesting morning. In fact, a fella I used to do a bit of business with probably feels the same way. Anyhow, I just now, as I was coming down the stairs... from... from somewhere, a kinda lizard thing wearing a gold sparkly coat whizzed by me, goin' up. You two know anything about that? It sorta looked like Elvis."

"Oh, yeah, do tell," says Jayderay. "RL has suddenly become an expert on that. He's been tellin' me all about what that lizard looks like," says Jayderay, giving RL a disgusted look. "Did you see where it went, Frankie?"

"Not really, it streaked past me too fast," answers Frankie, needlessly and dreamily turning to point. The back of his shirt and pants are plastered with dust and cobwebs, as if he had been rolling in a bed of them.

"Well," says a reluctant RL, "I guess we better go look for it."

"No! *WE,* are not gonna go lookin' for it," says Jayderay. "*YOU* are. It's you and that Satan thing that's caused this mess. Frankie and me are gonna stay down here. But first, you're gonna get that devil tool out of this house. And I mean *now*, RL!"

Jayderay issues orders downstairs, while upstairs, a very terrified lizard, who does look quite a bit like Elvis, is trying to climb through a shattered window. If Proby can just reach the vines below the sill, he can clutch his way to the ground. Down there where the iron-spiked fence waits for its next donor.

Behind the sparkling coated Proby, a woman of swirling greys, mists and shadows silently approaches. A woman of no color, only shifting hues. Except for the eyes, her eyes have color. The shadow woman stops directly behind Proby as he struggles to maneuver himself between the jagged glass. She reaches out.

Downstairs, standing in the kitchen doorway, Jayderay watches with fearful determination as RL sacks up the breastplate.

"You lock that awful piece up good, you hear, and I mean it, RL. But now I think about it, maybe your van ain't— isn't a good idea. You'll lie, and say you forgot about it, then it'll end up back in your house. That's way too close to me and Princess right next door. Mercy Sakes! Only the good Lord knows what Preacher Daniel is gonna say about all this."

"What's the big deal about it?" asks a still dreamy eyed Frankie, lounging against the kitchen counter. He looks as if he needs propping up.

"Oh, Jayderay thinks there's a sort of voodoo-hoodoo about it, and that... that lizard Elvis, or whatever it is, pops in and out of that breastplate like a genie."

"You on mighty thin ice, boy," warns Jayderay. "I don't think it, I know it! That armor thing puts out smoke or fog from hell, and out jumps a purple imp. It *grabbed* me once, and yanked me into—well, I don't know where, but I do know I ain't goin' back."

Frankie straightens from the counter hearing this. "Well it doesn't have to be evil magic to open into another place," he says, walking past Jayderay. "Let me take a look at—"

"NO! You two vultures are not gonna start playin' with it in here, and not outside neither. I don't want to be around it, and I'm not bein' left alone in here. Frankie, you take it outside and lock it up. RL, you stay in here with me. As good a liar as you are, you can help me make up some explainin' to tell my preacher."

"Let me take it, Mon Capitaine, I'll look it over, then lock it up in my car," says Frankie. "No need for, uh, any difficulties." He wiggles his eyebrows like semaphores, rolling his eyes toward Jaderay.

RL cuts his eyes over at Jayderay, and quickly says, "You bet Frankie, that's a good idea. You take the breastplate and I'll stay in here."

Caught in the jagged glass of the upstairs window, Proby works frantically to free his jacket from a glittering shard. A cold hand suddenly grips his neck, and a voice utters, "I am Roaton. I am the house."

Proby, having lived with shock, horror, and monsters all his long life, doesn't shriek, squeal... or shit. He faints. And falls out the window. He truly is human. Almost perfect.

CHAPTER 20

MEANWHILE, BACK IN THE SHIP

"HE DID WHAT?! HE'S GONE TOPSIDE?!," yells Lillith, her saliva splatting against Dr. Moto's screen image.

"Yes," answers Dr. Moto, standing at the Deck 19 control station. He's keeping his usual inscrutability of an oriental coconut. But he's certainly not happy; this is happening too soon for his plans.

"And just exactly where were you, Moto?"

"I was following *your* orders, Doctor Gaust. I was examining the Spill's body, which does indeed appear to be functionally hermaphroditic. It was not chipped nor branded so it was never one of ours."

"Now that is interesting. Could it possibly be— No, never mind about that for now. Are you sure Proby is out of the ship?"

"As I checked on the portal I saw him when he

went through. Evidently the Topsiders unmasked the Extender and it focused. Proby must've been in there when it happened and went through. *You* have never turned that functionality off, Dr. Gaust, and you're the only one who knows how." From somewhere behind Lillith, comes an agonized, low moan, which she ignores.

"I'm very well aware of that, Moto. If I did switch it off, this deteriorating crap of a ship may no longer be able to turn it back on. So the little shit is topside, with no tracker attached. Christ shit on a centrifuge. Could you get any indication of the Extender's location?"

"No," answers the coconut.

"Damn it, man! Give me an answer; is it in a house, on a flagpole, at the bottom of a volcano, up your ass, or what?"

"All I could see was a curving staircase. It looked old, high- end residential but abandoned for quite a while. Without increased visibility, there is no way to tell. Didn't Gosteen manage to do some bounces off the Extender the last time it was active?" Dr. Moto answers while looking closely at Lillith's image. ... *the lump seems to be getting larger, despite the inhibitor... I could cage her, and see what develops... but... I'm not ready... I still need this round-eye harridan... well, O' Honored Hyena-Bitch, your death shall just have to wait a while longer.*

"Yes, he did," answers Lillith, "and he should be able to find it again in the same manner. He'll have to, as I'm sending him on a seek and secure mission for the damn thing. I must meet with him."

"I could go," Dr. Moto says smoothly. And he hears that painful moan again. That assistant must truly be hurting to risk irritating Lillith.

"No, Moto. I need you here. Plus, I'm not sure you could survive topside air long enough to complete the mission." *And I don't trust you that much, you little yellow viper...*

Moto watches as his screen goes blank. And he smiles.

———·•·———

Far below these two lethal assholes, an ever-present haze drifts languidly about on a long-ago sealed deck. Fog like, it floats in clouds which stretch, dissipate, and form again. Ancient technology runs mechanisms made far from earth. Their muted whirring and dimly glowing, forgotten dials, add to the air of abandonment. Weak lighting comes from everywhere and nowhere. White stanchions disappear into the mists above, where dark bodies silently move and coil.

Like something spewed from the terminally ill, a patch of wall mold breathes with audible bubble exhalations.

It raises and extends a yellow pod out an inch further, settling quietly back. Where the growth has reached the floor, small animal forms show beneath the blight's skin. Some still make occasional movements, others are skeletal.

Wearing only a blood-stained lab coat, a figure sits at the decks long abandoned control station. One eye slowly revolves in its socket, forever seeking light it will never see again. A tapered finger traces the crude marks of bad stitching running below that eye. The finger then switches absently to an ear missing its lobe. The other ear bears bite marks that will never disappear. But all areas are healing well, which is all that can be hoped for under these conditions. The other hand taps and strokes lightly on the captured Uzi. The coat, torn and dirty, hangs open, completely unbuttoned.

On the opposite side of this control desk, stands one of Lillith's defected Almosts. The khaki wearing, near-human watches and listens intently.

"The reclaim crew that bitch Gaust sent in ran like fucking rabbits when the Coilers dropped in. And they did follow my orders, which you weren't so sure about," says Ton.

"No never no sure what Coiler savvy. They hard understand," answers the humanoid.

"Yeah, you're right, Seevee, they are damn hard to

read. Just squatting there on their coiled haunches looking back with all those clustered, burning orange eyes. Nothing but another Coiler could know what they're thinking. But the bastards are definitely smart. Maybe too smart. We mustn't forget that. It might help us if we knew how and when they were bred."

"Much long time ago sure, Ton. Maybe made… start life maybe by orig'al staff humans. No know even how they nest-stay up there," he says, gesturing upward. "No know much how many. Spills sure much 'fraid of them. Coilers eat them much."

Ton laughs, saying, "Yeah, getting ate can be a serious fucking drawback for friendship. But we need them cooperating with each other. We can't take and hold 19 without them."

Ton studies the Almost about a minute, and then asks, "Do you think they'll follow if you lead a group?"

"If understand… maybe. Sure to follow you."

"Yes, I believe they would, and you and I can herd them all in together. But once we are in, that's it. Then I'm going after Lillith, no matter what. The rest will be up to you. Well, we've got time; we're not ready yet. And we damn sure will work it out. Leave me now, I gotta think."

"Can, will… take—keep 19 when take?" Seevee asks.

"Yeah, we can, and yes we will. We'll take it, *and* we'll

use it. All Topsiders on the upper decks are terrified of Lillith and never drop to 19. I have a plan... and I have someone who will help. That's all on me, you don't need to try and think about that."

A slight noise comes from a wall, as the ship slides out a tray. Like it's been doing since forever, delivering some tasteless, crumbly wafers. Presumably, protein... of unknown origin. Presumably life sustaining, and definitely nasty and cramp causing.

"Oh, great, more Crap Cake," says Ton, looking over. "I can hardly fucking wait. Hell, the mold doesn't even touch it. That shit's made for little green bastards from deep space. You and the Spills will eat it, Seevee, but you're not all human, the rest of you and your bunch is part whatever monster Gaust pumped into you."

The Almost stands, unspeaking while the hurt wrinkles his face. Seevee hates to be reminded of his mutations. He wants the woman to see him as totally human.

"Damn it, Seevee, you've got to find me something else to eat. I know there's plenty of animals creeping around down here; I've seen them."

"Some much no good— make Spills bad much sick when catch eat. Make Ton maybe bad much sick."

"Then find me some that won't, goddamn it! I don't think I can handle many more gas attacks. What about those weird, sucking, egg frying sounds we hear coming from inside those locked areas? Maybe that's some damn animal I could eat."

"No know. Find way to open, Seevee much catch for Ton. Maybe can. For Ton."

"Well, that sure as hell doesn't feed me now, does it?" she snaps at him, yanking her coat closed.

Seevee silently, sadly, watches Ton, as she fiddles with the Uzi, ignoring him. His hidden mandibles moving inside the human jaws.

"Luff Ton," he finally says.

"Hell no! Not now, I have things I must do, and I'm fucking hungry. Why don't you get your knobby ass in gear and go find me some decent food."

"Ton not understand, Seevee," he says. "Seevee *luff* Ton. Luff much."

"Yeah, yeah, I know fucking well you do. And you killed all your friends for me. I won't forget it. Now go away." Her blind eye darts about in agitation.

As the Almost shuffles dejectedly away, Ton buttons the dirty lab coat across the bared breasts. They have done their job again; she doesn't want to over use them. The coat has a sewn-on name tag. The tag reads: Tanya.

No, Seevee, I won't forget... and I won't... I can't ever forget what the Almosts did to me, and who gave me to them... that good Dr. Lillith Sally Gaust... oh, you bitch, you fucking cunt... when I finally get my hands on you.

Not too far from Tanya, on this labyrinthine and shattered Waydowns deck, something still struggles inside one of the many locked areas. Despite long years of inactivity, it is powerful; yet its repeated attempts to rise from the strange bed, on which it has lain for decades, have produced very little freedom. And they have been agonizing. Its head and body seem somehow restrained, held down in a way it cannot understand.

Stretching and pulling against the bed has caused excruciating pain but has only gained it an inch or two of freedom. It collapses... but slowly... stiffly, dust rising slightly from the furred back, and sounds escape from it. Very odd, grinding, breaking noises. It must rest for the next try. Rest and hate. Rest, but not sleep. Rest, but it will never sleep again. Because the worms, the parasites that awakened it, continue to burrow, continue to eat. They never quit, they never tire, they have teeth.

It grinds out those sounds again, into its bed. What mind it has left doesn't know of parasites, of worms. But it has enough of a brain to know pain. And hate.

CHAPTER 21

DIRECTLY ABOVE THE SHIP

The large concrete building hides a secret. This structure, and its asphalt parking lot, sits on top of the secret. A secret it has guarded since a long-ago discovery. A deadly secret.

It was from here, not Roswell, that in 1947, a futile escape attempt had been launched. A desperate, doomed flight that only made it as far as that nearby town. A short flight made by unintentionally revived creatures from an ancient space craft. Terrified beings, gasping for breath in air not of their galaxy.

Sitting alone out in the New Mexico desert, the white building squats on top of a crash site. Block lettering on the thick glass entry read:

CONSOLIDATED CONCEPTS

And below all this... is an ancient starship. An enormous craft, entombed in radioactive green glass created when it screamed into the earth. This wrecked ship was there long before any white man set foot in

America. It was there before the Indians. Very long before. And inside that vessel... there was life; frozen, viable life. Some of that life is there still.

⁂

Thousands of years after the spaceship's penetrating crash, the Gitchiegoomba Indian tribe, while out slaughtering other Indian tribes (as was their custom), stumbled across the partially visible wreck. No vegetation had grown anywhere near the site, which appeared to be a blessing. This made the place a perfect spot for camping, as the squaws wouldn't have to do any clearing and could get on with their other work. It also glowed faintly at night, which also enabled the women to labor late into the evenings. Women's work is never done.

After thinking he knew a good thing when he saw it, the tribe's medicine man informed his fellow Gitchiegoombians that this strange thing sticking out of the odd green rocks... was from the Great Beyond. Therefore they must stay and worship it. Must revere it. Must be thankful and revel in its presence.

So the tribe camped at once. And began consuming peyote, chanting, and offering up their sacrifices of sickly children and old women. As was their custom.

It soon came to pass that the tribe's drugging, chanting, and blood offerings to the Great Beyond were not enough to combat the radiation sickness that the crash site bestowed upon them.

Soon, the new congregation started puking out their peyote... along with some of their innards. Then the peyote came out another exit... along with some of their innards.

A few of the Gitchiegoombians eventually managed to recover from the benefits of the Great Beyond. At least partially recover, but not totally... the shits continued. These survivors held council, chanted... and had more peyote. As was their custom.

After much communing and even more peyote, they scalped, castrated, and then gently sat the medicine man on a sharpened stake. As was their custom.

Leaving the medicine man moaning and calling to the Great Beyond, the depleted tribe moved on... with frequent stops for intestinal relief. Fuck the Great Beyond was the general consensus.

The fleeing survivors did not totally escape the benefits of worshiping at the crash site. Future generations gave birth to braves of damaged thinking, who would soon sign treaties with the newly arrived and tricky white men.

The Gitchiegoombian descendants of those treaty signing manure spreaders, now own oil fields, casinos, and are called Native Americans. It's a funny old world.

———•◦•———

Far beneath the large, unadorned one-story building and its asphalt parking lot, a man sweats, worries, and plots. A man who often contemplates his own mortality. He should. He needs to; time is not on his side.

After receiving his traveling orders from the increasingly, shit-your-pants hideous Dr. Gaust, Darren Gosteen glares at his now blank screen. Muscles knot in hairy forearms as he massages his neck. *That lump on the wicked witch's shoulder is getting bigger... she's probably growing a second head, then there'll be two mouths spewing commands. But this trip might be my best chance... hell, it may be my last chance, to get out of this cursed ship alive. I'll get over to Texas, grab the Extender... and run like hell... the thing has got to be worth millions.*

There are decisions that can irretrievably change a person's life. And their manner of death. *I'll take Patty with me, that girl's up for anything.* Darren keys the Rec Room connection. And Darren seals his fate.

"Patty, front and center. Now," he says. Without knowing it, Darren has started the process of lowering himself into a flaming pit of bubbling tar. He will soon realize this, and also realize... it ain't tar.

Death Head Patty arrives with a swaggering gait, a cloud of perfume and no makeup. She doesn't need it, her overpowering presence glosses over the average, so-so face.

"All fuckin' right, boss man!" she says, her forehead skull tattoo getting brighter. It always did when Patty got fired up. "Get over to Texas for a couple days; this is just too fuckin' good. Man! Have I been wantin' some topside time, like real fuckin' bad. Hey! Can I have my phone back while we're gone? Or ain't I supposed to call nobody?"

"We'll pick up a couple of burners while in transit, but they'll be for our communication, only. And Patty, wear some kind of cap with a bill you can pull down enough to hide the tat. It's a little too... uh... memorable."

"Yeah," she laughs, "that's why I got it. I just love it when I'm talkin' to some guy and his eyes keep bouncin' back and forth from my tits to the skull. Kinda like yours are doin' now. Nobody don't never even see my eyes! But yeah, sure, I'll wear a cap, boss. No sweat."

Darren watches this crazy feral woman a couple seconds, fighting hard against the urge to grin. "Okay, Death Head, go get your gear ready to go. We'll be leaving ASAP."

"All fuckin' right, Boss man! Texas here we come," she says heading for the exit. "Hey!" she calls, turning back. "You gonna fuck me topside, ain't you?" Laughing, she swaggers out.

He sighs, shaking his head. *...I imagine I will, but I suspect that by including you on this trip, I fucked someone else even closer. ME.*

Darren is right.

Later, miles east of Roswell, New Mexico, Darren speeds a maroon Ford-150 down U.S. 380, and Death Head Patty fools with the radio, maniacally jumping from station to station.

"There ain't never nothin' on but shit, and I bet we ain't got no CDs either. We oughta stop and buy some. Hey, does this thing got any way to stream movies? And how long before we get there, boss man?"

"God Almighty, Patty," he says laughing. "You're worse than a little kid. We haven't been gone an hour, and it's probably another five to Wichita Falls."

"Well fuck me, I don't wanna— Hey! You want me to drive? I bet I could cut down them hours."

"No way, Death Head! We need to get there alive. Besides, your license is revoked, for good reason I imagine. And there's for sure at least two warrants out on you."

"Yeah, well maybe... but fuck'em if they can't take a

joke. YOLO! And all that kinda shit. Hey, you want me to check out this map thing screen, you know, like be the navigator?"

"Nope, done that and it's all up here," he says tapping his forehead. Why don't you take a nap if you're so bored," he suggests hopefully.

"Fuck that shit, boss. I don't need no rest; I'll sleep when I'm dead," she says, pulling on the bill of her black cap. "This is the first time I been outta the ship since I got hired. That big deal cash sign on bonus— so fuckin' what! I ain't spent any 'cept playin' poker, and nobody wants to bet anything worth shittin' with. Hell, I brung it all with me hopin' to have some fun. You taking me on this mission is a total fuckin' life saver."

Darren didn't do the hiring, but he knew the terms: Twenty grand, paid in cash to the new recruit when they were delivered to the white building. Another twenty thousand a month, to be paid in lump sum, *upon completion* of their one-year contract. None of them ever collected; they never left. The dead and eaten don't tend to travel or spend very much. And those that didn't die... wished they had. Some wished it for a very long time.

"Yeah, I could tell you were definitely getting buggy, and when this order came up, you were my first choice, kiddo."

"I know everything is like fuckin' top secret shit, but what is this thing we're goin' after? Cain't I at least know what it looks like?"

"Tell you what, we're coming into Lubbock, we'll stop, get something to eat, and we can talk about it. What would you say if I tell you now— what we're supposed to bring back is worth more money than you or I have ever seen?"

Looking at him, blue eyes gleaming, an imp's smile twitching her lips, she pushes the bill of her cap higher, revealing the grinning tattoo.

"I'd say you was thinkin' about not comin' back. Hey! You gonna fuck me in Lubbock?"

In a restaurant on the west side of Lubbock, Darren and Patty struggle mightily with two fiercely resistant chicken fried steaks.

"Wonder if they skinned this bastard before they fried it; a fuckin' dinosaur couldn't chew this," says Patty reaching for her iced tea. Taking a drink, she continues, "and the same cow must've pissed in the tea. Let's send this shit back, and get something—"

A tired looking, fifty something waitress, walks up interrupting her, "You folks doing okay? Can I get you anything?"

"This is the best shoe leather I ever had," answers Patty. "Think maybe you could rustle us up a chain saw? And I wouldn't douche with this tea— Ouch! God dammit boss, don't kick me!"

"No ma'am," says Darren, flashing a smile at the woman, while reaching over and gripping Patty's hand. "We're doing just fine, don't need a thing right now, but thanks for asking."

Nodding uncertainly while giving Patty a wary look, the server trudges off.

"Look, Missy, we *do not* want to draw any attention to ourselves. We don't need you boiling over and pitching a bitch everywhere we go. Got it?" says Darren quietly, glancing around and releasing her.

"Okay, okay, you ain't gotta be such a shit about it. I wasn't gonna do nothin' and besides, she did ask." Rubbing her hand, she says, "You mad?"

"No, Death Head, but don't let that happen again... and pull your cap a little lower, Jolly Roger is about to peek out."

She grins. "You got it, boss. So does this mean you're still gonna fuck me when we finally get a room in Wichita Falls?"

Darren sighs. "I thought you were all fired up to find out what this trip is all about."

"Yeah, 'course I am. I just kinda figgered you'd

be easier to milk for info if you was all laid out and pussified.”

Barking out a laugh, Darren says, “Eat the rest of that shoe, or you’ll be whining your hungry an hour from now.”

“Okay, *Daddy*. But are you? Are you gonna fuck me?”

An elderly granny-type, tapping along slowly, leaning heavily on her cane, heard Patty. Particularly the ‘Daddy’ and ‘fuck me’ part of it. It affected her... like an icicle abruptly finding its way up a private area. More erect than she’d been in decades, granny sped away. She didn’t need her cane.

“We’ll see... maybe... if you’re good,” answers Darren.

“Good?! Why you don’t know what a good fu—”

“I said EAT!”

Getting an *unplanned* for motel room, *very* close to that shoe leather café, Darren finds that with Patty, there is no post coital bliss. Only the calm in the eye of a Type 5 hurricane. As she comes out of the bathroom, he’s relieved to see she’s finally slipped her panties back on. A tattooed tornado rises from her undies, whirling about her navel. He thinks it’s very fitting. Darren has definitely been pussified.

“Well, Big Guy, are you gonna tell me now? Or is it

gonna take more fuckin'? I already figgered out we ain't goin' back, so what is it we're gonna steal? Hey! You think I oughta get a tit job after we sell it?"

"What makes you so sure *we* are doing anything like that, kiddo?"

" 'Cause I'm 28. You know what that means? It means I sure as fuck weren't borned yesterday. I know *WE* ain't goin' back. For one, you said back on the highway, that the thing we're *'supposed'* to bring back. And for two, I don't think none of us grunts ever gets to collect our pay, 'cause ain't none of us is ever lives or gets to leave. If the Waydowns don't kill us, somethin' else will. And you ain't no different; you just get sent topside sometimes when there's some kind of illegal shit to do. So, yeah, *WE* are gonna steal the thing, and *WE* ain't goin' back. You gots a partner!"

Darren looks at her silently; looks hard at this wild child, realizing there's a pretty good brain behind the skull tattoo *...she's right about all of it... but have I escaped from the fire, carrying a lit stick of girl-dynamite in my pocket? ... Could she be crazy enough to screw everything up if I don't partner up with her?... Do I have a choice now?... Yes, I do, but only if I kill her.*

Making his mind up, he abruptly throws aside the sheets, swinging his feet to the carpet. Reaching for his pants, he commands, "Get dressed."

As they drive west on dry, deserted U.S.277, the maroon truck sails through dying small Texas towns. Darren rests his wrist loosely on the steering wheel and keeps the big truck five miles above the speed limit. Knowing no trooper will be so consumed with his duty that he'll get out in the searing heat to issue such a paltry speeding ticket. He certainly doesn't want Patty's septic tank mouth spewing at the law.

"Okay," says Patty, "I don't really give a fat geek fuck how it does it, but I'll buy into this shit; that the Extender thing can open a door into the ship from a fuck ton of miles away. Right? Hell, I done seen lots and lots of movies about shit like that."

"Yeah, me too, kiddo. But this is the real deal."

"So what's the plan after we steals it? Hey! If this thing can open a door into a ship that's all buried in radioactive sand and shit, AND underneath that building... fuck me, man! I'm seein' plenty of banks and jewelry stores."

"Cool your bike, Death Head. The Extender isn't magic, it's part of a machine. Actually, it's an attachment from a spacesuit, supposedly in sync with a specific ship portal. We can't just sit in a motel room and tell it to open us a door into a bank vault."

"You mean that's *all* the fucker will open? The ship? Well, piss on that! Then what fuckin' good is the bastard to us?" Patty flounces back against the door, crossing her arms on her chest. Her skull tattoo is beginning to stand out against the pale forehead. "Fuck me, boss, I thought we was gonna get rich."

Laughing, Darren says, "Trust me, there are people who'll pay big bucks for it."

"Like fuckin' who? And you say it looks like a piece of Sir Dick Head's armor, how in fuck do we prove what it is? If we do turn it on, and it only opens into the ship, we're ass fucked with no grease. Right back in the shit pool." Her tattoo is in danger of leaping from her skin. She starts plucking at her black tee's neckline.

"I'll be damned, Patty, there's a brain running that foul mouth. Yes, it's a problem, and let me stoke your boiler some more; I don't have a clue how to turn it on."

She looks at him like a turd was emerging from each of his ears.

"Then what in hell are we doin' even goin' after the mother fucker? Goddamn it, this is bullshit. Listen, I gots a Softail Harley in storage, and twenty grand from that sign on bonus. You gotta have brung your money with you, right? So fuck'em, let's get to the bike, dump the truck and just run!"

Darren nods silently. *Why not.*

CHAPTER 22

BACK AT THE ROATON PLACE

As Frankie carries the breastplate out the Roaton front door, RL turns to Jayderay.

"Listen to me a second, please, Jady, I —"

"NO, RL! Don't you dare call me no Amos n' Andy name!" The effects of the earlier, psyche shattering rape, finally hits Jayderay full force.

"If I let you start callin' me that, then I guess next time it's gonna be *SAPHIRE,* and then I really will be the silly nigger woman that can't hold a man and is always chasin' after y—" her voice breaks, and she runs to the kitchen back door. Yanking and pulling, her shoulders shake as she sobs. Of course it's as locked to her as it was to Bacon Lips Mable. *...Oh, please Lord, please open it... please don't do this to me...not after this morning...please.* She leans into the door, pressing clenched fists to the sides of her head and sobs.

A man unmoved by a woman's tears is no man. RL is beyond stunned. Jayderay could not have shocked him more if she had slapped and kneed him in the groin. He has no way of knowing about the morning invasion Jayderay had endured, or how hard she has worked at trying to appear normal. Speechless, he walks to her. It takes him three tries before he touches her shoulder.

"I'm, I'm—I'm so sorry, Jayderay. I never meant to, uh, to... I mean, I didn't think, I mean I, I'm an idiot and my mouth shoots out stuff without me knowing, or, or thinking, or realiz—"

"Oh hush, RL. Just please... please be quiet," she says, turning to him, wiping at tears. "You an idiot alright, always and always, but you got no idea when or why." As she wipes at the still flowing tears, RL finally does something right. He keeps silent... and puts his arms around her.

Outside the house, Frankie studies the breastplate, while marveling about the weed he'd smoked earlier. ... *man, talk about some good shit... a roll in the sack with a Miss Smokey Panties...that can't have been real... hell the only time I've been in a woman was when my mother was pregnant... and what about that lavender colored, sparkly Elvis lizard... man, oh, man, I gotta get some more of that crap...*

Sensing movement above him, he looks up in time to see that same lizard tumble from the broken upstairs window, its gold jacket glittering in the sun.

An arm shoots out of the window, barely catching the limp reptile by its ankle, and slowly lifts it back up. The crooked, maimed arm looks like it has reached out from a charcoal portrait; a matching arm appears and helps pull Proby back inside. The now empty window looks blankly back at Frankie, the remnants of ancient curtains shielding mysteries, telling no secrets.

Frankie stands open mouthed, holding the forgotten breastplate. *Oh, yeah... I definitely gotta get some more of that shit... unless... could all this be... real? Maybe it would be best if I DON"T get any more...*

Looking down at the piece of armor in his hands he slowly shakes his head, trying to dislodge Elvis reptiles and charcoal arms. Walking to his VW, he sets it on the roof, slowly turning it around, letting his fingers roam over the burnished metal surface. Its interior is black, with round indentions, like forge hammer marks, but there is a uniformity to them that doesn't fit with beaten metal. *Could this thing have been stamped out on some assembly line?... Jayderay is no fool... well except when it comes to RL... If she says it can become a door into another place, and that an Elvis lookin' lizard can pop out of it, then I'm inclined to believe her, no matter how high I'm flyin'... so wonder what else might come out of it?... and from where?*

Backing up several steps, Frankie studies the breastplate. Behind him towers the old, vine laden house. The broken window stares, its jagged edges of glass look like gleaming teeth.

The Extender is now stationary and uncovered. It can focus. The silly bastard looks at it intently. And in a ship's lab, hundreds of miles away, an old Asian man looks back at Frankie. There is nothing silly about Dr. Moto. Nothing silly at all.

Back inside, RL holds a rigid, still crying Jayderay against his chest, her clenched fists jammed to her mouth. Turning gently and pushing away from his arms, she steps to the kitchen counter, snatching at a roll of paper towels.

With her back to him, wiping her face, she takes a deep hitching breath.

"RL, I'm sorry for this, I had no call to speak to you like that. You didn't say anything wrong. I had something really— really bad happen this morning, really bad, and it's made me... snappish. Don't you ask— 'cause I won't tell."

"Is there anything I can do? Please, I'll do whatever it takes, just tell me. Please." At this moment, RL would eat a truck tire if it would help stop the tears. No other moisture in the world can so debilitate a man.

"No," she answers with a sour, forced laugh. "Only

the good Lord and showers can get me over... what happened. You just forgive me and let's forget about this. Mercy sakes! I blew up over a silly name, I'm better than that."

"There's absolutely nothing to forgive, Jayderay. But I'm pretty sure I'm not gonna be trying out any more nick names."

Really laughing this time, she turns to him and says, "Yeah, that might be for the best."

"YOU'RE TELLIN' ME, GIRL!"

"Oh, shut up, you. Let me get to that filthy bathroom and repair myself. And then, we've got to do something about finding that Lizardy Elvis thing that's sneakin' around upstairs. Or least ways, *you* can since you the gentleman responsible for it being here."

"Yes'm, Miz Scarlett."

This is a couple who should be married. Needs to be married. One of the two knows this. The other, being male, doesn't have a clue. Men: they are the most stupidest of things.

That "Lizardy Elvis thing" is definitely upstairs, but not sneaking around. He's still unconscious from his faint, and is reclining on a jumble of very soft, very dusty bedding and cobwebs. It could be called a nest. He is about to revive. He may wish he hadn't.

———••——

Outside the Roaton house of enigmas, the silly bastard ponders the breastplate. ... *If I believe Jayderay, which I do, then this thing is capable of becoming some type of doorway... and if that sparkly coated Gecko-Elvis can pop in and out of it... so can I... Wherever this gizmo came from there's a lot more crap worth tons of money... Okay, so what makes it open?... I gotta talk to RL about this.*

Frankie is RL's partner, no doubt of it. Never a thought about discovering another world, verifying the existence of other intelligent life, or of the technology that would unfold. To hell with all that; it's about money. Money is what makes the *worlds* go around.

He's right. It is.

———••——

As Frankie thinks about dollars, many hundreds of miles away, someone else is thinking about Frankie. Through the portal, Dr. Moto watches the silly bastard and tries to decide if there is any way he could use him. ...*I'd rather have had that huge lipped negroidal woman that ran in here... she would have made a most interesting specimen… But this male looks like he might be… silly… might get up to mischief and be more trouble than anything else.*

As Moto nixes Frankie as a volunteer, the voice of command that comes from everywhere echoes out: "Dr. Moto, report at once."

Ah, the Honored Gorgon speaks, and I must obey. Yes, I must obey… for now. But soon things will be different, Yes, O, Foul Lotus blossom…things will be very much different.

Moto smiles as he takes Lillith's private lift down to her quarters, her lair. The great Dr. Moto makes a house call. Moto wasn't his real name; it was what the American POWs had called him while they could still manage speech. He had a gleeful, delighted appreciation of the name's origin and relished the perversity of it: a B-grade American film series, starring a Hungarian Jew, playing a Japanese agent. How asininely American. How deliciously wonderful.

Dr. Gaust receives him, still sitting at her control console, naked. That sight alone would've felled most men. The blood spotted towel draped over her shoulder growth pulses rhythmically. It has grown to the size of a large grapefruit. The massively pregnant assistant still stands in the same corner. Silently in pain, sweat beading the face.

"The inhibitors have not worked, Moto," Lillith says calmly, her hands rubbing one another, caressing scars where nails once grew.

"Yes. I noticed," responds Moto, keeping his face unreadable as a frogs. "But without extensive testing we cannot know what we're fighting," he says, his eyes examining her. She's a cadaver that hasn't gotten the message; her facial skin is stretched to the point of splitting, and the eyes so sunken they look out from caves. But life still burns in those caverns, twin pits of malevolent fire.

"We are not going to fight it. I have decided to let it develop. And so I need meat, living breathing flesh. Bipedal only. Do you understand?"

One upward twitch of an eyebrow is Dr. Moto's only display of emotion. He thinks at once of the silly man he'd been watching through the Extender.

"I do," he answers.

CHAPTER 23

AND IN THE WAYDOWNS...

The Lab Spill lurches through the whisps of fog that perpetually drift about in the Waydowns. Mortally wounded, it's still conscious enough to stay away from the corridor walls where the mold continues its yellow, carnivorous spread.

Cradling a ripped off arm to its chest, blood runs thick from the jagged shoulder hole. It doesn't really understand the thought processes that urges it to keep the limb, only that Ton will fix. And Ton will have water; the Spill must find water.

Wriggling toe tendrils curl and reach, leaving whorled bloody foot prints on the deck. Staggering, the Spill falls to its knees but doesn't drop the arm. Water, it must have water. Sliding on knees, one leg forward, then the next, then the other, as the toes writhe and push. It aims toward a towering stanchion melded into the wall, knowing moisture sometimes trickles down the supports, pooling at their base.

Nearing the column, leaving a trail of smeared red life, the creature's sight clouds with visions. Long ago images... of soft soothing hands, caressing. Of a kind comforting voice. Memories of being held by tender arms. Dim memories of being loved.

Still advancing blindly, it bumps into the stanchion, shattering the stream of thought. Whimpering, the tongue flickers out to the beads of condensation, and it licks the way down, then sucks desperately at a small puddle of a faintly glowing liquid. As the Spill drinks, the bloody shoulder socket brushes against the adjoining wall.

The unseeing mold had sensed movement. It was ready.

Gently stroking Patty's abandoned Uzi, Tanya isn't startled by the anguished wail that bounces down the corridor entry. Screams are often heard in the Waydowns. Wronged, abandoned, and hungry creatures fight desperately, and life is short down here. But this particular screech had sounded like a word: Ton. A call for her using the pronunciation learned from the Almosts.

Putting the empty gun beneath the control station counter, she walks quickly to the hall, buttoning her lab coat. Entering, she carefully slips each hand into her coat pockets, drawing a scalpel from one, a combat knife from the other. The knife had been liberated from one of Lillith's exploration sorties. The former owner no longer needed it; he'd managed to get himself into the various stomachs of a Coiler.

Ahead she sees a struggling human form lying on the floor, up against the wall. *...that fucking Gunch... that shit is going to take this entire deck if I don't do something...*

Kneeling about three feet away from the Spill, she sees why there hasn't been any more screeching. The mold has already extended its bubbling yellow skin across the creature's mouth, one eye, and attached itself the full length of the body. *... one of Lillith's more recent discards... this poor shit still remembers it was once human.*

Still gripping the mangled arm, the Spill holds it out as far away from the devouring Gunch as possible, offering it to Tanya. Pathetically believing that it can somehow break free from the parasite and be repaired. A glistening yellow tendril slips across the bridge of the Spill's nose, closing in on the remaining eye.

Edging closer, Tanya nods to the Spill, and reaching out, takes the multi-jointed arm.

"Yes, Ton will fix, I will make you whole. You must

close your eye. Keep it closed no matter what you feel."

Obediently, the Spill closes its remaining eye. A tear trickles back into the shell of its ear.

"Be very still now, Ton is going to heal you." Tanya's hand flashes out with the scalpel, severing the jugular. It pumps the crimson weakly; the body has nearly bled out.

"Don't move, Ton is fixing."

"Yes, mama... Oh! Mama, I see, I see..." whispers the creature.

As the Spill dies, Tanya stands, leaving the torn off arm laying on the floor. She is not beyond kindness; the Spill wouldn't have smothered when the Gunch covered its nose. The mold would have imparted enough oxygen for the beast to live for a long time, keeping it fresh... as the body was slowly absorbed. Life is short in the Waydowns, but death isn't always quick.

Watching as the deadly gold organism crept across the carcass, Tanya has an absolutely edifying idea, an epiphany. She now knows what fate awaits dear Lillith.

Later, Tanya sits at the control console, once again idly stroking the Uzi with one hand; she has clips that will fit the gun, dropped by Deck 19 invaders not as fortunate as Patty. Or found in Coiler excreta dropped from above. The fingers of her other hand trace the ladders of the various healing wounds about her face and ears, the blind eye swivels. She slowly unbuttons her lab coat. Tanya isn't hot.

Standing at the counter, Seevee adoringly watches her. His khaki shirt sleeves fully rolled down and buttoned, hiding the extra joints. Not by any order, he simply knows Tanya finds them ugly. He was once proud of them, they made him more than human; now they cause him disgust.

"So, what do you think, is it possible? Can we get some pieces of that damn mold up to 19?" Tanya asks.

"Through main'ence tunnel. Can. Maybe. Who carry no may never come back. Gunch get on... take, eat."

Tanya waves the carrier's probable death away with a shrug and the flick of her hand. "Where on 19 could we put it? All we need is enough time for it to get a good start at growing, and as we know, that doesn't take long."

"What for... why?" Seevee asks.

"That's my department, don't worry about it. How about putting it in Proby's big room? I'd love for that that trouble making purple bastard to get into it. You know where I'm talking about?"

"Seevee 'member. Can put there. Yes. But only Seevee know place."

"Very good, I know you will do just fine," she says, flashing a smile as the now open coat flashes other attributes. "So now I've got to figure how to get enough viable Gunch for you to carry... and live long enough to get there... and come back, of course. I need to think," she says, arching her back as she stretches. The unbuttoned coat spreads. "Leave me."

"No luff? No now?"

"Oh, Seevee! I just told you I need to think, and I've got a splitting headache." Seeing the Almost's face and shoulders droop, she sighs. "Okay, alright, alright; don't pout. But not real love though— you can lick my feet for a little while."

Seevee brightens. Yes, love can be a hell of a thing. Even for an Almost.

The Almosts had been selected from the best of Dr. Lillith Gaust's failures. They weren't the Übermensch she was striving for, but they could pass for human... after their feet were trimmed. Intelligent and with varying degrees of speech, they were given many privileges, including cooked meat. And they had been fiercely loyal to Lillith... until she gave them Tanya to play with. Tanya changed everything.

First, the Almosts deserted Lillith and Deck 19, fleeing into the Waydowns taking Tanya. Actually, it was Tanya who took them, but being males, they didn't realize this.

Next, jealousy blossomed among them, and then

challenges to Seevee's authority erupted. With a tiny bit of behind-the-scenes direction to guide him, Seevee solved those 'who is the boss' problems. He killed all the others. Murder can often solve many of life's little difficulties.

Yes, without actually *doing* anything— Tanya had changed everything. Only a woman can have such an effect. Just think about the Garden of Eden! Adam, that bowlegged chimp, never knew what hit him.

Fairly close to the tender love scene unfolding between Seevee and Tanya, an awakened thing continues its fight to break free from its bed. Earlier, it had tried to rest, but the parasites had kept up their rooting, burrowing torture. It couldn't rest, it couldn't sleep, it hadn't enough mind to think, it could only struggle. And hate. It had enough brain for that.

Jerking upward a few inches, the restraints catch, and it collapses back onto the bed. It jerks again, back it falls. And again. And again. And on. Each upward thrust gains it more fractions of freedom and a lot more agony. Each collapse causes the dust accumulation of decades to loosen and spill from the furred back. It makes its crackling, breaking sounds into the strange bed. It hurts. It fights and strains. And it hates.

CHAPTER 24

AND AT THE ROATON HOUSE

Somewhere in the Roaton house, Proby blinks his nearly all pupil eyes, slowly recovering from his manly faint. His first sight reveals a woman made of shadows. She is ever-changing depths of silver and greys that blend and melt into each other. Except for her eyes, the eyes have color.

Having been created and reared in a laboratory where freaks were so common they weren't even noticed, Proby isn't frightened. And this woman is certainly no horror; she's quite pretty and quite favorably endowed, which usually turns any male's brains into cornmeal mush. Proby, if nothing else, is male. He had been quite deliberately engineered for it. She swirls mistily nearer, the gown's hem gliding silently on the dusty floor. Stopping beside the nest of bedding, she looks silently down at him for a few moments.

"What manner of creature are you? You are not one of the goblins and trolls that often scuffle their awful feet through the hallways of my home," she says with a liquid, whiskey voice.

Kneeling beside the bedding, her low-cut gown moves silkily, revealing light scars on near- white, marble breasts. Very ample breasts. With the faint scent of ancient roses, she reaches out a delicate hand, touching Proby's glittery coat. "What lovely clothes you do wear. Are you able to speak? Tell me, what manner of being are you?"

Proby's sight is bouncing like an epileptic ping-pong ball, back and forth between the woman's eyes and her cleavage. Her violet eyes are filled with shooting stars, as a film showing a galaxy traveled toward with great speed. The exposed upper portion of the breasts appear as molten candle wax. Soft, very soft, very lovely wax. Avoiding the mesmeric eyes, he speaks directly to the wax.

" I'm, uh, I'm Elvis... I think. Um... can't you tell?"

"An... 'Elv-is'? Is that a type of Elf, a pixie? That would not disquiet me. You are an oddly pretty, pretty boy." She reaches from his coat and strokes his cheek. "I like pretty boys, and I desire them in a most unchaste manner. I'm afraid I have been so lonely... so lonely for so many years, that it has made me untowardly forward."

Proby has known loneliness; he's known decades of

it. Years of only movies for company. His cheek tingles from her touch. It's a very good tingling, and he feels this encounter is certainly going in the right direction. Raising one side of his upper lip in the Elvis leer he's practiced for years, he says,

"Well, you're a real pretty kitty and, uh... and bein' chaste is a waste, so we're gonna get on really swell as a belle. And I bet we can chase those chaste blues away, what do you say? But, um, uh... wha— I mean, who are you?"

One dark grey eyebrow arches quizzically as she studies him silently, her violet eyes alive with those streaking stars.

"I must say, you speak much differently from any speech which I have ever encountered." The almost black lips smile, ghost-like dimples appearing in both cheeks. "But that is of no consequence, I believe our needs are alike," she says pointedly, her cheeks blushing darkly. "As to who I am; I am the house, I am Roaton."

Still fixated on the soft, moving, very soft looking, breast wax, Proby asks, "Well, that's okay and cool as a pool with me, but how can you be the house? Not that it matters," he adds quickly. It really didn't matter; he was visualizing those orbs that make the waxy cleavage. This woman could've said she was a kangaroo, and

Proby would still want to crawl into her pouch. A name is just a name.

As she watches Proby's eyes trying to expose her breasts, the grey mist woman's smile widens knowingly.

"As to your question of 'how can I be the house'— I cannot tell you what I do not know. I do believe I was taken out of mercy, for I was once married to a man who owned this dwelling. Ezekiel Roaton; a silent, horrid, and cruel man. A monstrous man who treated me badly and often. And the house finally... took me away from him. It took me for all time, in a manner I neither understand nor can explain. But I do not think that is overly concerning for you. Is it, Elv-is?" Her gown slides ethereally from the alabaster shoulders, revealing the breasts. Those exceedingly ample breasts. Their areolas are nearly black.

"No, not, not at all," he gasps out in a strangling whisper.

Proby speaks the truth. Whatever the house has done, or will do, or fucking well might do, does not concern him at all. It could sprout giant, fishnet clad legs and do the Can-Can for all he cares. His only concern is this gorgeous, scarred creature... and what's moving in the crotch of his black slacks. It's his other brain. He is so human. So male human.

———···———

Downstairs, beneath the budding tryst, Jayderay steps from the bathroom with a look of disgust. By tacit understanding, neither she nor RL will mention her embarrassing, emotional outburst. It's what real friends do. Married couples too.

"One thing's for sure, Uncle Wus sure didn't hurt himself none by doin' any cleaning in that toilet. Sakes, it's the filthiest place in the house, and that's sayin' a whole bunch."

"Thanks for the warning, I think I'll visit the bushes like us field hands is 'posed to do, Massa."

"Oh, yes RL, I'm knowin' you will, and I thank you for sharin' that! Gramma always said the whole wide world was a man's outhouse, and it's sure enough true. Okay, never mind about men's nasty bathroom habits, what we goin' to do about the breastplate and that purple man-lizard?"

"Well, I'm beginning to think you're right, somehow, the Elvis thing does come out of that piece of armor."

"Glory be to God; the boy has done seen the light! Of course I'm right, RL. I'm a woman. But to hear you admittin' I'm right, now that is mighty close to a miracle," she says, chuckling.

"Okay, *Miss* Wise Soloman, now what—"

"QUICK, RL! Get under something.' You referrin' to

the bible... hail the size of boulders is bound to start comin' down any second."

Laughing, he says, "Will you quit it and be serious. What about the lizard? If it does somehow come out of the breastplate, then it has to go back in."

"Yeah, and probably tryin' to drag me along. *Try* is about all it would do! Sakes, RL, at that black sinnin' Gunther's home, that thing grabbed my... my rear, and it called me its *Negro* Honey! And don't you dare laugh, I'm warning you."

Turning red, choking down the howl that almost escaped, RL says, "You never told me about that part!"

"And you not gonna hear it now, boy; you'd enjoy it way too much. Least you would 'til I got hold of you."

"I bet it'd be worth it," he says grinning. "But I wasn't about to suggest that you be bait for our scaley Elvis. But when it does go back through the breastplate to Venus, or wherever, if we see it go in, we can sack up the armor. It doesn't seem to work when it's in that garbage bag."

"That do bring up a very good point, RL. Just WHY did you uncover it when you brought it into this house?"

RL had been hoping this little insignificant matter wouldn't occur to her. Being male, he pretends he didn't hear the question.

"Do you want me to look for the Elvis lizard thing

now? If I find it, it'll probably run back down here, then what?"

"And me down here? That's not gonna happen, RL. You get Frankie and that tin can of devil back in here. He can hide and wait with the sack, while you go look. And I'm comin' with you. Right behind you."

"But I thought you said—"

"It don't matter what you thought, RL."

This pair really should be married.

Going outside, RL starts to explain the plan, but Frankie interrupts him.

"O, Fearless Leader of mine, this gizmo," he says, pointing to the breastplate still on top of his VW, "is ET, big time! I believe Jayderay; that Gecko-Elvis does come in and out of it; hell, *he's a spaceman*. And if he can somehow use it like a door, then so can we. I bet we can find and bring back tons of stuff worth lots more than that snazzy coat he wears." He giggles and adds, "But if I see one like it over there, I'll come back wearin' it."

"And what a surprise that is, Frankie. Calm down, because before you and I go shopping on Neptune, we've got to get our spaceman to go back inside the thing. If we don't, Jayderay is gonna revolt. And I doubt I could buy anything from that damn church without her. We sure don't want that; there's some way high dollar merchandise in this house."

"But just think what we'll find out *there*," says Frankie, pointing at the armor.

"Yeah, like maybe death, Frankie. What's *here* in this house is money in hand, not wafting about on planet Uranus. We get what's here, first. Then we'll see. Don't be so damn greedy."

Frankie looks at him a couple of seconds, as if wanting to ask where the real RL is.

"Right you are, O, Mighty One, you are absolutely right. I must remember that and not be greedy. Tell you what, I'll start imitating you, how about that?

RL bursts out laughing, "Point taken, Frankie, point taken! Okay, let's get moving on this reptile round up," he says, reaching for the breastplate.

CHAPTER 25

DR. MOTO FETCHES

Miles and miles away from the Roaton house, Dr. Moto stands at the portal screen, watching and straining to hear the two crooks. *My, my, getting the Honorable Dragon's lunch might be easier than I thought... If I activate the Extender right now, the silly round-eye will simply stroll in... he wants to...* Moto smiles gently. *Yes, just in time for dinner. If they both come in, I'll prod them, and keep one for her next snack.*

RL spoils the doctor's plan by abruptly reaching out and picking up the breastplate. To Moto, it appeared as if RL was stretching his hands into the control room, and suddenly the monitor screen went blank. The Extender was being moved and could no longer focus.

Moto shrugs philosophically, knowing things were rarely that easy. The rolling blankness of the screen only prompts him to consider the lunch alternative. The security and maintenance bunch tended to be on the rough and ready side. He could end up with his high voltage prod stuffed up his own Asian ass. That left only the labbies and geeks, who were still jumpy after Tanya's recent disappearance. Still, when need calls.

While often joking with the staff, Dr. Moto came across as elderly, kind, and quite jovial. Possessing the gift of gab, he used it often with the civies. Obviously incredibly old, there was no harm in the doctor; he was a really good person. Really a nice man. This good and nice old man also had the empathy of a trombone, and the emotional capacity of a maggot.

Moto, having spent most of his lengthy service time in the same cold sleep areas as Dr. Gaust, only looked old. The ship's ancient, sporadic time-treatments still functioned in those rooms. The time rippling effect had provided Moto the same extended life that it had given Lillith and Proby. It had also changed Dr. Moto's... wants. Made his needs more... *earthy*.

Assuming the stoop shouldered, old codger shuffle he used when around employees, Moto arrives at 19's central station. Nodding and smiling at Tanya's replacement, whose only important function was keeping an eye on various warning lights. And several switches that had clear plexiglass boxes affixed over them. These were labeled UNKNOWN. Some of these were actually *known*, but defied civilized terrestrial description. Particularly those that had enabled the ship's original occupants to relieve themselves. Previous experimentation with these switches had produced interesting results... along with screaming and very fast trips to the infirmary.

Casually checking the duty roster, he then shuffles off, heading to Lillith's private lift. Rising through the upper decks, he gets off on the ground floor of the nearly deserted building squatting above the ship. Opening a door onto a long, white tiled hall way, Moto carefully leaves the door open. The door has no hall- side knob. Nor do any of the others.

Walking springily now, Dr. Moto follows the white flooring into the reception area. He smiles, nodding at the lone man busily pecking away on a computer behind the sparkling clean and bare counter. Seating himself on a chair not designed to encourage waiting, he gazes out patiently through the thick glass and lettering. Watching heat waves rise from the baking asphalt lot with its sprinkling of cars. Smirking, he notes that most of the vehicles are from Japan. *And who was it that had supposedly lost WW2?*

Rewarding the patience, his prey arrives, parks, and heads for the entrance. Moto stands, assuming his old man slump and benign face. *Oh, very good, a chubby one.*

"Why, hi there, Dr. Moto! Man this a/c feels good,"

says the young woman, entering, fanning a hand in front of her face, and shaking a bouncy pony tail. "It's hotter than a fryin' pan out there! And you're kind of a surprise; I've never seen you up this high before, aren't you afraid you'll get a nose bleed?" laughs Debbie.

"Well, Debra, that blasted staff elevator has gone glitchy again. So, I've been chosen by the powers that be, to lead everyone *Down To The Depths Of Labor*," he intones, grinning and waggling snowy white eye brows.

"Then lead the way, O, Kind Sir. I can hardly wait to put on my cool and fashionable lab coat."

"Believe me, I know exactly how you feel," he says, trudging toward the hall with its waiting open door. "I've worn mine so many years, I feel positively naked without it, though I shudder at the vision that might bring up."

They both laugh gaily, passing through the one knob white door, chatting the few steps to Dr. Gaust's forbidden lift. Moto makes a little bow, extending an arm and allowing her to enter first. Debbie says, "Oh, my! Such a gentleman you are, and thanks for showing me the way, I would have never been able to fin—"

She collapses as Moto jams the prod into her spine. *Ah, so! The Honorable Rotten Cunt's luncheon is ready, warm, and breathing. But first, there is the little matter of ME.* The lift descends, and when the doors slide open, he seizes Debbie's pony tail, lifting her top half effortlessly, and drags her away.

With Lillith's growing wound keeping her office bound, there is no problem finding a place of privacy. Dr. Moto has his requirements, his needs, and they are best met without an audience. He very carefully strips the young woman, with much admiration and touching. Using the prod again, when she gave signs of reviving. Turning her face down, his breathing becomes increasingly harsh and labored as mucus runs in strings from his nose. The swaying snot curls and loops about on Debra's pink skin. His mouth drips.

Moto's desires are not sexual. No, not really, they're not exactly, precisely sexual. But they are extremely, extremely perverse, repugnant, and... ingestive.

CHAPTER 26

BACK WITH DARREN AND PATTY

Hunting a motel in Wichita Falls, Darren drives by a billboard advertising Dignity Funeral Homes. There are few things that pass by Patty without a comment. This is not one of them.

"Well fuck the fuck out of me! What kinda goddamn dignity is there in bein' gutted like a fuckin' fish and then dumped in a hole? Buryin' is bullshit. I watched a bunch of that show 'Six Feet Under,' and what a crock of fuck all that funeral shit is. Don't you think so?"

"I've tried not to think about it, kiddo. The job we're leaving held a lot of promise for death, but none and less for getting buried."

"Ain't that the shittin' truth! Okay, so I've been thinking of what all you said about that Extender thing," says Patty with her usual lightning quick change of subjects. "I guess we could at least check out where it is and see if the fucker is easy to steal. You DO know where it is, right? You ain't got any more of them surprises, like not knowin' how to turn the son of a bitch on... do you?"

"Yeah, Death Head, I know where it is, and the directions are right up here," he says, tapping his temple.

"Well if it ain't, I might do some of that tappin' on your skull like you're always doin,' but I ain't gonna use no finger. Hey! There's some kinda Air Force Base here, ain't there? Hell, they're sorta connected to outer space shit, they'd probably jump on gettin' a chance at the Extender. Right?"

"Maybe. And I've thought about that quite a bit. But what they'd probably jump on, is us. The organization we work for, and plan to steal from, is somehow connected to the military, and has been since... well, I guess since way before WW2. I'm sure it's hidden under all sorts of privatized fake companies, and only known by some of the high up brass. Anyway, if we just show up trying to sell the thing, IF they thought it was real, then word would go through some very quick channels. And we'd end up in a cell, trying to answer all kind of sticky questions."

Darren suddenly brakes, swerving to avoiding some idiot who, like most, shouldn't be driving anything more complicated than a stick-horse. Patty helps by spewing out a stream of complementary phrases at the driver, with appropriate friendly finger gestures. She turns back to Darren, the idiot driver immediately forgotten.

"So fuck those Air Force cocksuckers. We don't show it, we just tell'em about the Extender, what can they do? We got it, they ain't, and if they want it, they can put there fuckin' money where their mouths is."

Darren sighs. "Well they sure wouldn't believe us if we didn't show it. But even if they did, they'd react the same way, and what they *would* have would be us, you and me, kiddo. And all the time in the world."

"Well, yeah, I guess there is that. But hell, we could hire a bunch of lawyers, and they could spring us, right?"

"And how are those lawyers going to know about us? We're not going to be allowed any phone calls—Oh, screw all this crap, missy. Let's first see if the Extender is gettable. If we get it, then we go from there."

"What if it ain't? What if we cain't get the fucker? Are we gonna still be... still be like partners?' The skull tattoo is beginning to stand out on her forehead, and the neck of her tee neckline is getting rubber-banded again.

Darren heaves a deep breath, looking over at her. "Do you want that? If we don't get a bunch of money, would you still want us to stay together?"

"Yeah, I would. Either way." She keeps plucking and pulling on the neck of her tee. "Look, we already gots a fuck ton of money, and you... you— you the only guy I ever gave a fuckin' shit about that's smart and knows enough manners to keep his mouth shut when he eats." She throws herself back in the seat, the tee's neck is stretched like a tempted priest's libido, and the skull tattoo dances.

Darren bursts out laughing. "I swear, that's the—"

"DON'T YOU LAUGH AT ME!" she screams, hitting him full in the face with a round house slap. "You son of a bitch, who the fuck do you—"

She's slammed forward as Darren brakes hard, narrowly missing a turning car in their path. Their truck jumps a curb, careening across a sidewalk and into a parking lot. Before he can fully stop, she lunges back at him aiming for his neck.

Darren grabs both her wrists as the truck comes to a full stop. The muscles in his forearms knotting into ridges.

"God damn it, Patty, what the hell!?"

"You think I'm some kinda fuckin' joke? You gonna laugh at me?" Spit flies with the words, as she fights to free her hands. She's strong, insanely strong, her teeth bared, lips red, wet and dripping saliva.

Darren is losing his grip on her arms. He has no

doubt she means to claw his face off. He has seen her fight.

"I ain't some white trash whore you can fuck and laugh at, and then dump as soon as you—"

Darren shakes her so hard the back of her head bangs repeatedly into the window glass, knocking her cap off.

"Shut up, goddamn it; shut up and listen to me! I was NOT laughing at you— only at what you said about me eating. Understand?" He gave her another hard, head banging shake. "Do you understand me? Jesus Christ, girl."

Slightly dazed from the window smacks, she stops fighting his grip. Beneath the spikey thatch of straw-colored hair, her forehead tattoo still throbs purple, but the madness is fading from her eyes. Her mouth hangs open, lips and chin shining, running wetly with spit.

"Patty," he says, looking everywhere for police or anyone else watching. "I'm going to let you go and get us the hell out of here before the law pulls up. DO NOT jump me again. If you do, I swear I'll break your jaw. Do - you- understand?"

She nods without speaking or taking her glazed eyes off his face. As he releases her, she sinks back into the seat, and Darren quickly drives across the lot, turning on a side road. And got them out of there. Fast.

Constantly darting his eyes over at her, Darren plays a guessing game at getting out of the neighborhood they're in. Patty silently watches him. Lucking his way out of the maze, he gets back on the main drag, turning in at the first motel he sees. Parking far in the back among a scattering of vehicles, he takes a deep breath, and turns to her.

Before he can begin, she speaks for the first time since he had released her.

"I'm sorry," she says, still staring at him. It's the first time he's ever heard her use the phrase. She turns, wipes her mouth on her arm and looks out through the windshield, fighting inner demons. "You can dump me here if you want. It don't matter none to me." There are no voice tremors, no tears, no emotion.

Darren studies this psychotic woman for several moments, maybe more. Seconds can last a very long time.

"No," he finally says. "We make a good team, Death Head. I think we should stay together... if you think you can keep from tearing my head off— at least while I'm driving."

Turning back toward him, a grin struggles to appear. "Yeah? Really? Huh! Well, fuck me! Then I guess you better let me get us a room. 'Cause you got a big ol' slap mark across your face."

"Get the room," says this man with the big ol' slap mark across his face. Darren is doomed, he knows it, and he's come to the realization that he really doesn't care. He'd made his choices and received a death sentence long, long ago. There are roads that have no exit; once taken; travel it. Ride it. Ride it to the end.

Patty travels that same road; the road of the damned. She was on it years before they met. There is no getting off. She can't.

There had been no childhood trauma in Patricia's life. None. Born to an average, lower middle-class parents, in a reasonably quiet neighborhood, with fairly good schools. There had been very little trouble at home or in the classroom, just the usual back talk, not doing homework, not minding or paying attention, etc. There were no warning signs.

And then came age thirteen. And then, Little Patty became... fried tits crazy. It's a medical term.

— • • • —

Much, much later, they arrive back at the motel after a late dinner. And too many drinks at an armpit dive. A place that Darren felt Patty would feel comfortable in... and not cause trouble. Like ripping some smart mouthed fool's face off. He didn't bother her with his reasoning for choosing the spot... it might not have been good for one of them. Parking among the other vehicles, they fail to notice the only lighting is a full moon. Management was evidently conserving on electricity.

Darren hurries around, opening the door for her, and she laughs at this, but thanks him, easily sliding her arm around him. Both are alcohol unsteady, weaving and chatting their way through the parked cars. Stumbling, talking, laughing, they pass by a long semi-tractor trailer, taking up several parking spots. Two men creep from around the huge rig, silently coming up behind them.

Patty leans into Darren, and says, "Hey, you gonna fuck me again when we get back to—"

A pistol smacks into the back of Darren's head, knocking him down but not out. As the second blow lands, the other man grabs Patty. Throwing her against one of the massive tires and twisting her arms around to her back, he swivels his lower body sideways, pressing his hip into her. She cannot knee his groin, and he pushes her arms higher up her back, sending a sharp pain shooting through both shoulders, totally immobilizing her. He's had practice. But this is Patty.

She can see Darren a few feet away, lying face down, the gun wielder towering over him. The man pinning her against the semi, grinds his hip into her. Shoving a fat whiskered face closer to her, his eyes gleaming with delight and malice, his voice is a high, stinking whisper.

"No, whore, he ain't gonna fuck you, but we sure are, and we don't need no room for it. You be a good, quiet piece of ass, don't make us no noise, and maybe we let your boyfriend live. We got us a nice comfy cot in back of the cab, and you're taking a little road trip with us. Gonna get a real ride, you are."

The other man, wearing a snap button western shirt, still points his gun at Darren. Bending over, he starts working Darren's wallet out of the back pocket.

Turning her head away from the whispering fat lips, Patty sees Darren try to rise. The mugger straightens up and kicks a point-toed boot into his temple.

With a low guttural sound, Patty turns back, plunging her open mouth into the fat bastard's neck, teeth sinking in, tearing and jerking at the sweaty meat. As the jugular is torn open, bright arterial blood spurts across her face and the big man staggers back, with his life spewing out. Clapping both hands to his gushing throat, he lets out a whining moan, sinking to his knees, eyes wide with shock and disbelief.

Hearing the moan, the gunman looks over incredulously at his blood spurting partner. Stunned beyond thought, he just stands there, the gun forgotten in his hand.

And Patty is on him.

Grabbing the pistol barrel, she forces it back, snapping the man's trigger finger, while her other hand claws deeply into one eye, nails ripping downward. He screams as the gun is wrenched from his broken finger. Still gripping the barrel, she swings the pistol, crashing it into his jaw. Stumbling back he claps a hand to his ruined eye. He raises the other hand trying to fight Patty off; the splintered finger sticks out at an impossible angle, showing the sickly white of bone.

His own wetly glistening bone is a sight that's too much for this pistol packing tough guy. This toughie who silently attacks unarmed people from behind. He's had enough entertainment for one evening. Deserting his dying partner and their tractor trailer, he skitters away through the parking lot, disappearing into darkness.

The fat mugger, swaying on his knees, with blood drenching through his fingers onto a flannel, plaid shirt, slowly topples over. And dies. He too has had enough.

Stuffing the automatic into her waistband, she kneels beside Darren. Rolling him over, his eyes flicker several times and then remain open. Looking up at Patty's blood smeared face, his first thought is: *What now?*

Taking his face between both hands, Patty looks into his eyes.

"Baby? Darren? Honey, can you hear me? Can you?

Listen, a couple of fuckin' shit kickers tried to rob us. They clobbered you from behind and you been out. But we gotta split really quick, like fuckin' now, 'cause I sorta killed one of them."

"How nice for him," croaks Darren.

CHAPTER 27

GOING FOR GUNCH

Back in the Waydowns, the mold is proving to be quicker than Tanya had thought it could be. A lot quicker. After losing two Lab Spills in attempts to capture a viable specimen, she now directs a third, terrified volunteer. She's using the captured Uzi as encouragement to keep the volunteer... volunteering. It has no way of knowing the gun isn't loaded.

"You have to get close enough for the shit to get into the glass," she says in exasperation. "Goddamn it, you! Quit jerking back, the fucking Gunch isn't going to leap from the wall and bite you. You're safe."

The Spill rolls its eyes downward, looking at the still struggling forms of the two previous Gunch wranglers. Those two squirming figures are almost totally enveloped by the shiny, bright yellow fungus. Only the tips of their still wiggling fingers protrude from the mass. It glances over its shoulder at Tanya and Seevee, looks back down at those wiggling fingers, and finally at the test tube it's holding. The creature makes a couple of low unintelligible grunts. It's the Lab Spill equivalent of: "Yeah. Right."

"Ton," says Seevee, "maybe get, push chair… can pull back, Gunch will stick, maybe can."

"Yeah, that's a good idea, but I doubt the crap will attach to a chair any more than it has to that test tube. That shit must be able to sense living tissue, but if we could tie the Spill in the chair…"

Quite a screeching struggle later, Seevee pushes a wheeled stool toward the mold festooned wall. An exceedingly unhappy Lab Spill sits, securely lashed to the seat. Tanya had finally gained the creature's cooperation by gesturing with the Uzi and telling it the alternative was being shot and given to the Coilers. Threat of the Coilers did the trick.

Seevee maneuvers the stool closer, as the Spill extends one trembling, multi-jointed arm toward the wall, clutching the glass vial. The fact that Seevee is holding on to the chair, is a slight comfort for the Spill. At least it can think it will be snatched away from the wall as soon as it has scooped some mold. And, yes, it will indeed be yanked away… after *enough* Gunch has been obtained. Seevee wouldn't bet on the creature's future. Life, like love, can be such a bastard. Even for monsters.

Safely watching from a distance, Tanya holds a glass specimen case, it's about the size of a shoe box. It's perfect for holding a severed, mold dripping wrist and hand.

Behind a locked door not far from the Gunch gathering trio, a nearly mindless creature continues its fight. It's still struggling to break free from that bed it has lain across for so many years. The odd bed that has such a tenacious hold on it.

But this thing has managed to buck and jerk its way free another inch, increasing its distance from the bed's surface, allowing a little more room for more powerful upward thrusts. With every straining effort, the dust of years shifts on the coarse, matted fur of its back. Grinding sounds come from deep within the creature as it gains, it hurts, but it does not quit. Hate drives it, consumes it. It will be free. It must.

CHAPTER 28

MORE MEANWHILE AT THE ROATON PLACE

Somewhere in the Roaton house, Proby lies amid a tangle of dusty sheets. He doesn't mind the dust. Not at all. Beside him, propped on her elbow, a woman of mists and shadows languidly strokes his lavender cheek. He has no memory of removing his clothes. He has a very clear memory of the woman removing hers; the gown had cascaded off the marbled body like a waterfall. A waterfall of swirling greys... and ecstasy. Proby's ecstasy. The body she'd revealed was as tarnished silver, its hues constantly moving like liquid. Proby's hands had also moved. Constantly. Like liquid.

Leaning in closer, glossy ringlets of her black hair brushing his chest, she peers closely at Proby's skin. "What amazing coloring and skin you have, Elv-is. Why, it is as if you have another layer of skin beneath, perhaps like... oh, I cannot say, I cannot think of the words. It is of no consequence. You make me most happy, and *that* is of great consequence."

Proby saw no reason to tell this passionate, ashen goddess that he did upon occasion shed his upper skin. That just might be of *consequence*. When those times came, they had usually occurred when he was tubed, put in a tortured, deep frozen sleep for endless months. Bombarded by movies and advertisements from a bygone era. They had played continuously. He had been raised on, educated by, and nurtured by them.

But there had been a couple of shedding's during his playtime. Looking in his Groomer mirror, he'd been horrified seeing a huge lavender frog inside a loose-fitting condom. And even worse, a blight beyond words: his hair fell out. That's true terror for any species of male.

"Jeepers Creepers, you cool as a pool, pretty kitty, you sure make me sappy-happy," he says, looking down her body's mist colored length.

"My disfigurements—they do not offend you?" she asks brushing her fingers across the dark grey scars that crisscross her breasts, stomach, and thighs. They match those across her back and buttocks. She raises a crooked arm, further showing her damage. Her shame, her deformities.

Proby looks sadly into those star- shooting eyes.

Proby knows of being hurt. Before answering, he moves and gently kisses the badly mended arm, and the dark scar across her face. Laying back, he again looks directly at her. Dropping the 50's cool cat jive, he speaks.

"No, they make you real, and they only make me mad. Mad and wanting to kill whoever did this to someone as wonderful and beautiful as you. Who did these awful things?"

"My husband. He whipped me and my daughters often. And he hurt us in... other ways. We were blamed for the lust that drew him away from God and made the poison rise in his loins."

"Where are your daughters? *And where is HE?*" Where is he right now?" Proby asks, his voice becoming guttural, his eyes totally black, skin darkening; a very pissed, purple reptile.

Proby is in danger. A danger from that most pernicious of all dangers. A danger he has never before experienced. Ever. It's called love. It can kill.

"My girls became infected with a foul, bleeding disease that I can only guess came from those Troll creatures that sometimes appeared. The house took my daughters, but in a manner different than my taking. They are still here, and I can sometimes feel their presence, but I have never seen them."

"And the man? Where is the man?" Proby asks again, his eyes smoldering, glittering.

"He passed on many years back," answer this beautiful, violence marked woman. "He departed by his own hand, and beyond anyone's reach. He looked to the ants to rid himself of carnality by way of pain. Parts of him may actually still live, but only in crawling pieces. I have occasionally seen those that I knew to be *of* him. But I've not found one of those small beasts in—" Stopping suddenly, she cocks her head, listening.

"Elv-is, I heard—"

Proby sits up suddenly, interrupting her. "Yeah, me too. Something's coming up the stairs. I think there's two of it. What'll we do?"

Downstairs, Frankie waits in the Roaton kitchen, holding the garbage bag in readiness to sack the breastplate if Proby returns to it. *...but what if that purple Elvis thing doesn't run back to the gizmo? Besides, the thing didn't look dangerous to me. Hell, it looked terrified... I bet I could make friends with it... at least long enough to find out where the goodies are at when he goes back in...taking me with him.*

As the silly bastard, looking like a greedy boy scout, thinks about pilfering treasures from another world, RL and Jayderay climb the winding stairs. Slowly. Quite slowly, since she's hanging onto one of his belt loops, and he isn't just real keen on finding the man-lizard. ... *Maybe it bites. Maybe it's poisonous. Maybe it's got big fangs. Maybe it's... hungry... maybe...*

"RL, we want to get up there sometime today," she whispers.

"Well... you're holdin' me back," he hisses.

"Yeah, I guess that's why I keep bumping into you. You want me to wait here?"

"NO! Uh... you might get... frightened."

"Frightened of what? You runnin' over me galloping back, or dyin' of old age on these stairs?"

"Oh, do be quiet, it might hear us!"

"I 'magine the thing has already heard all this loud thumping."

"What thumping?"

"Your gizzard, RL. Now, how 'bout you try and at least *move,* like maybe once an hour or so, okay?"

He doesn't answer but manages to mount the next step. He's helped by Jayderay lifting on the belt loops. In his mind RL is seeing: Fangs, big Fangs, hideous Fangs, huge, poison dripping Fangs.

Upstairs, that terrifying lizard with the huge, hideous, poison dripping Fangs... is cowering beside his shadow woman. With lowered voice, Proby bravely asks her where they can hide.

"Do not fret, my pretty Elv-is; they cannot find us. Nor are they likely to hear us... unless you do some more squealing as you did when we loved. Even then, they would only hear our sounds as if from afar."

"Oh! Okay, then... but are you sure... uh... Shadow? Gee, I just realized... I don't even know your name."

Laughing softly, her midnight lips kiss his ear. "Yes, I am quite sure they cannot find us, you brave and pretty boy. My name is Anna, or it was before that existence became more than mind could bear. However, I do think 'Shadow' is ever so nice; it has a soft resonance. I shall be Shadow if it pleases you."

"*YOU* please me... Shadow, everything about you pleases me. You're so soft, so beautiful, so wonderful," says Proby, looking into those fabulous, those heart capturing eyes. Placing a hand on her shoulder, he slides it gently down her back. Feeling the scar welts beneath his fingers fills him with sadness for this woman. He knows much about mistreatment. Too much.

"You are only being kind, Elv-is. Of the few people that come here, most scream and run at the mere sight of me. Loneliness has long been my only companion. I look in the mirror and know how I must appear to—"

A crashing noise from the hall breaks in on them.

"I, uh… I believe those somethings are getting closer," says Proby. "How can they not be able to find us?"

"Elv-is, this house is… my home is… 'I'… am a mansion of many rooms. Not all appear to everyone or can be entered, except by me… and mine. Is this confusing to you?"

"No, I can dig it,' he answers without hesitation. "I got here through something called an Extender. It can open into places not seen, but only for certain people. Sounds like the same kinda thing to me, so yeah, I get it."

Her eyes widen, arching the charcoal eyebrows. "You 'dig it', what amazing speech you have, yet I see that you do understand. I must hear more of this… Ex-tender and how you came to—"

More sounds interrupt her as a heated exchange comes from the hall outside. Proby can barely hear them, but Shadow hears perfectly. Holding black tipped fingers to his lips, she listens.

"I wouldn't have fallen if you hadn't pushed me," says RL in a stage whisper.

"I didn't push you; I was helping you along. You movin' so slow, I thought you must've stepped in some glue. And I 'magine you just now tripped over your nerve," answers Jayderay.

"It's called being cautious. We can't rush into—"

"*CAUTIOUS!* Is that what you call this? RL, there's spiders weavin' webs 'tween us."

"Okay, okay, I'll go faster." And off he sprints... like a terrapin.

"Yeah, I *see* you doin' it; I don't know if I can keep up," says Jayderay, still aiding him by his belt loops.

Listening as the two bicker and sneak about in her home, Shadow turns to Proby. As her smile creates grey, ghost dimples, she says, "I have listened to those two who are now exploring. They have been in love for the longest of time, but I don't think the man knows it."

And one of these two strange beings is also in love but doesn't know it. How typical of life and love; they're always a big pain in the butt.

CHAPTER 29

NOT PATTY'S FIRST BIKE RIDE

Back in town, the very dead fat trucker that Patty had 'sorta killed' lies in a spreading pool of his own worthless blood. He's still leaking from a ripped jugular and is making one hell of a mess on the asphalt. Not to mention littering the parking lot, and even at night, being just a little noticeable. What an inconsiderate piece of shit.

"Boss—Darren, honey, we've got to get the hell up and gone. Can you make it?"

Brain addled Darren, who has managed to sit up, looks blankly at Patty for a second. Then, despite the spinning comets and bursting bombs in his head, he nods.

"Yeah, I can make it; there's no choice, I've got to. Are you sure he's dead?" he asks, motioning with his chin toward the body. The movement causing large mallets to pummel his mushy brain.

"Well, if he ain't, I can sure as fuck fix that," she answers, blue eyes gleaming from her blood-spattered face. She looks maniacal... and plenty happy about it.

"No, I'll take care of that if he needs it. Then I'll try and roll him under his semi, while you get up to the room and grab our stuff. Don't run! And don't leave anything."

"Fuck me! This ain't exactly my first bike ride, you know."

"So? Then get going, girl. And wipe the blood off your face, you look like you just killed someone. Move it! And don't step in the blood."

"Yes, *daddy*," she grins, hopping over the body and moving off through the parked cars. Wiping at her cheeks, she manages to smear enough of the red gore around to look like she's in war paint. She is, she's Patty.

Back in the room, she smirks at herself in the mirror, then washes her face and hands. She does not leave any traces of blood in the sink or counter top, nor does she use a towel. This definitely is not Patty's first bike ride.

Before she begins grabbing and stuffing, she checks Darren's brown leather carrier. The carrier she's noticed that seems to be heavier than it should be. That bag she's been wondering if she should ask him about. No, don't ask, just do.

Dumping its contents on the rumpled bed, and finding it still too heavy, she pries at the inside seam around the bottom. And finds the mother lode! Beneath the false bottom, nesting quite innocently, are rows of banded hundred-dollar bills. Each paper band is conveniently bank stamped: One Thousand. There are over three hundred of them.

For most of her life, Patty has been plagued, ruled by temptations and impulses. Emotions that drown all else. She feels them right now, sailing about through the valleys of her brain, soaring above the peaks. And she feels herself getting wet and ready. *Holy fuck me! Why in hell is he even thinkin' about that shittin' Extender? Well I sure as fuck ain't thinking about it no more.*

Down in the parking lot, Darren drags the pig-fat trucker's body out of its blood pool. After seeing the gaping, savagely torn neck, he doesn't bother checking for a pulse; a zombie couldn't recover from that wound. *Besides, who's this turd going to tell if he is alive ... Damn! How'd she do it? Best I don't think about that.*

Working from his knees because he's too dizzy to stand, Darren's head throbs like a gorilla's hemorrhoid as he rolls the dead porker toward the huge rig. Nausea roils through him, and he doesn't bother turning his head to puke. Giving the guy a little something to take along to the morgue. Bon Voyage, shit hook. Getting to the edge of the truck steps, he pauses long enough to take the man's wallet and watch. *It's too bad, you poor fat bastard, just tough luck that you got robbed and murdered while trying to earn an honest living... Just what is this world coming to?... I don't see how—*

"Oh, Honey Pie, I sure do hope my little ol' thumb doesn't hit the last number to this 911 number I'm callin.' I'll bet you do too, huh Lil' Sweetie?"

Darren snaps his head toward the woman's voice. The whore doesn't have a phone in her hand. It's a stubby nosed revolver. This is Texas for sure. For dead sure.

Back in their room, Patty makes a final check for anything belonging to her. Having left her cap in the Ford, she ties a bandanna around her forehead, hiding the skull tattoo. With the short blond hair sticking up and out in every direction, she looks like a haystack in heat. A very dangerous, very deadly haystack.

Leaving Darren's clothes laying on the bed, she grabs his carrier, her duffle, and heads for the door. And pauses with her hand on the knob. *Okay, I got a gun,*

I got his money and mine, I got the world by the ass. I can hitch a ride to the bike easy... Okie City is close... hell if I got to, I'll take the bus with all the niggers and Meskins... Yeah, I got the world by the fuckin' nuts... and I'm gone!

And out the door Patty goes.

Bend over Darren, your life is making a delivery.

CHAPTER 30

HIGH SPEED SEARCH AT THE ROATON HOUSE

With the eyewatering speed of caterpillars, RL and Jaderay explore upstairs. He leads... cautiously... for her safety. She helps with whispered commentary and gentle encouragement. Encouragement by way of keeping her hand in the small of his back and pushing.

There are more rooms than they had thought. Too many, even for this Victorian mansion of a house. A house that has absorbed life, human life, and the lives of some... that are not. Faint light creeps sickly in through tattered, decaying curtains. Everywhere has layers of cobwebs, sagging from light fixtures, draping over furniture, coating beds, and stirring slightly from odd scratches in the ceiling. Closets are filled with relics and rotting clothes from forgotten lives, and all the rooms seem to have extra doors opening into yet another space. And everywhere the lonely desolate dust lies heavily.

"Sakes RL, this house is sure enough awful, no wonder I've always been scared of it," she whispers.

"Well, I'm sure not blaming you; we're definitely not visiting Mr. Roger's neighborhood. I'm surprised you're not praying."

"I *am* praying, RL! You just not hearin' it. What do you think those funny swirls in the floor dirt are? I saw them downstairs too."

"Yeah, I've been wondering about that. Maybe somebody tried to sweep up here, you think?"

"Oh, RL, don't be a donkey butt... if you can keep from it. Nobody's done any cleaning in this place since Moses was floatin' in the bulrushes."

"Well, I was trying hard *not* to think about how those marks only show in areas that somebody would walk along. Somebody or some... *thing*."

"You shut up, RL! Okay, that did it, you done finished me! This is enough of this crap, we bound to have been everyplace up here there is. I think we somehow got turned around and been checking places we done already looked in."

"You're right. Our Elvis lizard must've crawled out that broken window back in the hall and climbed down those vines."

"RL...that hall. Just where *IS* the hallway? Seems like a long time since we were in it and seems there's several doors for each spooky room."

"Yeah, the builder was plenty big on exits, but I did see the hall a few places back."

"Then don't just stand there, let's get back to it, find the stairs and go on back to Frankie. I bet neither of us gonna need any help gettin' down there."

"You right about that, and it'd probably be best to not get in my way," he says grinning, grabbing her hand and leading the way.

"And if you don't move faster, you gonna feel me trottin' on your spine, boy."

No, they haven't found anyone. But there are many dwelling spaces in the Roaton house other than its rooms. And other dwellers. And they can be found. When they want to be.

————— • • • —————

"It's about time you two got back down here," says Frankie. "I've been thinking I'd have to give up on Elvis catching and come searching for the searchers."

"Well, it's a hell of a lot bigger up there than we thought, Frankie. Did you do much looking around upstairs when you were up there?"

"Uh... no... not, uh, not exactly, Great General of

mine," answers the silly bastard, getting a dreamy look on his face. "It seems like I saw... well... but I can't seem to remember which room it happened in... uh... I mean which ones I wandered into. Anyway, I haven't seen that sparkly coated lizard come whizzin' down the stairs.

"We didn't see him neither. RL thinks he must've climbed out through that broken win—" Her phone trills, interrupting her.

As she fishes it out of her jeans, Frankie catches himself marveling at how tight they are, how they mold to the very opulent figure. *Damn! I gotta stop this, what in hell is wrong with me?... the first time I saw a vagina I thought it was a Venus Fly Trap and been avoiding them ever since, but now I'm ogling Jayderay?... maybe I don't need any more of that Suga' Boo weed... maybe I better lay off dope for a while. Nah, probably not, mustn't get paranoid and fanatical about things.*

Preacher Dan starts speaking before Jayderay even gets out a syllable.

"Hello, Sister J, Daniel here, and I just wanted to apologize for my abrupt departure. I realized that Sister Mabel must have had another attack of those visions Our Good Lord in his wisdom sometimes sends her, and I, of course, didn't see a thing but I knew she needed my guidance. While I've been comforting the poor woman, I've been doing some serious thinking about that house

Brother Wus has blessed the congregation with. I never did see any need to supervise you while you inventoried the contents with your business friend. That was all Sister Mabel's idea, and while we all know that her heart is in the right place, the truth is, she sometimes can't see the goodness in others. I, of course, know that anyone as devout as you are, would not, in fact, could not, in any way cheat my, I mean, Our Church. Why, good heavens! That would be like defrauding our Holy Savior Jesus."

"Sakes, Preacher Daniel," Jayderay manages to get a few words in. "I never thought for a minute that you were—"

"Of course you didn't, Sister! There's no need to apologize to this servant of the Lord. So, why don't you and your friend put together a price for the entire contents from the home of our dear Brother Wus, and when you're ready, just give me a call. I trust you, and the Lord trusts you, so there will be no need for any intrusions by Sister Mable, or myself. You and I can conduct this business for Our Lord over the phone. And, to save her any embarrassment, let's not mention this to poor Sister Mable. With my, and of course, our ministry, needing funds so badly, I'm sure that you will come up with an acceptable, fair, dare I say, even a generous price. I'm sure you can do this for our Lord in, let us say... in a couple of days. I'm sure you can. And, when you bring in the payment, I would like to speak with you about this play I'm going to star in...um... for our church's benefit. Well, Sister, it's been really nice talking to you, I must check on poor Sister Mable, and I know I'll hear from you real soon. God bless you and keep you. Goodbye."

Jayderay stands a couple of seconds with the lifeless phone still held to her ear. "Mercy, but don't that man leave me breathless."

When RL had heard Jayderay get out her first and only brief "preacher" comment, he'd given Frankie a disgusted, sour look. Frankie had simply nodded.

"And just what did His Holiness have to say?" *That grasping, bible thumping canary is greasier than yesterday's fried chicken.*

"Oh, RL, don't be like that. He a Man of God after all, and 'sides that, you gonna like what he had to say."

"Well if that's so, then we probably better get ready for the snow storm that's about to hit, 'cause all hell has froze over."

"What Preacher Daniel pretty much said, was that he trusts me, don't need to come back here, and wants you to take the entire contents... at your price."

Frankie lights up like 500-Watt bulb and starts laughing.

"You know, I always did like that guy," says RL, matching Frankie's wattage.

"Now RL... I AM NOT going to let you cheat my church. I WILL keep you honest.

"Honest? Well sure I'll be honest, what else? There's plenty of honesty in me."

This statement is too much, even for Frankie, and he collapses against the kitchen counter, his giggles becoming shrieks of hilarity.

RL looks over at him, assuming the look of someone deeply wounded.

Jayderay looks at the pair silently, fighting down her own laughter.

"Yes, RL," she finally says, "There is honesty in you. It would fit real easy in one of my gramma's thimbles. Fit real easy, and there wouldn't be none sloppin' over the rim, neither."

"Well... I'm always straight with you when you sell me stuff!"

"Yes, you are, and I'm thankful for that. But you about the shape of a bent bed spring with everybody else. '*I*' am gonna go through all this house with you, and *I'm* the one that will arrive at a dollar figure."

"But—"

"Don't start RL. The only 'buts' here is you two, and

I ain— I'm not having any of you two's magic math on this."

"Yes'm Miz Scarlett," says RL, with a long-suffering sigh over such an injustice.

"Hey, Bossman, we don't really want everything," says Frankie, glancing around disdainfully. "Let's face it, a bunch of this is junk, I mean real junk, not our kind of crap.

"Hell, Frankie, that's not a problem. I'll give Manny a call, he's been driving me crazy wantin' to get in here. This will be right up his alley."

"Oh, Lord, give me strength; that nasty old man," says Jayderay. "Well I guess I can stand him if it'll get us quit from this place. And speaking of 'this place,' it's gettin' late, and I'm not in no mood to ride herd on you two greedy-gut vultures underpricing everything."

"Yeah, night is about here, but what about that Elvis lizard?" asks RL.

"I'm telling you both," pipes in Frankie, "he's a spaceman. I flat out know he is. Him and that breastplate he abracadabras himself out of, can make us rich. Let's lock this place up, leave the thing sittin' right where it is. Let him find it and go back in. Then we'll have them both.

"Well... *wherever* in God's universe it come from, it ain't— it is NOT coming back to your house, RL. Or mine!" says Jayderay. "I don't even want that awful thing back in town."

RL is uneasy about leaving the breastplate unguarded. Somebody like RL might come along.

"I really don't like leaving the breastplate out here by itself. How about you stay out here with it, Frankie?"

Frankie glances quickly toward the stairs. "No, Mon Capitaine, I don't think that's a good idea, I kinda get... well... I sorta get some real funny ideas when I'm alone out here."

"RL! You afraid that thing is gonna get cold and lonesome? It's got that purple people eater lizard to keep it warm and happy," says Jayderay. "Frankie, you leavin' with us, period. Don't nobody need you gettin' funny ideas and up to something, 'specially with that devil's toy."

Jayderay has settled the matter for RL, regardless of what he thinks. She is a woman and, of course, knows best. Like in a marriage.

So, after receiving this decree, they all roar away, down the weedy, darkening drive. Leaving the Extender sitting on the old velour recliner. All alone, uncovered and waiting for activation. It won't have long to wait.

Soon after RL and crew depart, a shadow drifts to the upstairs railing. A beautiful, scarred shadow. She and her gown are made from ever shifting hues of blacks and grays, like winter clouds and harbor water. Only the eyes have color.

The shadow's partner makes up for her lack of color. More than makes up for it. Holding her hand is a lavender... lizard. Sort of. It bears a strong resemblance to a fifties Elvis. Its golden jacket glints in the dim light, the eggplant colored, duck tailed do, gleams with grease, and the blue suede loafers really set off its black satin shirt beautifully. Truly a stunning couple is Shadow and Proby.

"It is as I told you, Elv-is, they have left my house. You need not have any fear of them, my pretty, pretty boy, for it is they who are mightily afraid of you."

"Yeah, I guess you're right, Shadow. Everyone does seem to go Screams-Ville when they see me, but golly whiz-biz, pretty kitty, I don't know why."

Her sable eyebrows arch and eyes widen at this statement. The ebony lips smile gently, slightly dimpling both marble cheeks. She nods, knowingly to herself.

"Do not let it cause you distress, Elv-is. It is only that they have not ever seen any man as strikingly handsome as you are."

"SURE! That's it! I should've realized that. After all,

I *am* Elvis, and except for that, why... I'm just like any other guy. And you—you're like any other girl, except more beautiful. We're just like... we *are* like everybody else. Right? Aren't we?"

"Yes, my pretty boy... my Elv-is," she answers, with a look of infinite sadness, this woman the color of swirling smoke, ashes, and scars. This woman who has merged with, has become, the Roaton house. "Yes, we are very, we most truly are, like everyone else, you should not think otherwise. Why, look! I believe I can see below this device of which you spoke. This thing which allows you to travel so strangely, much as I do in this house. Come, show me." Hand in hand, this odd, but strangely beautiful couple descend.

Standing at the worn, liver-colored recliner, Proby picks the Extender up, turning it about before her. Its front surface shines dully with the dim light, highlighting a series of thirteen small indentions that form a slightly raised rectangle on the chest area. Swirling damascene patterns flow from the raised area, fading out at the outer edges of the metal. The interior is forge-black, somehow menacing.

"It does indeed look like a piece taken from a suit of armor," says Shadow, "As one from the days of knights and chivalry. I now know why I've heard the others naming it a breastplate."

"Well, it does come from a suit, but a spacesuit. You dig? Like in outer space, you understand about that?"

"Oh, yes, Elv-is. I know of such things. I... dig. There was a Negro caretaker who lived here after my family were all... gone. I often watched the tele-vision when he did. Of course, he didn't know of my presence; I think it would not have given him comfort," she smiles gently. "I learned much from the watching."

"Then you probably know as much as I do," he says grinning. "I've kinda been, uh... cooped up a lot. I don't really even know how this thing works, only what it does."

Reaching out, she runs her hands over its surface, feeling here and there, tapping with black nails that are not painted. Her fingers pausing and feeling the thirteen small depressions. A slight haze begins to form in the dark interior, the vapor spreading out, and a webbing of blue light, briefly flashes out across the Extender's front.

"Wow! You can... you can turn it on!" says a shocked, wide eyed Proby. Quickly pulling it away from her, he sets it back on the chair. The fog begins disappearing.

"Did I do wrong?" Her reflexes from years of abuse cause her to step away from him when he takes it, as if expecting to be slapped.

"No, honey bunny. *You* couldn't *DO* anything wrong, Shadow. You're too beautiful," he adds, giving her the much-practiced Elvis grin, one side of his upper lip lifting. "It's just that, for years and forever, it could only be activated from inside the ship. And I don't think it oughta be turned on right now. People... or things might come out of there." *Probably after me, but I better not tell her about that just yet...*

Both dimples show at the compliment, her black lips curving slightly. "I have a quite similar effect on a type of strange metal doorway that's in my basement closet. Come, Elv-is, let me show you."

In the basement, they walk to the closet with its clawed bottom door.

"I do not know whence it came," she says, pointing at the back wall, but it seems to have somehow became part of the house. No one ever sees it, nor could I, until the house took me. Perhaps that is why I have such an effect on the Ex-tender."

"Well, I can't see anything but the wall. Show me."

She reaches out, lightly touching the wall's surface. Instantly an elevator door appears, enmeshed and occupying the same space as the plastered wall. It shimmers, glowing with energy from the ancient ship.

"I do know that this is where the horrible goblins and trolls that sometimes tramp through my home come from. I do not fear them, but I have never entered; I do not dare. "

"Lab Spills... The Waydowns..." mutters Proby. "No, Shadow! Please, don't ever go in! I've never been in that place, but I've heard terrible, awful stories about it. It's really, really dangerous in there."

"How truly sweet it is to hear that you care, Elv-is. But do not fear for me; I will not go out, for I cannot. In ways I cannot explain or understand, when the house took me, when I became the house, it made me as such that to go beyond these walls is to cease my existence."

He nods, understanding more than she realizes. Proby has been told much the same thing about himself. Told repeatedly that he cannot live in topside air for any extended period. He will die. These warnings had always kept him coming back into the ship. Fear is always the best minder. But not any longer. He will not go back to the ship; he will not leave this beautiful, scarred and lonely woman. He can't bear to even think of leaving her. Better to die.

"But tell me, Elv-is. Lab-Spill? Way-Downs? You speak of things I know nothing of."

"Well, there's a lot I don't know; I've heard scuttlebutt, uh, rumors, that once, long before I... uh... I... came to the ship, that an experiment blew up, and caused other Extenders and some lift doors to vanish. This door is definitely one of those, and it's somehow been... teleported here. I think that's the word, I've seen movies about this kinda stuff. Anyway, it's become part of the house. If those trolls you've seen come through this, then they're Lab Spills— terrible monsters, and this door leads directly into the Waydowns. And that's a bad, bad place, pretty kitty, we don't even wanna think about what's in there!"

"Then we shall leave all these things alone, if that is your wish; we need not ever come down to the basement," she says, taking his hand.

Giving her his Elvis grin, he says, "Yeah, that's the best way, we just won't ever come in here. And it would be cool brain waves to go Splits-Ville outta here and get back upstairs. Tell you what, buttercup, let's go get the Extender and I'll sack it up so it can't focus or open up to let anything in. Then we'll take it with us back upstairs and talk about all this. How 'bout that, kitty cat?"

Her eyes of violet look intently at him. One sable eyebrow arches high and the stars in those eyes shoot faster. Glistening dark lips curve into a smile, dimples appear, and then melt into her mouth as she speaks.

"Talk? Only? Will we only talk, my pretty, pretty Elvis?" A faint scent of rose petals drifts about, and the gown cascades off her shoulders like flowing mercury.

CHAPTER 31

AND BACK TO THE WHORE

Bypassing the parking lot side exit, Patty heads down the hallway to the motel's front doors. With Darren's money. All of it.

What a damn stupid shit Darren is... I gived him a chance, the dumb son of a bitch... I told him I'd get out of the pickup without no fuckin' bullshit and he could leave me there... This is his own fault... and he sure ain't no boss of me no more... he's nothin' to me. Fuck him! I can already feel that Soft Tail bike throbbin' and rubbin' on my twat...

In the motel's parking lot, Darren stares at the hooker and the gun she's resting on top of a shoulder strap purse. The gun isn't shaking, not a bit. Even in this poor light, there's no doubt of her profession; she's much too old, but still flaunts it. The slathered on turquoise eye shadow matches her fish nets, and the crusted eyeliner looks drawn on with a fat Magic Marker. Those thick black lines surround crow footed eyes that are harder than the gun. Much harder. They have seen much too much for way too long.

"Now don't you worry none, Honey Bunch. I know that fuck-slime you're stuffing under there because I know his truck. He's been a customer of mine... when I was desperate, so I don't give a dead rat's ass what you've done to him. But what you took off him... well, he's usually got a wad on him and that's mine now. I've earned it."

"Okay, it's all yours," says Darren. "I'll lay it right here, and back away. I really don't want any trouble."

"Oh, Honey Child! I *know* you don't. I can see the big ol' nasty puddle of blood you rolled that fat shit out of, so if he ain't dead he's hurryin' in that direction. And that means I've caught my little self a murderer, and *that* means you're mine. I could score all kinda 'Get Out Of Jail Free' points by calling the law right now. The law around these here parts does remember favors, and a workin' girl needs those from time to time. Now get off your knees, darlin'— I'm not in the mood."

Darren tries to rise, but stumbles back against the rig's huge tire, and has to lean there, still clutching the trucker's wallet and watch. Nausea boils out of him and he's sick again. And once more the blubbery bastard gets a spew splattering. The dead bastard is good about it and doesn't object.

The whore grates out a chuckle, "Why goodness gracious me, Puddin' Pie; I just don't believe you've got the stomach for this kind of thing."

"Don't... please don't call the police... I can pay you."

"How much? Having the law owe me is worth quite a bit, Sugar. Me letting you skate away from a homicide charge is worth a fuck-ton."

"I got a few hundred on me, plus whatever's in his wallet." Darren nods toward the puke drenched corpse.

"Well shit, fuck and piss, Honey Bunch! I'm sure enough gonna have all that anyway, *and* still get brownie points for callin' this here murder in."

"Look, listen to me, please. I got a room here. There's about... about three thousand cash in there, how about that? Come on, be smart, let's get away from this mess."

The whore stares at him a few seconds, thinking.... *he's tellin' the truth about the money, or some of it anyway. But he paused before he said how much... so there's more... maybe a lot more...*

"All righty, Sweetie Pie, you're on. And here's the way we're gonna do this: I'm gonna snuggle up just real close and lovey-dovey to you, and you'll put your arm around my shoulders. You and me are gonna be in such a real bad fucky-heat, we're gonna just be absolutely panting. And I'll have this little ol' snubby barrel rammed in your god damn fucking armpit. Oh, and Honey Bunch, you better hope to God there's money in that room."

Arriving at the room's door, she pushes the barrel in deeper. "Now before you swipe the card, you knock first. Li'l ol' me don't like surprises, and I'll make sure as fuck you don't."

"I told you, there's no one in there—"

"I said knock, mother fucker, and it sure better not sound like a signal."

With his rectum so tight a nail couldn't be driven into it; Darren gives the door several hard raps. ... *if Patty is still in there, then things are gonna go to hell real quick, but if she's not, then there won't be any money... and things are gonna go to hell real quick... Either way, I'm screwed...*

There's not a sound from inside the room. He tries again with the same results.

"Okay, open the door, Sugar Puss. If there ain't no money, I've decided I'm puttin' a bullet in you, fuck the law," says the sidewalk sweetie. She repeatedly jabs the gun barrel deeper, accentuating each word.

Darren feels the barrel digging in. She didn't need to emphasize her statement; he believes her. He believes every word. He's always wondered if there's anything on the other side of life. If there is, he suspects his posting over there might be a bit warm. And it looks like he's about to find out.

CHAPTER 32

SERVING DEBRA ON DECK 19

Following Dr. Lillith Gaust's terse directions, Moto dumps the naked body beside her chair. Debra collapses in a heap of loose flesh, arms and legs flopping about awkwardly, her slack-jawed mouth drooling. Her eyes, wide and staring into eternity. Moto idly thinks maybe he'd been a little too enthusiastic while enjoying the volunteer. But that's acceptable, she is at least still warm. He does take a furtive look at the *assistant*, still standing in a corner, trembling slightly, sweating in silence. Dull red spotting shows at the surgical gowns crotch area. Despite the pregnancy, it's an oddly sexless face. *From where do I know this round-eye female?*

Without a further glance at his Debra handiwork, he turns and walks to his usual spot in front of Lillith and her control station. The lump on her shoulder, hidden by a draped towel, is definitely bigger, rolling around a bit when she moves. Or moving on its own.

"It would appear you did an exploratory examination

of this delivery, Moto. I hope you got what you needed. Is she still alive?"

"Yes. The subject was most cooperative, Dr. Gaust," he answers, maintaining a bland unreadable look. A wooden monkey would show more emotion. "She should be fresh enough for—" A weak moan from the floor interrupts him.

"Ah, yes," says Lillith. "So she is... quite fresh enough. This will not take long, you are to remain." And Lillith lowers her head and shoulders to the body. Debra doesn't live long; the throat and breasts are such tender areas.

Even for Moto, Dr. Gaust's ensuing meal is a bit too much for pleasurable viewing. Fortunately, most of it takes place behind her console. He notices she occasionally takes bits from her own mouth and slips it under the towel. Evidently the lump is very hungry as well, as she always yanks her hand back quickly.

The sounds of feeding finally end, and Lillith sits up, leaning back in her chair. The blood drenched chin and lips move with a last bit of chewing while she looks at Moto. She belches, and as the blood drips, she says:

"My ability to sustain the growth is waning fast, and I doubt it can yet ingest enough solids to continue development if removed. You must acquire a volunteer for surgical attachment very soon. And quit giving me that pie-eyed look; with your ancestry it makes the pies look squeezed."

Her command had indeed surprised Moto, and he is mortified that he'd allowed his eyes to show it. He recovers quickly, resuming his normal inscrutableness. And his silence.

"Use whatever means necessary," Lillith continues, "but the volunteer should come from topside. After Debra is discovered missing, taking another member of staff is to be absolutely avoided. You're to keep a watch on the portal screen, and the next time the Extender focuses, secure a suitable host. They must be large, female, reasonably young, and very healthy. There is no way to determine how long the partial implantation will be required, and *WE* don't want some weak-pussy, slip of a girl dying until the growth is complete. If that were to happen, I might cause the procurer to feel... some regret." She actually smiles at him while delivering this last part, baring blood-stained teeth.

"As you wish, Doctor," answers Moto, displaying the facial readability of concrete. *Yes, Honored Dog Feces.... your every wish is my command...* "Are you sure you're strong enough for the anesthesia?"

"There will be no anesthesia, *Doctor* Moto. And I will be quite strong enough, thank you for the concern." ...

No, you little squinting oriental pig, I will not give you the chance to murder me...

"None? No anesthesia whatever?" asks Moto, shocked but quite delighted. *I will certainly enjoy that!...* "Not even localized?"

"None," answers the Honored Dog Feces. "And you can take these leftovers away," she adds, gesturing downwards with her glistening red chin toward Debra's remains. A mercifully quite dead Debra.

From the pregnant assistant comes an almost inaudible groan. It sounds like a word. It sounds like... "Please."

CHAPTER 33

BACK AT THE MOTEL

With the whore's gun barrel encouraging him not to dawdle, Darren pushes the motel room door open. As they enter the room, the whore kicks the door closed with a turquoise clad heel. And together they see his clothes tossed on the much-rumpled bed. What they don't see is his leather carrier. Darren takes keen notice of his missing bag, which means there's no money, and hell is only seconds away.

Keeping the gun in his armpit, she shoves him a couple more steps in and takes a quick look in the bath area. Seeing an open and empty shower, Darren's razor, deodorant, and nothing else. She sighs, and Darren is silent.

"Well, Honey Bunch, believe me when I say it, I know the look of a fuck-bed, the smell of pussy, and a run-from room. Been there and done that, Sugar, way too many times. Whoever she is, she has left you high and dry. I sure do hope you're stupid enough to think she was a good fuck." She blows out a long breath, heavily scented with peppermint.

Besides the very hard gun beneath his arm, Darren is also feeling the much harder devil's pitchfork... as it slides up his ass. With absolutely nothing to lose, he decides he has to try.

"You're right, I've been had. Look, there's some more money out in my pickup, let's—"

"Shut your fucking cum trap! Even if you did have something in your truck, your bitch has it by now, Sugar Pie, and your fucking ride. You know what I'm thinking? I'm thinking I'm tired, and you're just not worth the hassle of calling the cops. This little ol' gun of mine, all cuddled up in your pit, won't make as much sound as one of my farts. I believe I'll just pull the trigger, and watch you die. I've killed a few other stupid, double-crossing fucks like you, and you know what? I really liked the feel of it. And I need to feel something good tonigh—"

She lets out a gargling sound as her head is yanked back, and a knife is thrust beneath her jawbone. It's pushed hard, hard enough to draw blood... and it stays there.

"I'll shoot him," squawks the whore. "I swear to fuck, I'll kill him, I'll kill him right here, right now!"

"So what, bitch? Go for it. You think I give a shit?

I only come back 'cause I smelt your rotten gash and sticky thighs way on out to the motel front; so I just had to come see what kinda pig's pussy could stink so bad. I shoulda knowed it was just some old, petrified, wore out whore," says Patty, her teeth clenched in a feral smile. The blond thatch sticks out in every direction from beneath her bandana. Her forehead tattoo is peeking out, absolutely pulsing. It looks as maniacally gleeful as she does.

"I said I'll kill him, I mean it, I'll blow his heart out, my gun's jammed in his pit and I—"

"I heard you the first time, bitch, and I told you to go ahead, you asphalt cunt. I was ditchin' his ass anyways."

"NO!" Darren says, who has an intense, deeply personal interest in all this. "Patty, listen a second, if she shoots, there'll be cops here quick. Let's buy her; let's just pay her off, and we can all get out of here."

"You bet, Sugar! I can be reasonable," says the whore, who has also taken an intense, deeply personal interest in all this. Feeling her own blood trickling down into her bra has had a clarifying effect on things.

"FUCK ME! I ain't payin' this pussy pimple a fuckin' dime. I'm gonna slit her—"

"No, Patty! Don't, please, don't. Let's talk a little, we can work this out," says the panicking Darren. He can already feel the bullet tearing through his heart.

"Damn right, we can talk," squeaks the increasingly desperate whore. "Take the knife from my throat, honey—and we'll work something out." With one of Patty's hands still clenched and pulling back on her hair, she's talking upwards at the ceiling.

"C'mon Patty," pleads Darren. This can end in a good way; there's no need for any of us to be a hard ass."

"Listen to the man, Sweetie. Just a little money can solve all this, and how about I throw in a blowjob for both of you? Believe me, this ol' gal can really lick and suck."

Patty slowly nods her head. Her lips are shiny with spittle, the skull tattoo dancing, pulsing purple, and her eyes jitter in time with it.

"Yeah, Darren, I think you're right. This can end in a good way." Still nodding thoughtfully, Patty eases the blade away from the whore's throat, and the woman visibly relaxes.

Patty drops the knife, and with blinding speed jams the heel of that hand against the woman's chin, while yanking her hair in the opposite direction. The already strained neck snaps, and the whore collapses like a rag doll. Dead on arrival at the floor. Her gun bounces on the floor once, and then is as still as the body.

"Yep, you sure were right, Darren, it did end in a good way."

Darren looks down at a very tired, very old, very dead Pavement Princess. The woman lies there on the dirty, cheap carpet, a perfect resting place for a dirty, cheap life. Still brain addled from his recent clubbing, he slowly shakes his head. Looking up into the crazed, and deadly face of Patty, he asks:

"What now?"

"Well, fuck me! What do you think, honey? '*Now*' we're goin' out to that fuckin' old house. And then we can see if that precious shittin' Extender, that *you* want so God damn bad, is there. By sayin' *now*, I mean like TONIGHT. How's that for *now*."

"Yes, okay."

Patty starts laughing, "Just fuckin' listen to you! If I'd knowed a couple raps across your head would make you all milky and polite, I would've done it myself. So move your ass and pack your gear." She tosses his carrier onto the rumpled bed and scoops up her knife. "And your money is still in there."

Darren stands there, arms hanging limp, gazing down at the whore's body. The woman's turquoise fishnets glaring up from legs white as maggots. He's a man who has seen so much death, so much, too much. Some of it by his own hand, a lot of it by the doings of others... like this poor woman. Death, always death.

"Darren!— Honey... that bitch is dead, and we gotta

get out of here. Man up! You seen plenty of dead before, and that fuckin' lot-lizard wasn't no better than a Spill. You just remember, there's a dead as fuck, tub of guts layin' in the parking lot just waiting to be found, and that's where our truck is. And we sure as fuck need to be in it and gone before any flashin' blues show up."

"Wonder how old she was," he says in a vague 'this hasn't happened' voice. He still stands over the body, unmoving, still looking down.

Patty's hand moves in a blur, slapping him across the face, her skull tattoo throbbing. "Move, big man, and move now or I'm leavin' your ass here," she says in a quiet, harsh voice. "I ain't goin back to fightin' dykes in no prison."

The slap does it, jarring his brain for the fourth time in less than an hour. He starts gathering his belongings.

"Leave Miss Turquoise Pantie's gun where it lays," he orders, "and don't touch her purse. That should give us a little more time; she was armed and not robbed; it'll slow the law down some, trying to figure what the hell has gone down. We'll go out through the front, skirting the parking lot, and come up to our truck from the back. That way we'll bypass that bled out tub of lard."

"Welcome back, lover," grins Patty. "Hey! You gonna fuck me at that old house?"

MEANWHILES

After leaving the Roaton place, RL and Frankie take their vehicles to the shop. Entering, they start all their usual checking.

First they check for break-ins, which is something all thieves fear even more than honest people do. To lose something of value to some *other* low- life is unbearable. In RL's case, the fear of theft is even worse than for the average crook, after all, he or Frankie, had to labor hard to cheat the steaming Jesus out of somebody to get the crap.

Next on the checking list are phone messages. Most important are those from the police, who always want to talk with the owner, to help them in an investigation. Which is cop speak, translating into: looking for stolen merchandise. Knowing dealers in antiques quite well, the calling officer never names what is being looked for. That type of unspecific, ambiguous message can cause a flurry of frantic hiding of things that the shop owner knew damn well was hot when they bought the flaming piece. The police know this and love it; the crook can't sell what he's hidden in Aunt Grannie's outhouse. There are no cop calls.

The second most important call messages are those from beloved souls who want to sell something, i.e. they need a really good screwing. Those calls are always answered. Promptly. It's the kind thing to do, and kindness is a byword of the trade. Unfortunately, this evening, there are no sellers who would've soon needed KY Jelly. And later, Preparation H.

During the checking, they talk, planning the next day, establishing that Frankie will run the shop as usual. To hell with dodging a possible visit from the police and the rude, Hila Monster seeing, Yankee couple. And RL will return to the Roaton house, so he can get back to chasing that Gecko Elvis.

Frankie spots the box RL had bought from the seed. RL actually *had* bought the stuff, as in paid good money for, not the usual penny on the dollar. Frankie doesn't know this. Yet.

"Damn! This must've came in while I was off... visiting." Frankie sees no need to enlightened RL about the call he made on Suga' Boo. RL can be a little prissy about some things, and besides, that particular adventure would require some explaining. And Frankie wasn't about to betray Jayderay's trust.

"Hey, O Chief of Mine, this is some damn good merchandise!" he says, picking up the motel fan. Giggling, he asks, "What'd you have to pay out, a whopping ten bucks?"

RL mumbles something, not wanting to have this conversation.

"What? I must not have heard you right. It sounded like you said—"

"I said three hundred," snaps RL.

"Dollars?!" Frankie asks, his eyes growing huge with incredulity.

"Yes, damn it. Dollars, big fat dollars." RL hisses the answer out, shuddering at the vile memory.

"OH, FUCK NO, BOSS! Tell me it wasn't from another waif- eyed, makeup smeared, runaway?" Frankie asks, having awful, dreadful visions of another pouty-lipped Deena Lynn; fleeing her molesting father, Gunther Dawson Fly. (Who is currently missing, according to the news. How odd.) Frankie didn't think he could handle another of RL's mid-life love seizures.

"No. It was from some hillbilly seed. I could've had the entire box easy for a twenty. But the rotten, no good, filthy, bastard, son of a bitch just had to let slip he was taking care of a bunch of strays."

"Ah," says Frankie, and nods knowingly... and feels immensely relieved. Helping animals is fine, but he and the shop most definitely did not need another pulchritudinous teen, twisting and torturing RL's brain. And other parts.

"Well, boss, maybe it won't be too bad. The fan should bring in an easy $350, and the two Cream Tops should fetch about thirty each. And what are these little round tins with women's faces and names? Must be several dozen in here."

"Those are Merry Widows; they're condom tins from way, way back. Don't find those much anymore, should bring about fifteen bucks each."

"Hmmm," muses Frankie, doing the math. "Well... we're sure not gonna be able to get our normal profit margin on the three hundred, but as you always say, 'sums are better than nuns.' I'll get it all out on the floor ASAP... priced accordingly." This last about pricing was a given. Pricing diminished the asking of that asinine question: 'how much is this?' Hell, if they have to ask, they can't afford it. Everything in the store is clearly marked. RL absolutely insists on that; the sucker needs to have an idea how deep the penetration will be. Then, if that bending-over pigeon still wants to talk about the piece... reach for the Vaseline.

"But RL, really, you..." he clears his throat before

continuing, "you need to reign in this Florence Nightingale Disease you're afflicted with. Before it bankrupts us."

"Yeah, I know," says RL, shaking his head sadly. Running all fingers through his hair, and not improving it, he thinks for a moment.

"Frankie, you need to plug that fan in."

<hr>

After leaving the Roaton house, Jayderay drives home in the dark, dreading having to face the scene of her morning assault. Parking in the detached garage, she has thoughts of Suga' Boo hiding in some corner, with plans on taking a second helping of her. Given the man's current condition, that would indeed be a remarkable achievement on his part. And Frankie would be absolutely, positively astounded.

She hesitates before walking to her back porch, trying to think of some believable excuse to call RL, or just wait for him at his house next door. *NO! I'm not gonna pull RL into my mess. And I will not let that... that rapin' nigger ruin my life and home. I won't!*

Straightening her shoulders, she starts with determination for the back door... and something wonderful happens. Princess starts her high-pitched yelps of ecstatic greetings. And Jayderay actually laughs.

"Oh, my baby girl hears her momma! And I'm so glad to hear you too, Princess," she calls out, breaking into a near trot.

Then came the requisite hugging, petting, face licking, baby talk and other asinine silliness. Only people who are lucky enough to love animals can understand. Afterwards, a still limping Princess accompanies Jayderay as she checks all the windows and the front door. The woman fights back tears at the door where Suga' Boo had shoved his way through. But Suga' Boo had paid. He had paid a high price, but overall... a just one. Especially considering this is Texas.

Frankie had been on the right track with Suga' Boo's punishment. But the silly bastard really needs to keep the whole affair from RL. There is no doubt, RL would've certainly agreed with the execution. Heartily agreed. Gleefully agreed. He would probably even agree that Frankie cutting off the raping bastard's private parts was indeed justified. But RL *might possibly* feel, that Frankie stuffing them down the still living Suga' Boo's throat, had been a bit much. Sort of over the top... even for Texas. RL can be a bit stuffy and prissy about some things.

With everything safely locked, Jayderay feeds

Princess, and as the once starved dog eats, she goes to her bedroom. And prays. Kneeling, hands clasped like a child, her brow resting on them, this woman gives thanks to her God for all that she has. She asks forgiveness for all her shortcomings. She asks blessings for her friends. So she prays, does this woman, who had been knocked unconscious and violated by a bestial man in her own home. Less than six hours ago.

Later, while eating a light supper, she talks to Princess, who sits worshipfully at her side. In bits and pieces, the dog gets fed about half of Jayderay's food… while being told that she shouldn't be fed from the table. Pet owners, what silly, lucky people they are.

"Just what a wonderful, wonderful baby girl you are, and yes, momma does know how lucky she is to have you. You one of the best things RL ever done for me." Princess thumps her tail at the mention of RL's name. "Yes, baby, I see you waggin' when you hear your daddy's name," she chuckles. "Well, he is a good man, it's just a shame he don't know it or show it more. But I promise to make sure you get to see him tomorrow, honey."

Yes, RL will see the dog tomorrow. And both of them will be terrified. Very terrified.

"Princess, I've got all my Tidy Tinas ready for tomorrow, 'cause I really need to get back out to that awful old house, first thing in the morning. What a way to start a day, going out there. I'd sure love to take you with me, but I better not. I just don't trust that foul place, it's not... not right, not good. But I'm word bound to the church to tend to their business out there, so I'm goin.'" She sighs, shaking her head.

Jayderay will go to the Roaton house tomorrow. Tomorrow will be a day like no other.

A day when death can be a blessing.

CHAPTER 35

LATER THAT NIGHT...

After finding the Roaton place, Darren and Patty repeatedly cruise back and forth in front of the vine cloaked house. Moonlight does not improve this eerie two-story place. Their headlights flash on the black windows, making them look like malevolent blinking eyes. While below, the vine leaves appear as small green, clutching hands, pulling some monstrous green body to those windows.

Darren's head has finally cleared from all the thumping, banging... and murder. So he asks the question Patty's been waiting for. Not dreading, just waiting.

"Why did you come back, kiddo?"

"You complainin'? I come back 'cause I figgered some guy as dick-headed as you needed me around. You know, like to keep you from fuckin' up and gettin' into trouble."

"Yeah, right. I thought that must be it. Thanks."

"Fuck me, Darren, ain't we ever gonna park and go in? We been checkin' this place out for a fuckin' hour."

"Cool your pipes, Patient Patty. We've been checking the place out for about 20 minutes, and good recon has saved many a mission from disaster."

A good distance down from the house he pulls into an overgrown dirt drive, parking at the barbed wire gate stretched across it.

"What's this? You wantin' a blow job now? Or you figger we need the exercise walkin' ten miles before we get there?"

"Listen, Death Head, the drive up to that house is narrow, and we don't want to get blocked in by some gung-ho Trooper, who thinks he saw a light waving around in there. We leg it in from here. "

"Damn! I was hopin' for the blow job, honey," she chuckles, adding "Maybe you'll let me when we get inside."

"With the night I've had, I don't think I could survive it. Come on, Death Head, let's get it done. And if any Samaritan happens by, we say we're on a long trip, and just need to stretch our legs."

"What the fuck's a 'Samerton,' some kinda patrol?"

"No, it's a type of idiot. Now be quiet."

Besides having to cross a couple fences, the way to the back of the house is easy. The kitchen back door lock is even easier. With both their flashlights sweeping, they move quietly into the living area.

"Fuck me, honey," Patty hisses in a stage whisper. "Look at this staircase! It's even hauntier than the outside of this dump."

"Hush, girl. I know damn well you're not afraid of any spooks."

"Well, 'course not, but maybe one of them might want that blow job. I cain't seem to get no action outta you. Maybe we should split up, you know, like in a horror flick? Then something will grab me, and I can scream, so you'll come runnin' to the rescue. And then I'll reward you with a fuck."

"Oh, do shut up, child. I've still got such a headache," he winks. "And no, we're not splitting up... you might find *something* to reward. Let's do the upstairs first... and no blow jobs."

Both grinning, they start up the curving stairs. But they have been heard.

<hr>

Hours after Jayderay's prayer, Amy drives her little peach colored Honda out U.S. 287, headed to the Roaton house. She's not old enough for a license, but her dad can't say no to her, and she's supposed to be overnighting at a girlfriend's home. Yeah, right. That hoary lie told around the world. Even in Muslim countries.

That very same *girlfriend* is currently sitting beside Amy. *He's* fondling his Nunchuks. The very weapon he'd knocked out his bottom front teeth with while practicing. Now he whistles and lisps when he talks. And Hector also has a black eye— he's been practicing again.

Of course, the teeth story everyone got at school was that three Black guys jumped him as he was walking to the rec. center to shoot some pool. They were some mean 'mutha fuckas', but he'd been lucky enough to have the deadly Nunchuks with him, he'd said, telling everyone who would listen. And he had whipped their black asses until two ran away, leaving the third behind, unconscious. Sure. If three guys of any race had actually jumped Lisping Hector... he would've learned how delicious Nunchuks were. And maybe penis as well. Plenty of dressing provided.

"Like I've already told you, *Hecky*, I am not gonna stand there at the front door of that old ookey-spooky house waiting on you this time. I'm staying in the car, 'cause you'll probably get all fraidy-cat like you did last time and knock me down runnin' away."

"I WASN'T SCARED! Only for you, I was only worried for you," whistles and lisps tough guy Hector.

She giggles. "Is that why you went wee-wee in your pants, 'cause you were so worried?"

"I DINT GO WEE— I dint piss myself! I just... uh, I spilt something inside the house."

Amy laughs but doesn't comment. She knew he had wet himself, because when she finally got back to her little car that night, brave Hecky was sitting there, ripe with the smell of urine. It took days and days and a can of Lysol to get it all out.

"Okay, Amy, you just go on and laugh. You'll see. I'm gonna show you tonight, count on it. I got my Nunchuks with me this time, and ain't nothin' in that house gonna dare fuck with me. And I'll come back with pics and whatever else I wanna take. You'll see, count on it." *Yeah, you'll see, and then I'm gonna pump your virgin gringa ass, no matter even if you fight... ain't nothin' you can do about it, you won't tell nobody 'cause you ain't supposed to be out.*

Hector, sitting beside the petite, spoiled 15-year-old blond, is aware the only reason she's agreed to this trip is to keep from being called a racist. Gringo girls are so stupid. He smiles, thinking of the upcoming Amy sex. He hopes she does fight and cry.

"Oh, yeah," he says, "I scored a big fat joint for us, you want me to fire up?"

"NO! My dad might smell it and he'd raise all kinds

of hell. He might even take away my car. 'Sides, I'm driving; otherwise I sure would." Amy hasn't tried weed yet, but naturally tells everyone she has.

"Well, baby, we can rolls down the windows, and I'll drive."

"NO, Hecky! You're not driving my car, and if you light that thing, I'm turning around.

Hector grins, nodding good naturedly. He will fire up on their way back, Amy won't object; she'll have other things to think about. Count on it.

He continues smiling and fondling those deadly, Black guy beating, teeth shattering, lisp causing Nunchuks. Holding one of the two 11-inch sticks in each hand, he swings the connecting chrome chain back and forth. The clicking sound it makes as it flips over and under striking the octagonal wood fills him with power. It's going to be a great night. Count on it.

It will be a great night... and a memorable one, Hector. Count on it.

Pulling down the Roaton drive, Hector's nerve plummets; it is a scary looking place. Amy parks behind the vine covered iron fence. The house towers above, seeming to lean over, its upper windows leering down at them.

"Okay, toughie guy, here you are. I'm staying in the car and locking it."

"You sure you don't wanna smoke a little good shit before I go in?"

Amy sighs theatrically. "Hecky, if you're gonna go, then go. Now."

Hector makes a big, slow production of getting out. He's already about to piss himself, and that would be such a shame, since he's wearing some really bad, bad pants. They're black to match his wife beater tee, they've got huge gang banger legs, and ride very low, showing off his boxers. Plus they have some simply marvy white stitching along all seams and pockets. They're more than bad... they're awful. An unusually flamboyant Peacock would kill for these.

Hector creeps along to the front door, taking comfort from the deadly Nunchuks he's clutching. He wishes to Holy Saint Somebody, that he hadn't bragged to Amy about how easy the door lock had been to jimmy on the trip before. Now, any 'I couldn't get in' excuse won't work. Worse yet, the damn thing isn't locked. Taking a shuddering breath, in he goes.

Pulling his phone from the voluminous pantaloon's pocket, he starts filming. Panning the camera up the stairway... he nearly shits himself.

Up there, leaning against the landing post is another blond. Standing beneath the domed skylight, the full moon puts her on display. Her arms are folded beneath some pretty good-looking tits, ankles crossed, and she's smirking. Hector knows an easy white slut when he sees one. Hell, this one here has even got a skull tattoo on her forehead. His fear evaporates; if there was anything to be afraid of, this gringa bitch wouldn't be leaning there smiling. She's wanting it. Hell, she's begging for it. The way Hecky sees things, he's going to get two pieces of white ass tonight.

As he pockets the phone, Hector intentionally shoves the pants even lower, exposing more boxers, and some pubic hair. This guy is so, SO bad. He struts to the base of the stairs, swinging the Nunchuks, saying,

"Hey, Blondie Girl, I likes that tattoo. I gots one that's lower down, a whole bunch lower down. I bet you know exactly what I mean. I'm gonna show it to you, you gonna be big impressed... and I do mean big. Count on it."

Patty doesn't straighten, unfold her arms, or uncross her ankles. But her smirk broadens into a welcoming smile. "Well now, just supposin' I don't wanna see nothin?"

Hector, mounting the dusty, debris littered steps one at a time, slaps the beloved Nunchuks into a palm with each step.

"Oh, Blondie baby, you do wants to, this bad Chicano can tell. I gots a tamale you just dyin' to taste, 'cause I know a hungry slut when I sees one."

Patty doesn't move. Except for her eyes narrowing slightly. And her smile changing, it's showing more teeth now. Her lips are also getting redder with saliva. The tattoo gets brighter.

"Nah, I don't like no fuckin' Meskin food, and from lookin' at you, I figger your *tamale* wouldn't fill a Chihuahua's ass."

About now, even a blind turtle would sense danger. Hector ain't a turtle. He releases one of the Nunchuk batons, letting it swing before him like a pendulum.

"You lissen to me, you fuckin' white trash whore," says this blind and stupid turtle. "You gonna suck me and like it. Count on it. If you does it real slow and swallow, then maybe I won't put no bruises all over your Lilly-white ass." Hector advances... with the feared, deadly Nunchuks.

Patty doesn't move. Not one bit.

Hector bursts through the Roaton front door, crying. He blasts through the vine covered gate, screaming for Amy to start the car.

Amy, already frightened, starts the car but doesn't unlock the doors. Hector is *naked*... and the moonlight glistens on his urine drenched legs. He pounds on the glass, cursing and threatening her. The now terrified

Amy shakes her head, NO. And the weeing, nekkid Hecky takes off running for the highway.

Amy backs the car around, spraying gravel as she speeds out. Hector has already left the driveway. Count on it. As she turns onto the blacktop, her headlights spot him jogging up ahead. *Something* is moving on him.

Getting closer to Hector, both of Amy's hands abruptly fly from the steering wheel, covering her mouth in horror. She's seen what's on him that's moving.

As Hector runs, a single baton from his Nunchuks moves on him with the pounding of each foot. It bounces on him... it's dangling from the chrome chain... it's dangling out of Hecky's rectum.

Passing the manly Hector, Amy drives toward home, thinking about what she had seen. She thinks about the fact that Nunchuks have *two* big sticks. Two, *long,* big sticks. She starts laughing. She can hardly wait to go to school.

Back in the Roaton house, Patty is laying on the floor... chortling with glee. Darren looks down at her, weakly smiling and shaking his head.

When they'd heard Amy pull up and park, both had rushed to a window, and knew right away there was no danger from the Peach colored Honda Fit. Seeing bad boy

Hector get out from the passenger side, they'd quickly analyzed his clothes. This was just a bit of burglary.

"Oh, fuck me, it's just a wannabe gangbanger, he's probably showing off for some silly assed girl; that's a chick's car for sure. Let me take care of this, Darren." Patty had whispered. "I'll scare him off, and I promise I won't kill the fucker. Well... I won't unless he really asks for it. Now you just stay back in the hallway and be quiet." She had taken her stance at the railing post. Hector had entered, and totally lived up to her expectations. And she had totally taken care of Hector.

Now, as her laughing dies down, she gasps, "How I love fuckin' with bad asses, and I tole you I wouldn't kill him." A most magnanimous gesture for Patty.

"Okay, honey, so what do we do now? That God damn Extender thing just ain't here, Darren, we done looked plenty enough." They had both quit the stage whispers. Why bother? After all the extreme and thrilling noises Hecky had made, there couldn't possibly be anyone here. Darren and Patty would have heard them laughing.

Darren blows out a heavy sigh. "Okay, Death Head, you get your way: Okie City it is." *Wonder if I'll live to get there.*

"ALL RIGHT, LOVER BOY! Now you're talkin.' Hey... you gonna fuck me now, or when we get to the truck?"

CHAPTER 36

AND IN THE WAYDOWNS

Seevee scuttles, crawls, and worms his way back through the Waydowns' long forgotten and unused maintenance tunnels. He'd hidden the glass encased Gunch in Proby's cavernous playroom himself, rather than trust a terrified Spill with the job. He has risked capture by Lillith's security people, who are on the lookout for any of the deserting Almosts. Getting caught would have guaranteed a long and horrendous death. An agonizing end, or worse... the pit. The danger was worth it, Seevee did not want to fail Ton. Not out of fear, not out of duty, but out of love. It's a hell of a thing.

As the exhausted, renegade Almost climbs out of a crawlspace flap, Tanya watches, but doesn't bother to help— and her lab coat is securely buttoned.

"Well? Did you get it done?" she asks without any stupid questions about his welfare. Yes, love really can be hell... especially when it's one sided.

"Yes, Ton. Seevee do good, hide in room of Proby

room. Hide much good, no find, plenty room for Gunch grow, get big. No not find 'til too much late," he answers. His multi-jointed arms repeatedly folding and unfolding as he brushes his maintenance khakis, simultaneously front and back. Trying to look his best, not realizing he's looking like a big spasming bug.

"Good, well done, Seevee," Tanya says, looking away in revulsion from the gangly creature's attempts to make itself presentable. *Jesus, just look at him! He's like a giant fucking Walking Stick. Makes me want to puke... I don't know how much more of this can I stand... but he's all I have. He will have to do. For now.*

"While you were gone, I met with Dr. Moto at the lift again. Damn, I wish the controls on our side of that door weren't ruined. Anyway, the plan is going forward, but we have to give that mold time to spread."

"No trust Moto, he sneak snake," says Seevee, who has just completed some sneak snaking of his own. But that's different, that was for Ton. "Coilers more much trust than Moto."

"You're right, I don't trust that Slant bastard, either. But he does hate Lillith, he hates being under her thumb. So he'll go along with my plan, but I'll have to be very careful. I— we aren't ready to take 19. Not yet... but I— we, will get there. And with the Coilers," she chuckles. "Yeah, maybe they are more trustworthy than

Moto. Maybe. But they would also like to eat us. Let's don't forget that."

Seevee stands silently, watching her, awaiting his next orders. Being tired, hungry, and thirsty are all pushed away. They do not matter. Only Ton matters. Which is exactly the way Tanya sees things.

"I heard some more of those sounds again from another of the locked areas. That same vacuuming, slurping noise; it sounds just like frying eggs. Anyway, I followed the noises, and found a door they were coming from. I swear those sounds are not machine made, not made by some function of the ship. And whatever it is, it was sucking... or *lapping,* all around the door seal. I knocked on the door with the butt of my knife, three times, hard, and it stopped. Then it rapped back... three times, and then nothing more."

"What Ton do? Is maybe much be much danger back in locked!"

"Yeah, that's why I got the hell away; all I had with me, was my knife. Seevee, I think it's intelligent. All those places have been in lock down since the mutiny, Jesus Christ, there could be descendants of the original human staff in there. They may still have knowledge lost when these fucking Waydowns were formed. Shit that could be important to us."

"No much know, Ton."

"You're right," she laughs sourly. "You 'no much know' a lot, don't you. Well, *I, do* much know— I intend to open that door." *And just maybe I can replace your ugly ass.*

When that long ago experiment with two Extenders had so disastrously backfired, creating the Waydowns, many areas became locked. Barricaded by staff against the ensuing mutiny, madness and cannibalism. But they had not been immune to the mental and physiological changes the colliding Extenders had wrought. No, not immune... but some had survived. And they had bred.

"Ton? Seevee do lot much good; Seevee brave for Ton. Luff? Real luff now?"

Successfully hiding a grimace, Tanya looks at the Almost. This almost human who had murdered his brethren for her, often risks his life for her, and guards her sleep every night. *I knew this shit was coming, God damn it... Guess I better not put him off again... Damn it.* And here is love, being hell... again.

Flashing a smile, she says, "Of course we'll love now, Seevee! I've really been so eager for you to get back!" Women can be so resilient... and so practical.

And off the happy couple go, to Tanya's private quarters and domestic bliss. Those rooms that Seevee sleeps outside of, in the hall... usually. He sleeps there on a pallet unrolled in front of her locked door. It is hell.

———

Fairly close to Tanya's cabin, behind a different door than the one she had been listening at, a thing still fights. It continues its struggles against the bed. It rages against the tenacious bed it has been on since this area had been locked... decades ago.

As it thrusts, strains, and pulls, years of dust billow off the creature, and it does make incremental gains. Its freedom is gradually increasing against whatever restraints hold it. And the parasites inside this being constantly chew. And multiply. And add to its madness.

But this thing is gaining, and each gain gets it a little more space, a little more space of movement for the next try. And it will not quit. It will never quit.

This raging, hating thing has a *need*.

CHAPTER 37

BAD DAY FOR JAYDERAY

On the morning after Hector received his insertion, Jayderay prepares for her trip out to the Roaton place. All her Tidy Tinas are headed to the various homes and companies, Princess has been lavishly petted and fed, and lavishly petted again. She decides on a quick look at the daily paper, to which she does still subscribe. This is indicative of her age, as she is rapidly approaching the Big Four O. She also thinks another cup of coffee would be good, but knowing it'll mean having to use the filthy bathroom out at the Roaton pile.

"Oh, Princess, I know what I'm doin.' I'm just puttin' off going out to that awful house," she says, unrolling the news. "But I've got to go, somebody has sure got to keep an eye on your crooked daddy and his so called apprais—" She breaks off, her eyes widening as she read the headlines. "Land of Goshen! I need to call RL about this, some of this might come back on me!" she says, yanking her phone from a tissue stuffed robe pocket.

———

RL, is already at NEAT STUFF, he and Frankie oozing greed while pricing things. And often as not, urging each other to a higher mark up. Both are paying eager, and very sincere, homage to the God of their choice: money. Maybe it can't buy happiness but being poor damn sure doesn't either. RL would much rather cry in his Jag, than on a city bus with lint in his pockets.

Frankie has whined a little about not getting to go to the Roaton house and play with the space-lizard-spouting breastplate. RL wisely suggested that he could come out with him... but they'd lose a day's shop profit... and the chances of buying. Frankie is staying.

Answering his trilling mobile, RL gets a barrage of news:

"Sakes RL! Wichita Falls is becomin' a terrible big city; there was murders done last night! Some trucker, a woman at a motel, and Shanaqueela, that worthless girl I fired, she done been arrested for killin' her man, Suga' Boo. And they found a lot of drugs at her house. You don't suppose the police gonna want to question me, do you?"

"Calm down, Jayderay. Good Lord woman, if the

police do bother with you, it'll only be to find out if you witnessed or knew of any trouble between them. From the stories you've told me, the cops will have plenty to investigate about those two without pestering you. Relax and go on out to the house. I'm gonna be heading that way in a few minutes."

Hearing the words Jayderay and cops, Frankie's ears grow a little. They're now about the size of a large elephant's. As RL pockets his phone, Frankie asks casually what's up. He's a tad concerned… for Jayderay's sake.

"Oh, not anything really. Jaderay said the paper is plastered with a story about that girl she fired being arrested for killing her husband. We sorta know him, calls himself Sug'a Boo. That low life has been in here a couple of times selling crap that's so hot it's melting. Which caused us the trouble of having to hide it after he left. Good riddance."

"Yeah, seems like I remember him," says Frankie. "Not much of a loss," he giggles. RL doesn't ask.

Arriving at the Roaton place, Jayderay unlocks the door, not realizing that action wasn't necessary. Hector, having penetrating thoughts last night, had forgotten to relock. Besides thinking, the bad boy had also been busy with screaming, crying, and weeing. Count on it.

Talking aloud for the comforting noise, Jayderay bustles in with her canvas tote hanging off a shoulder. "Lord, please don't hold this too much against me, but I got to confess; I'm *glad* that awful man is dead. I know I shouldn't be, but I am. And I'm kinda wonderin' if that girl could really do mur—" She stops, seeing the empty recliner.

But she has not stopped speaking in time. Something has heard her. Something intelligent. Something very intelligent. Something very hungry.

Sakes! Where is that breastplate? Good Jesus knows I want it gone, but RL will have a conniption fit if it's been stole. Did RL or Frankie move it before they left? They did come out after I did... but why would they move the thing? No sense callin' RL, he's sure gonna know soon enough...Wonder if that purple Elvis thing took it?

She wanders, looking around, the canvas carry-all bouncing on a hip. Jayderay starts talking again, just for the sound of a human voice, anything to dispel some of the haunting, eerie loneliness in the brooding house.

"If I find the cussed thing, I'm not even gonna touch it, but if it's still here, I would like to know, least that way I can keep RL from havin' a heart attack." She chuckles lightly. "I can't have that man dying from loss and greed... though there's some might say, such a thing would be a right fittin' end for him."

Walking down the steps into the day basement, she glances into the closet. Nothing. Turning, she surveys the room, not seeing the breastplate. Behind her, the closet wall flickers, the elevator's face appears. The door slides silently open. Something crawls toward her. Quietly undulating nearer. Closer.

"Well, that's enough lookin', I sure ain— I'm sure not gonna go look upstairs, Mr. Greedy, can just do that for himsel—"

Jayderay screams as a scaled, web-draped tentacle wraps around both ankles, yanking her feet from beneath her. Slamming into the floor, her nose bursts, spurting blood across the dust. Desperately clawing at the wooden floor, kicking frantically to free her legs, she's drawn into the yawning blackness of the closet. Grabbing the edge of the elevator door, she pulls with all the might of her terror. Her shrieks echo out into the house:

"HELP ME, LORD, PLEASE, OH GOD, HELP ME, HELP ME!" Her grip is torn from the door as she's jerked inside. The door slides shut, biting off Jayderay's screams of prayer. It becomes as one with the plastered closet wall. The house is silent.

Upstairs, Shadow's eyes fly open, raising her cheek from the sleeping Proby's chest, she listens and then sits up. The scars across her face and breasts darken.

"Elv-is, Elv-is... you must awake," she says shaking his shoulder.

Proby lazily opens his eyes, sinuously stretches, looking at her. Seeing her darkened scars, he bolts upright.

"Baby! What's wrong, are you hurt?"

"There is trouble in my... in our home, Elv-is. Nothing happens in this house that I do not feel an awareness of. That odd door in the basement, the one I showed you. It was opened and has now closed, there were screams also. All my broken places do now ache," she says rubbing her crooked arms. "I believe something terrible has happened; someone has been hurt, someone I would not hurt, nor would I want hurt."

Proby swallows, but does not hesitate, saying, "I'll go down, I'm... I'm not afraid."

"I know you are not frightened, Elv-is," she says gently, touching his lips. But the things that have come into this house from that opening, I do not believe they can hurt me. I am not sure they can always see me. I will go down and—No! Wait... someone is coming to the front door."

RL, buoyant with thoughts of looking through Roaton treasures with Jayderay, enters the house. As they both love the old 'I Love Lucy' shows on the rerun channel, he calls out the famous line, "Looocee, I'm home!"

Pray you are *not* home, RL. Pray this does not *become* your home. It could. It easily could.

CHAPTER 38

MEANWHILE, WITH MERRY MANNY

Once upon a time, Manny's mouth looked like a hamster's butt. Sort of pursed, sort of pinched and sort of surrounded by dingy white fur; his van-dyke beard. Now it resembles an old horizontal vagina — stretched, hairy and worn. Gazing in the shop office mirror, he shakes his head. *God almighty I need to trim this thatch, it's beginning to look like a side-ways pussy... sorta like Fluffy's, 'course there ain't no mystery to that, it's sure as shit sure, been down there with it enough. Maybe I'll trim it today... if I can manage to keep Fluffy from clamping it between her thighs long enough.*

Today, SHE had decided was to be her bingo and shopping day, so HE should open HER shop. Marriage... it's a hell of a thing. It would be the first opening in many days. The first in many, many, fuck filled days. All those 'Fuck-Manny', fuck filled days.

Manny was actually looking forward to being open. And looking forward to a deep delving into that favorite bottom drawer... from which joy, charm and intelligence flowed like an amber fountain of youth. Most days lately, he often didn't have the strength to unscrew the cap. Yes, today would be different; today would be great.

But today would also be the day of the Frenchman.

From his bed beside Manny's desk, Sparkles watches his tired old human. *Poor old codger... that he continues to survive the female's attacks is miraculous. How she GOES at him. Those massive flexing thighs jackhammering him, trying to squeeze him in half, when that fails, then comes the smothering, and downward she jams his head... shrieking like a Banshee while she tears at his hair...* The little dog lets out a long whimpering whine of sympathy.

"What in the cornbread fuck is wrong with you, Sparks?" asks the old man, stepping to the desk. "Can't decide which piece of furniture to piss on, you damn walkin' bladder? Well, here in a bit, 'She Who Must Be Fucked,' will be off for the day, and you can anoint anything you want. I, sure as shit sure, won't bitch none, 'cause I'm gonna be tending to business," says Manny, with a toothless vagina smile, while sliding open that wonderful, soul saving, favorite drawer.

Suddenly, the entry door of the store opens, and its wired on, rusty cow bell clangs with ambience, announcing a customer. Enter the Frenchman.

It will be a memorable day for this son of France.

CHAPTER 39

PORT OF LAST RESORT

RL gets no answer from his smarty-pants, Ricky Riccardo greeting he's called out to Jayderay. The Roaton house is silent. The furniture's carved faces mutely stare. Dust motes drift about in the rays beneath the stained-glass skylight. It is a silence that seems loud. Ominous.

Walking further in, he spots the empty recliner. No breastplate. Apprehension begins to seep in. *She wouldn't have moved it. Absolutely she wouldn't... won't even touch it anymore.*

"Jayderay?" he calls, loudly. Nothing. Moving quickly into the kitchen, glancing out the window, checking the bathroom, and finding nothing. *Can't' believe she'd go upstairs... it's even spookier than down here. No, she wouldn't.* "Jayderay!" Shouting this time but still there is only silence. Nothing but the dead, dust laden, empty silence.

Stepping down into the day basement, he freezes at the sight of her canvas tote, sprawling in the closet. Her hairbrush, cell, and a small box of tissues lay spilled from its mouth. Kneeling slowly, his hand reaching to gather her things, stopping. Goose flesh ripples across him as he sees the bag's strap... it disappears *into* the wall. Imbedded in the wall. Touching the strap, sliding his fingers along it to the plaster. Rubbing the spot where it goes into the wall, he shakes his head, pulling at the canvas. *This is crap...total bullshit. Is she playing some kind of joke? How'd she stick the damn strap into the wall... she wouldn't waste this much time just to tease me.*

Against evidence of his own sight and common sense, RL wants to, desperately wants to believe this is all just a really good practical joke.

"All right, Jayderay," he calls out, "you got me, okay? Hear me? You really had me goin' there for a—" He stops, his eyes widening in horror.

Close by the open bag is a spray of... red. The bright, harsh, glaring red of blood. And above that, wedged in a crack between the floor boards— is a ripped out, bloody fingernail. With bile rising in his throat, he grabs for his phone, but manages to stop before punching 911. *No, what could the law do? Waste a lot of time, questioning the crap out me... hell, after seeing that fingernail, they might even haul my ass in... No. No cops... not yet.* Being in a profession usually looked at with a cold, steely eye by law enforcement, RL has had a few run-ins with them. Justifiable ones for the law's part. RL fears he has no time to waste fooling with the police.

Grabbing a wooden ladder-back chair from the room, he smashes it against the closet wall. Again and again and again, until it splinters, coming apart in his hands. Slinging the pieces down, he looks frantically for some other tool.

An awful, horrifying thought blossoms. *Suppose there is nothing behind this closet wall? What if there is no cleverly hidden secret room? What if there is only... the outside. But there has to be a room, a shed, something, that damn strap has got to go somewhere.*

Running for the door, tripping on the steps, skidding on one knee, he makes it into the kitchen. Yanking at the still locked back door, he backs up, kicking till the jamb splinters, and pulls it open. Looking out along the exterior wall, his heart sinks, shoulders slumping, panic rising. The wall is smooth; there is no added on, secret room. Nothing. And there damn sure isn't any canvas strap sticking out.

Like a cartoon lightbulb appearing above his head: *THE DOG! The dog can track her.* He grabs for his phone again, hitting speed dial for the shop. He starts in the second Frankie picks up. "Frankie! I'm at the Roaton place, something bad has happened to Jayderay, she's missing, there's blood. Go to her house, get the dog, and bring it out here. Now!"

"I'm on my way," is all that Frankie says. There are no questions, no silly remarks, no giggling. If there's any woman he's ever loved, it's Jayderay. She's the woman he wishes his mother had been, rather than the cause-spouting, alcoholic, liberal academic he'd been cursed with.

Hanging up, he brusquely rousts a couple who've been turkey-necking around for an hour, not buying. It wouldn't have mattered if they'd been excreting hundred-dollar bills. Get the fuck out.

Back at the Roaton house, still gripping his phone, RL sinks to his knees beside that disappearing strap, and the terrifying spray of red with a bloody, unpolished fingernail imbedded in the floor. Jayderay's fingernail. He knows it is, he feels it deep inside. So deep, he doesn't waste time on some frantic and futile search upstairs. She's gone. Taken by this house. *She was right, there is something awful about this place... why did I let her come out here? Where was I ? Where was I? Where was I?*

Slamming his fist into the closet wall, he leans forward, pressing the top of his head against the plastered surface. Holding his injured hand to his chest, he looks up. Driven to a last resort, he prays... as best he can. It is an extremely rare occurrence. RL despises God and has since childhood. But when he does pray, it's with a vengeance, with passion, and never for anything for himself. Not even money.

"All right you son of a bitch, I'm here, you've got me on my knees. Like you had me when I was a kid. Don't you hurt— don't you take this woman, this kind, this, this *GOOD* woman; she truly worships you, she goes to your fucking shit church, she *gives* to it. Don't do it, you bastard. Put me in her place, ruin me, cripple me, kill me—do anything, anything, anything to me, but don't you take her. I beg you on my knees... and how I hate you for the shame of it." What deity could possibly turn a deaf ear to such a plea?

RL had prayed as a child. Prayed as a crying little boy, shivering beneath his bed on a hard cold floor. Praying that the nightly shame of wetting would stop and put an end to that stinging morning belt. Put an end to the words of ridicule and disgust that came with the blows. The prayers were never answered. The child had quit praying, cursed God, and outgrew the shame. The belt had continued for other wrongs. Had continued until RL killed the man, murdered that good Christian nightmare.

———•◦•———

Above this praying, desperate man, a hand-holding couple stand at the upstairs railing, listening. One silently pulls the other back and down the connecting hall.

"Elv-is, they will not find the woman. The door will not appear, not open for them. I have listened to her and this man. Conversations that are beyond your range of hearing. I wish to help. The woman is a good person; the man... the man feels toward God as I do. I must help."

Proby squirms and frowns before speaking. All he knows of God is from old movies. God created. God was all powerful. God was good. Down deep where Proby pushed and kept everything he knew, but could not face, were some hard facts. Dr. Lillith Sally Gaust had created him. Lillith was all powerful. And Lillith—was not good. So what did that make him? *PUSH IT AWAY!... that does not matter... push it away. Only Shadow matters.*

"I'll do whatever you want, Shadow. I'll do whatever you ask, but to help, don't we have to... to go down there? Show ourselves? Isn't that dangerous for you?"

"No, Elv-is. That man, nor any of the others, can hurt me. Knowledge of my... *our* existence might cause later trouble, but remember, these people have already seen you."

His lavender complexion turns purple as Proby

remembers how he had ran from them, scrambling away, squealing with fright. *Had Shadow seen that?... of course she had... I must, I will be brave now...not for them... but for her, for Shadow.*

"Uh... yeah. Well, Shadow... I guess I kinda forgot about all that. So, um, do you want me to go down? I'm not scared. I am really not afraid. Really not."

Shadow smiles slightly, saying, "No, my pretty, pretty, and brave Elv-is, that doorway will not work for you. It is now of the house, of me, it is no longer of your world like the Ex-tender is. We shall go together— but only if you wish to come."

There is no place, anywhere, in any world, that Proby would not follow her.

———— ·•· ————

Still kneeling at the wall, RL gazes down at the simple canvas strap. A piece of coarse cloth that pierces his heart on its way to nowhere. *To nowhere... How can this be? It's not possible... it can't be...*

RL feels rather than hears the couple walk up. He's too worried and heartsick to give a constipated cat's crap about the appearance of a spook or some lavender spaceman. Rising to face them, he speaks.

"I've seen this damn lizard thing before, but what the hell are—"

"He is a *MAN*," hisses Shadow, abruptly leaning toward RL. Her eyebrows arching, the shooting stars in her eyes becoming so rapid, the eyes become totally white.

The sheer force of her wrath pushes RL backward, his eyes widening; he hits the closet wall. He had been too desperate and worried to even consider being frightened of the two. He has reconsidered.

"And he is my *HUSBAND*," she continues, taking a step forward, her eyes glowing with white heat. "You *WILL* address him with respect. His name is Elv-is. Hear me! His name is Elv-is. I bid you say it, I bid you to do so." Her words and breath are as steam rolling through the ebony lips. The scar across her ashen face pulses.

Proby at once straightens, lifting his chin higher. *Husband! Wow...*

"Yes," RL quickly answers. "Yes, he is a man, and he is your husband. His name is Elvis. And—my, mine is RL, and I, I apologize to you both for being rude. It's just...I'm dealing with, with an emergency, and I—"

"And we've come to help," interrupts Proby, speaking for the first time. "She can, Shadow, my wife can get you into— into where the woman has been taken." *Wow! I'm married...like in the movies...*

RL steps forward, eyes glinting with hope. Unconsciously extending his right hand to shake, he asks, "You know where she is? You can take me to her?"

No one had ever offered to shake Proby's hand before, and he's nearly too shocked to respond. "Well, yeah—kind of I know... RL... sir," he says, taking the hand.

"Elv-is only *knows of* this place, he, nor I, have ever entered into it," says Shadow. "I can gain you access into where your woman has been taken, but I cannot enter. You need to understand, there are monstrous creatures and great danger; you must take help with you. I cannot bear for Elv-is to go— "

"I've called for help, it's on the way," RL interrupts. "But I'm not waiting, if she's there, I MUST go, I have to go. I'll go in now, and the guy I've called will just have to follow."

Watching RL and Shadow, Proby thinks hard about Lab Spills... and The Waydowns. That place of dark rumors, a place of unknown horrors and death. He thinks of capture by Lillith. His mouth is dry, he fidgets, he palms his duck tails back, he finger combs the sideburns, he smooths his sparkling jacket; he's scared shitless. AND most of all, he thinks of Shadow... his *wife*. The wife who has seen him running scared. Has seen him scuttling and squealing in fear... like a fucking lizard. He is a man now, he is Elvis. Shadow has said so. Proby says the only thing he can possibly say.

"I will go with you."

Shadow looks over, reaching for his hand. "No, Elv-is, please not. You must not do this thing. You must not leave my side—"

"I have to go with him, Shadow. I can't just stand here with you, and let him—"

"No, Elv-is! I could not bear it should som—"

"GOD DAMN IT!" explodes RL. "Open the fucking— I'm sorry, I'm sorry… but please, please, open that place up—"

And Frankie arrives.

CHAPTER 40

ON THE WAYDOWNS SIDE OF THAT CLOSET

As Jayderay screams to her God for help, the Coiler pulls her past the elevator door— into the Waydowns. It stretches another scaled arm out, delicately tapping the door controls, shutting it.

Looking down past her tentacle wrapped legs, Jayderay sees what has caught her. And her dithering God finally shows a little mercy; she faints into blackness.

Filling a full third of the wide corridor, is a pulsing, wart sprinkled, bulbous, variegated green body. The Coiler sits on three coiled tentacles, while many others lift and writhe in the air about it, constantly in motion. Several bright orange eyes, clustered on top, angle in all directions. This is one really ugly fucker.

Gliding on the rolled-up, flexing tentacles, the Coiler pulls itself and Jayderay closer together. Her head lolls from side to side, and blood drips from her nose. Lifting the woman into the air, her limbs flopping, it slides silently away from the elevator door; the Coiler wants to avoid any surprises coming through from the house. It doesn't like interrupted meals. They're not good for the digestion.

About 200 feet away, it stops, with Jayderay's body dangling and swaying, her nose draining life. From one of several vertical lipped openings spaced about the lower portion of its body, a beak appears. A beak for ripping and tearing meat. The Coiler begins lowering the limp, bleeding woman. That sharp beak reaches upwards, gnashing, snapping, eager.

———————

Elsewhere, on this same twisted and forsaken level of the Waydowns, a long, agonizing struggle ends. And something finally breaks free, ripping itself loose from the bed it has lain on for so many years. Painfully lain in, and slowly grown, like a tree, like an oak. The thing is now huge, massive. It rises, pulling roots with it from the alien soil; roots it has grown. The bed it had been fighting to free itself from... was made of dirt. Soil taken from a planet far away by those who once flew this ancient ship.

Standing slowly, its body making sounds like breaking wood, the beast towers high in the room.

Pieces of rotting cloth fall away from the bark-like skin and furry moss on its back.

A square piece of metal glints in the always present light, something that is still imbedded in the thing's waist. Moss and bark have grown around but not totally covered the two stamped letters that are still visible: A. M. It is a belt buckle. This creature had been a man, a member of staff.

This former man, Arthur Matheson, had once been in charge of the ship's botanical lab. He had been a dedicated, resolute, and intelligent man. A loyal employee. When the disaster of the failed Extender experiments and the ensuing quarantine came, he had kept to his tasks of tending the alien seeds, nurturing sprouting plants, and regularly checking the nutrient enriched fluid the ship's auto feed supplied. He did not falter. Not ever.

Then came the mutiny. Arthur had remained loyal, dedicated, and had labored on. As insanity and cannibalism began sweeping through the staff, this man had kept his head, still being true, steadfastly guarding the lab and plants in his charge.

While fighting off a marauding, blood smeared labbie, Authur had suffered a severe blow to the head. Managing to lock the lab's door, he had staggered toward the first aid supplies. But his bleeding brain took him into a black void, and he had collapsed on top of his beloved plants growing in that strange, alien soil. Those very foreign, sprouting seeds— with their constant auto-feed of nutrient rich fluids.

And there, in a coma, Arthur Matheson had stayed; stayed on that bed of extraterrestrial soil and plants. Stayed through many, long years, being liquid fed by the ancient starship, developing roots. And the body grew slowly like an oak. Grew until very recently, when the burrowing parasites had awakened what little was left of the once human mind. He was no longer intelligent. He was no longer a man. He was no longer anything that had a name.

This once a human, was now just a thing. A very big, deadly thing. But it still had enough brain left to hate. Enough left to know that loyalty and devotion had been repaid with abandonment and treachery. Yes, enough mind remained to hate. And enough mind to have a mission.

What had once been an eye is now a protruding, gnarled, dusky pink root, one among many that had grown from its body; and one of several that had held it so firmly to that bed of dirt. The thing tries to rip out the eye-growth, as a thick pink discharge seeps from the socket. Screaming with a sound like a wood chipper, it gives up on the root, and lurches to the decades locked door. Tearing it from the hinges, Arthur tosses it over the massive shoulders as if it were weightless.

How much this thing hated; how much it hated anything that moved. And this former human, this former faithful employee, is going from this room. It has a mission: A mission to kill.

Quite a distance from the raging, former Arthur Matheson, the Coiler hears something, but not Arthur. It stops lowering Jayderay, listening intently. Perhaps another delicacy? It often hunts and captures several creatures during these forays down from the nest. When needed, it can produce webbing from the beak, securing prey alive for future dining. The snapping beak withdraws, and it lowers the limp body, dumping her carelessly onto the corridor floor. Quietly gliding toward the noise with all eyes swiveling, it spots a Spill coming from the endless warren of halls and passages.

Seeing the pulsing green body and waving tentacles, the Spill keeps coming. Seevee has said it was safe from Coilers; they were now allies. Fearing attack from the many limbed creatures is no longer necessary.

A tentacle shoots forward, wrapping about the Spills torso. *Allies my ass*...thinks the Spill. Throughout history, allies have often thought this about allies.

Screaming, the Spill tries to sink its fangs into the ever-tightening serpentine arm. Being one of Tanya's recruits, it is armed with a knife, and shrieking "Ton" repeatedly, it slashes, cuts, and rips at the squeezing tentacle.

If a Coiler could yawn, this one would. It casually smashes the uncooperative Spill head first into a wall, stunning it into silence. It's best if Ton doesn't hear one of her minions being caught and had for lunch. That might not be too good for their incipient alliance.

The dark, gripping tentacle brings the feebly struggling Spill closer, positioning it directly above. The food lowering process starts again, and the beak reappears, snapping away greedily. The Coiler has decided to eat this lively one now. It has plenty of time, since the other prisoner appears to have died, and isn't going anywhere. Its hungry, and still moving meat is so much better.

Jayderay's limp body lays close by. The Coiler is right; she isn't going anywhere.

—————— ♦ ——————

Above the Waydowns, on Deck 19, Dr. Moto thinks of his clandestine meeting with Tanya. He naturally has no intentions of actually cooperating with that little upstart of a labbie. She'd been nothing but a glorified secretary, guarding a console of lighted and blinking buttons. Until she had fallen into disfavor with the Honored Shit of Dragons. Moto chuckles about that. *What a time the fair Tanya must have had when the Almosts took her. And what an Empress Pussy the round-eye slut must have! To have gained control over them in such a short period of time is indeed an impressive accomplishment.*

And Moto did have admiration for the most exceedingly wonderful ending Tanya had planned for Dr. Lillith Sally Gaust. Most wonderful indeed. If he didn't beat Tanya to it and kill the foul bitch first. A very strong possibility. She needs it badly.

Yes, Dr. Moto might temporarily go along with Tanya's little plan, she and her ragtag band of Lab Spills, and whatever other monstrosities she might dredge up. But Moto has a scheme of his own. A scheme that could be greatly aided by something he'd seen in the Waydowns during their meet. Something she was too ignorant to know the uses of. A device that had been on that deck before the chaos, before it became part of the Waydowns. *I must pull up some old files, try and determine if it's what I hope it is. And perhaps another quick trip into the Waydowns is called for. A bit of reconnoitering without that bit of fluff Tanya being present. Yes, I must.*

Even someone as brilliantly devious as Dr. Moto can occasionally think askew. Even the most calculating can get a crimp in the brain, can think wrong headedly about things. Yes, anyone can— fuck up. Chance can trump all plans... including those of a Moto.

CHAPTER 41

FRANKIE ARRIVES

Getting into Jayderay's home was no problem for Frankie. Hell, he's an antiques dealer, they're always prepared for locked doors. Providing there's no one home, that is. They're always very careful and considerate about that part, mustn't disturb anyone. Or someone of great value might get their ass blown off. This is Texas, after all.

Princess, though knowing Frankie, wasn't quite so easy. He talked to her and petted, but not for long. Jayderay was in trouble, and he wasted no time. Finding the dog's leash draped over a chair, and while speaking softly, he snaps it to the collar, then quickly wraps it around her muzzle. Picking her up, he carries her out to the waiting open door of his car, the seat pushed back and ready.

Frankie doesn't bother with going back and locking the house. The clock is ticking, and time is running against the only two people he cares about. The only two people he's ever cared about... besides Frankie.

Princess is an angel about it all, and quietly sits still, minding her manners. Whining a little, she occasionally looks over at Frankie with that quizzical expression dogs do so well. While driving, he continues talking softly to the dog, stroking her neck, and finally unwraps the leash from her muzzle. And except for getting behind some inconsiderate butt plug who was determined to obey the speed limit, they make good time.

Being pulled into the house by a yelping, straining Princess, both she and Frankie immediately see Shadow and Proby walking from the basement. Holding hands. Halting, the dog seems mesmerized by the two, practically going on point. Who wouldn't? They *are* quite a couple.

Frankie stares as he slowly kneels beside Princess, keeping a hold on the leash, and laying a hand on her back. *My God, the woman is real, and holding the lizard's hand. Well now, won't this meeting be just a trifle awkward.*

RL, closely following the couple, sees Frankie, and quickly thinks of his own faux paux of a few minutes ago. He also thinks of the silly bastard's loose, quick, and smart aleckey mouth. Disaster looms!

"Frankie!" he nearly shouts, trying to avoid imminent

catastrophe. Gesturing toward the couple, he continues frantically, "Let me introduce Shadow... and her *husband,* whose name is *ELVIS*. This house is *their home,* and they have offered to help. They *know* where Jayderay is," continues RL, putting great stress on the salient words, his eyebrows flapping like a diarrhetic bat.

Frankie, being Frankie, has necessarily been a quick study since his earliest years, catches all the emphasized words. *Husband, oh dear... a married woman. I might've known my first time would prove perilous... I better watch my mouth, or RL's eyebrows will lift him into space.* He flashes his most disarming boy scout smile.

"So happy to meet you two! And I knew right away you were Elvis, guy! I mean you'd have to be, who else could possibly have such a beautiful wife."

Shadow, being a woman, was *born* a quick study. Her dark lips smile demurely, producing the ghost of a dimple in each cheek. And she nods graciously, remaining silent.

Proby has suddenly grown about three inches taller, and he positively beams. It's not hard for him to do, being lavender and all.

Frankie, wanting to follow success with success, unclips the leash and Princess runs straight to Proby, her tail a wagging blur.

"Gosh! I always, always wanted a dog," he says kneeling to meet her. His grin is as big as the dog's.

———••———

Back in the Waydowns, the Coiler drops the remains from its dinner of Spill; the discards amounting to very little. It must get the other captive now; the human might not be dead and try to escape— but not bloody likely. Moving toward Jayderay, it picks her up. It will web this one and carry it up a stanchion to the nest far, far above. It's been thinking during its meal, thinking about having this surplus body. Which had made it start thinking of Zthruskaing.

Whichever Coiler brings the food offering, gets to be the Zthruska-*er*, rather than being the Zthruska-*ee*. While both roles are quite enjoyable, whichever is the Zthruska-er can't become pregnant. That's kind of a big deal... laying those eggs is a real pain in the ass. Plus, the recipient of the food offering was required to do that ridiculous damn acceptance dance. Twirling about repeatedly on tippy tentacles... really now, just how did that embarrassing shit come into play? But if a Coiler wanted to Zthruska, it was either bring the grub... or do the dance. Sort of a put up, or put out, proposition. Courtship can indeed be such a problem. For all species.

———— + + + ————

That former man, Arther Matheson, throws the ripped off door aside, sending it sailing across the room to crash against a counter. This thing must get out, must get into the passageway. It must. It does not hunger, it does not feel, it hates. It hates anything that moves.

The Arther monster bends to get through the opening. Its back creaks and splits, leaking a viscous milky-pink sap. Growths from Arther's body crack and splinter as he fights through the opening, and he screams the wood chipper sound. Breaking through into the corridor, he slams up against the opposite wall.

Finally free from the lab he had once tended, the former Arthur slowly forces his body erect. He is immense, the knot encrusted head towering into the hazy air, roots like horns extend out at twisting angles. Its remaining eye rolls wildly in the socket, as pink sap and red parasitic larva drip from the sagging lower lid. But it can see... and it is free now, it can move. And it hates, hates anything that moves.

CHAPTER 42

BACK IN TOWN: SACRE BLEU TO YOU TOO

As Manfred ponders trimming the whiskers surrounding that horizontal vagina his mouth resembles, he's also taking some small medicinal gulps of Jim Beam. Lubrication for the day. Supposedly a Fluffy free day; a good, restful day. But then the cow bell clangs. The one she had insisted he wire to the door... for ambience.

Being in high spirits, he saunters out of the office, just in time to see a Pierre mincing into the store.

Pierre Francois Conyea is an antiques dealer from France. He looks it. From his jaunty little beret perched to one side, on down to some darling, soft, dainty shoes. In between is a three-piece, nightmare-colored suit; the type of color an intestinally disturbed bird might produce.

The very sight of this beret-wearing popinjay immediately gnaws into Manny's vitals. His hemorrhoids become engorged, inflamed— erect even. Yet, being in an upbeat mood with a day before him without Fluffy, or Fluffy fucking, and very much *with* a bottle... or two, he doesn't run the foul twerp off. Leaning against the cracked, glass topped display counter, he watches. *I, sure as shit sure, need to keep an eye on this trike-seat sniffer. Where in hell did he find those clothes? Sick Cunt, China most likely. Looks like the type to piss in Spark's water dish... and then drink it.*

The visitor does not speak. After giving Manny a slow look up and down, Pierre sniffs delicately, and then starts picking merchandise up, examining the item and price tag. Each thing he picks up results in an exclamation and a bit of theatre:

"Mon Dieu!" clapping his hand to a cheek, roughly putting the item down.

"La Nausée!" clutching his stomach, carelessly tossing another thing aside.

"Le Vomit!" slapping two fingers over his lips, cheeks blowing out, flinging another item back.

"De Merde!... Le Sheeet!" shaking his head, dropping yet another.

And on around the shop Precious Pierre continues, leaving a trail of "Mon Dieu, La Nausé, Le Vomit, Le Sheeet" each comment accompanied with histrionics... and a lot of mishandled property. Manny's property.

All antiques and junque shops get this type. Bad potty training during the customer's formative years is probably responsible. Or none. If ignored, they usually wear themselves out with their own repetitions and leave. And of course, loudly complaining about worthless merchandise and poor service. Some shop owners help with the exit. Shop owners like Manfred Claude Wetzel.

Sparks trots out from the office and takes a position beside Manny. Silently watching Pierre's progress around the store, he glances up at his human, then back at the diseased shopper. *This shouldn't take long... wonder if this one will make it out with his hat and ass? I should find out any minute now.*

Manny looks down at the dog, silently willing it to go hike a leg on the Frenchman. *Why not, you little turd rustler? You piss on everything else in the store. 'Course I don't much blame you, I ain't very keen on gettin' too close to the tiddly-wink neither; and this jelly-dick is wearin' perfume that's gotta be called Eau de Queer Nuts. I bet that silly bastard Frankie would just love the shit... all Root the Fruit smelly.*

Giving out a snort of disgust, Manny walks back to the office. And downs a bit of Beam's Buoyant Bliss... about three fingers worth from the quart bottle. Large fingers. Just a little fortification for the pleasantries he feels sure are coming. Shit sure, in fact.

As Manny gulps down the modest sized three fingers, Fluffy starts her decent from their apartment. All 360 luscious pounds of her, with each stair step creaking groans. She's intending to model her latest floral tent dress for Manny. And just maybe, she'll show him how quickly she can shuck out of it. She ain't wearin' a stitch underneath. Nothing... nothing except the hearts she's drawn around each nipple. Cherry red, matching her lipstick.

Fortunately, Hot Nipples Fluffy sees the Frenchman down below before she can say something intended for Manny only. Something demure, something like "Hi, you big, wienered devil!" or some other tender endearments. But she does spot Pierre, and stops, deciding to wait in case Manny is about to make a sale.

Not seeing Fluffy, who's still at the stop of the stairs, Pierre does see the freshly lubricated Manny coming from the office. How fortuitous. The Frenchman has been saving his best ejaculation, his top-choice expression of shock and disdain. Picking up a milk stool from beside the bottom step, he readies himself, looking closely at the price tag. Any price will do, even free.

As Manny walks up, both are now standing at the foot of the stairs. Pierre looking at the tag, then slaps a hand to his forehead, yelling "Sacré Bleu!"

"WHAT?! SUCK YOU BLUE?! WHY YOU FAGGOT

SON OF A BITCH!" screams an enraged Manny. And he plants a bony fist in Sacré Bleu's eye. The stool flies through the air, lands, bounces, and snaps off a leg. It doesn't matter, Penis Pulling Pierre, wouldn't have bought it anyway.

Fluffy starts down the steps. Silently bristling, quietly burning. Swelling.

The Frenchman, like all Frenchmen, consider surrendering the natural, the only thing to do in any battle. Let someone else fight for them. They always have. But Pierre is much younger than his assailant, bigger, stronger, plus the old man smells as if he's drank a barrel of hooch. A big barrel.

Also, though Pierre doesn't know it, Manny has had the very soul fucked out of him. Daily. Several times daily. He is drained, he is milked, he is terminally weak. Perhaps this is that very, very, very rare time for French valor. It would be a first for Pierre, possibly even a first for France.

So, Pierre Conyea delivers a round-house slap to the old man's face, sending the drunk codger reeling back against the sales counter. Viva La France! Manny tries to catch himself, but slips on the glass, collapsing to the floor.

Sparkles rushes in, biting at the brave Frenchman's ankle. Pierre squeals, aiming a kick at the dog.

"I saw you attack my husband! And now you're kicking my poor little dog!" shouts an angry voice. A very large angry voice.

Pierre spins about to face... a very large floral tent dress standing on the stairs. Filled with an extremely large florid woman. Fluffy stands on the next to the last step. A mere couple of feet away. Redly glowing and glowering with rage.

"I, I, I calling Gendarmes!" Pierre squeaks. The time for French valor has ended. "I sue! I have you all—"

Fluffy flies. Launching herself in a dive, she lands on top of the lawsuit threatening, cop calling, scion of French manhood. All of her. All of her on top of him. All of her.

"What you are going to do," informs Fluffy, raising up enough to grip both lapels of his coat, and glaring ferally into his eyes, "is get out of my store. Do you hear me? Do you? Do you hear me?" she accentuates each question with a shake, bouncing Pierre's beret wearing head against the floor. "I saw you attack my poor frail, sick husband, and then kick my tiny dog who was only trying to defend him. What you are going to do is GO! Do you hear me? Do you? Tell me what you are going to do, little man. TELL - ME - NOW!"

With Fluffy on top, Pierre can only wheeze, but

wheeze he does. With all his heart he wheezes. With every fiber of his being, he wheezes:

"I, I go... I gone- went, I gone- went... now."

" Yes, very good, you squeaking little shit. See that you do and see that you do it NOW!" orders Fluffy. Rolling off the wheezing Pierre, she crawls over to Manny, and pulls him to her behemoth bosom, cradling him. Cradling him in tender arms... arms like Anacondas.

"Oh, Manny! You were so brave, and I was so afraid, but Lordy, Lord, Lord, didn't you just take care of that horsey butt! Oh, my Manny Man, my Studly-Wudly."

Behind the embracing couple, a French pancake ripples slowly, painfully toward the exit. Pierre Francois Conyea reaches out, pulls himself forward, his face dragging against the floor. He reaches out, pulls himself forward again, his face furrowing the carpet. And again, and again, and again. With each pull he gasps into the rug:

"I go... I fucking gone- went... now."

He reaches, he pulls, he gasps: "I go... I fucking gone- went...now." Reach, pull, gasp: "I go... I fucking gone- went...now." And on and on went the slow retreat of this valiant Frenchman. Perhaps if Joan of Arc had been more like Fluffy, the French wouldn't have betrayed her. All in all, it has been a most memorable day for Pierre.

Quite some time later, after the pancake had finally undulated and gasped its way out of the store, Sparks hikes his leg over a new item. With expert aim, he drenches a jaunty beret. Viva La France.

CHAPTER 43

AT THE ROATON HOUSE: INTO THE WAYDOWNS

Inside the Roaton house, the three waiting men and dog steel themselves to enter the unknown hell of the Waydowns. Princess yelps, straining at the leash in Frankie's hand. At a nod from RL, Shadow takes a deep breath, reaches out and touches the closet wall. It glows, and the door at once flickers into view, sliding open. And they rush into the awaiting corridor, Princess leads, tugging against Frankie's grip.

A couple of hundred feet away, the very full Coiler is casually preparing to web Jayderay's body... and still thinking of Zthruskaing. One of the busy eyes spot the door sliding open, and it stops being casual. All its eyes glow and swivel as the group rushes in. It quickly starts gliding silently toward them, tentacles reaching out. Just look at this! A self- delivering feast. Jayderay's body lays behind the massive creature, obscured from view.

And then *they* see the Coiler. All but the dog freeze, even Proby, long used to horrors, has never seen anything like this monster awaiting them in the hall.

The thing is fast, the coils it sits on rapidly flexing, and with only a few yards to travel, it is coming. The snapping beak appears.

Only Princess is beyond fear, catching Jayderay's scent, she tears the leash from Frankie's hand, lunging to attack the Coiler. RL dives for the dog's strap, going to his knees, barely catching its end. Trying to drag the dog back, scrambling to get on his feet, he slips, falling backward.

Now less than twenty feet away, the Coiler streaks toward them, and starts emitting a high-pitched piercing squeal, the dark tentacles waving, tips clutching at air, the beak snapping.

RL, still on his butt, fights to hold the leash, and scoot backward into the closet. The thing is less than ten feet away, the writhing scaled coils fully extended.

Proby darts forward, scooping the dog into his arms, as Frankie grabs RL, dragging him back into the closet. Proby falls in through the opening, catapulting Princess inside, screaming, "Shut it, Shadow, shut the door!"

Shadow slams her hand into the wall as Proby scrambles inside— but she isn't quick enough.

Just as the door closes — the end of a tentacle snakes in, wrapping around his ankle.

───

The newly freed monster that was once Arthur Matheson, starts down the corridor. It has no thought as to a destination. It has no plan, it has only hate and its mission to kill. It only wants to slaughter. It wants to rend, to shred all living flesh. To murder all that can move.

As it crashes from one side of the hall to the other, splintering growths crackle and break, leaving thick pink smears. The one eye rolls up and down, back and forth, as wriggling worms crawl from behind it, falling into the sagging lower lid. They spill out onto the moss like tufts growing on the face, and a dusky pink, twisted root protrudes from the other eye socket, like a horn. Its bark encrusted hands pound like mallets into the walls and whatever is near.

As the hall tees into yet another corridor, the creature lurches into the far wall before turning, punching, and pounding on the metal. Ricocheting, wall to wall, back and forth, splintering its growths, and hammering at anything, at everything, at life. This thing that was once a man shambles and rages on.

───

As the snaking tentacle wraps around Proby's ankle, the elevator door zips shut. And it meshes with, and immediately becomes the old, plastered closet wall. The door has not severed the tentacle. The years ago teleported elevator door has done exactly the inexplicable thing it had done with the strap of Jayderay's canvas tote.

RL scrambles to his feet as Shadow utters a small cry, dropping to her knees beside Proby. He sits with one leg drawn up, his other extends toward the wall. That wall that has a tentacle coming through it, gripping his ankle. Frankie gathers the leash as Princess whimpers, bristles and growls at the tentacle.

Putting a crooked arm around Proby's shoulder, the ash and mist colored woman reaches down and without hesitation touches the scaled coil. It spasms, tightening, Proby moans and she jerks her hand back.

"Please don't touch it again, Shadow. I'm afraid it'll keep tightening, and maybe break something, or... " He stops, too horrified with the thought of having the foot squeezed off, to finish. The lavender skin has bleached into a fish-belly pallor.

"Oh, Elv-is," is all she says, a tear spills from one eye, rolling down the scarred cheek.

"Jesus Christ Almighty," says Frankie, "what IS that thing? What IS that place?"

"It's part of a, part of a... the ship, a starship," answers Proby, in a dazed voice, still looking in horror at his caught ankle. "That place is called the Waydowns, I don't know what that creature—"

"A spaceship!" exclaims Frankie. "I knew it! Where does—"

"God damn it, Jayderay is still in there with a monster!" explodes RL. "And now because this, this damn Elvis thing was too slow we can't get—"

"SHUT UP, RL, SHUT UP!" yells Frankie, as Shadow slowly rises from Proby's side. Her eyes pulsing totally white, her facial scar darkening, and the ebony lips peeling back from bared teeth.

"You shut your fucking mouth, RL," Frankie says, softening his voice this time, laying a hand on RL's shoulder. "You're not hearing yourself, boss; you're talking God damn crazy." Gesturing with his chin towards Shadow and Proby, "They didn't have to help, Elvis didn't have to go in. Without them we would never have even found out about the door; Jayderay would be gone. Gone fucking forever, lost in hell. Understand?" Turning toward Shadow he says, "He's in love with that woman and too stupid to know it or know what he's saying. I apologize for him."

"No," says RL, in a strained hoarse voice. "I do know I'm in love with her, I'm just stupid, too damn stupid to tell her and too stupid to know friends." Standing there, hands clenching, looking directly at Elvis, "I'm, I'm sorry for what I said... no, no, I'm *ashamed* of it, I'm ashamed of *me*. I didn't mean— I don't— oh, God damn it!" he breaks off with a sob, turning away.

Proby, sitting on the floor with his foot gripped by a thing from hell, caught because he had helped, says, "It's okay... RL, uh, sir. Really, sir, it's alright. I know you didn't mean it." He looks like a little boy who'll say anything to get his parents to stop fighting. Then looking at his wife, he says, "Shadow... it is okay, honey, really it is."

Shadow silently kneels back down beside him, placing a hand to his cheek. "Oh, Elv-is," are her only words. She had not spoken to RL. But she will not forget what RL has said. She is woman and her memory is forever.

"No, it's not alright, Elvis," says RL, his back still to them. "It was inexcusable, and I know it. And I also know you saved Princess; I won't forget that." He runs all fingers through his hair, sliding both hands back down to his face, scrubbing at tears. Turning toward them, he says, "But I'll try to make up for... for being me. I'll try and not be such... an ass." He gives a sour, humorless chuckle, and adds, "Sometimes, that's pretty hard to do. So, how about while you and I work on getting you free, Elvis, Frankie runs to my house to get the guns, then all of—"

"Boss," Frankie breaks in, "let's think about this. Either that thing knows how to operate the door, or it got lucky when it grabbed Jayderay. I'm guessing it was more than luck, so it's smart. And right now, it's thinking of the best way to get its tentacle back. It knows there are several of us, and it doesn't want to slither into a trap. That's probably the only reason it hasn't just opened the door and yanked Elvis back in or charged in here attacking."

Hearing the words "...yank Elvis back in" Proby lets out a small cry, and both of Shadow's arms leap around him.

"Let's try and get that tentacle thing off him," Frankie continues, "then all of us can move further back, and we can plan some kind of rescue."

"Okay, you're thinking straight. While you're at it, got any ideas about how to get him loose?" asks RL, pointing at Proby.

"Well, I just sorta happen to have this," Frankie answers, pulling an Ivory handled straight razor from his back pocket.

RL is not surprised. He knows the silly bastard.

<hr>

In the Waydowns, on the opposite side of that closet wall, sits the Coiler. It's not trashing about, mindlessly yanking at its imbedded tentacle. More importantly, for RL and crew, it has not raised one of its other scaled arms to the controls. Two of the orange eyes stare intently at the door, while the rest swivel about, keeping watch, looking around, as eyes are supposed to. Humans might do well with such an arrangement.

The Coiler is indeed smart, as Frankie had suggested. It's very smart; and it is thinking, thinking hard, sitting there quietly analyzing the situation. This is its version of 'look before you leap.' Most humans never learn this valuable practice. Politicians and leaders seldom mange it either. It knows it has a firm hold on one of the four, and rightly figures the other three are there, close by. And they may have armed themselves. So it sits and thinks.

Only a couple hundred feet away, lies Jayderay's body where the Coiler had dropped it. Her arms and legs are twisted awkwardly, and the brown skin has grown much lighter, too much. The burst nose no longer bleeds, and crusts of congealed blood have formed in both nostrils. The beds of her ripped nails no longer seep. Trails of dried tears, saliva, and blood show across the cold face. That prayed to, and worshipped, and obeyed God of hers... must be busy.

⁕

Quite some distance from Jayderay and the Coiler, a different type of creature is not thinking. It no longer can. Nor is it sitting. It is hating. It is berserk and rampaging.

Something once human careens back and forth between the corridor walls. Fists like wooden sledge hammers punch and pound. These white walls of metal from another world take no damage but give off huge dull thudding sounds as the blows land. Tree trunk legs stiffly march the beast along in a staggering goosestep. Every surface the thing crashes into or hits shows smears of a thick pink syrup, its sap, its blood, and it leaves a trail of snapped, torn off debris from itself. Hate. Hate. Hate emanates from the former Arthur Matheson, that once dedicated, loyal and intelligent employee. It lets out an occasional reverberating scream, the sound of a chain saw.

From an entrance to yet another room, a conference table sticks out into the hall. Dropped long ago by members of a terrified, uninfected staff, trying frantically to barricade themselves from their friends and workmates — who now wanted to eat them. A little above this table, a Spill peeks around the openings edge, curious about the noise. Not a good idea. A cat might've told it that curiosity can have consequences.

No, the peek was not the thing to do. For that quick look has revealed a towering, root and tumor encrusted, raging... *something*. A plant monster, and that's quite an observation coming from a Lab Spill. Had the Spill worn any clothes, it would have ruined them, or at least the pants. The Spill rises to the occasion and bravely makes do without pants. It shits down both bare legs.

The rolling, parasite-drooling eye of this former dedicated man, spots the peeking Spill. The Spill, no fool, jerks its head back into the room. Too late.

With a grinding roar, the plant monster lunges forward. Grabbing the table, it hurls it sliding across the floor toward the fleeing Spill. The table rams into the creature's back, knocking it to the floor. What had been Arthur, shambles into the room.

No, the Spill shouldn't have peeked.

Seeing Frankie produce the straight razor, Proby produces a moan, absolutely certain they're going to amputate his foot. Shadow hugs him closer, quickly moving her body, shielding him from the razor. "You will not cut him," she hisses.

"No, no, no, you two!" says Frankie, correctly deciphering the moan, the terror on Proby's face, and Shadow's feral hiss. "This," he continues, brandishing the deadly razor "is for that fat worm wrapped around your ankle, Elvis."

This does not comfort Proby, who immediately thinks of the tentacle squeezing his foot off. "Can't we let Shadow start the door opening, and... and the thing will probably release me, then you two can snatch me inside as soon as it does. Right? And then she can, real quick like, start it closing? That'll work, sure it will. Won't it? Please?" He's nearly babbling.

RL, dropping to a knee beside the two, looks closely at the tentacle wrapped ankle. "Elvis, I doubt it will let you go when the door opens, and I don't think me and Frankie could pull you away from it. It's more likely that Octopus monster would surge in here with us."

Proby looks at RL, at this man who had actually shaken his hand. This man who has lost his love to the Waydowns. "I'm sorry for being so much trouble and holding you up, I want to help, uh, RL... sir. I want to get her back too, but what if... I'm afraid it might..." he breaks off, unable to finish. He looks at his wife. "What do you... what if... what...," he takes a deep breath, and his next sentence comes out in a rush. "Shadow, will you still want me if I'm a cripple?"

The woman tightens her broken arms around him, "Elv-is, if you had no feet, if you had no arms, I would want you still. I love you." It is the first time she has told him. It is the first time anyone has ever said those words to him.

Holding her, he simply says, "Then I want them to cut... no matter what happens."

Shadow removes her arms from him, worry and tears etching the scarred, alabaster face. Still kneeling at his side, taking his hands in hers, she says, "I think this is correct to do, Elv-is. Let them sever the beast's arm. But I promise you, I swear to you, if you should say to stop, I WILL make them stop." No one doubts her.

"Hey everybody, listen, I've been thinking," Frankie says, "IF that Octo-puss can operate the door, then why won't it open up the second it feels me cutting?"

"Damn it," says RL, "we've got to DO something! Jayderay is in that hell hole. Maybe the thing did just get lucky in opening the door when it grabbed her. Why else hasn't it opened the door back up? Why else hasn't it at least tried to free itself?"

"That's a point, Boss. But you're right about Jayderay. We've got to do something and do it now."

Sitting there, his ankle in the grips of a monster, his mouth too dry to swallow, Proby looks into Shadow's star-shooting eyes. *This really is just like being in a movie... but I don't like this one.*

"Okay," says a frightened little boy's voice. "let's just do it, just cut it off quick, and I'll be ready to jump back."

Frankie, beginning to regret ever suggesting this, drops to one knee, razor in hand.

CHAPTER 44

OL' ARTHUR

The plant monster, that former Arthur Matheson, shambles after the table it has just thrown into the fleeing Spill.

Knocked flat and stunned, but still conscious enough to see fast approaching death, the Spill tries to scramble away.

Ol' Arthur steps on one of the Spill's legs, grabbing the other in massive, moss and bark covered hands. Ripping the leg from its socket and tossing it aside, the raging monster snatches up the other leg. Lifting and swinging the screaming Spill in an arc, he slams it back to the floor. As blood spews from the smashed body, Arthur stamps a huge, gnarled foot into its chest, creating a bright red, star burst pattern around the carcass.

Careening about the room, smashing, throwing, destroying all its path, this former man, with one nightmarish eye, sees an opening to yet another corridor. Emitting its grinding chittering wail it stomps through, bouncing off the walls, raging on.

———•◦•———

The Coiler still sits, studying the door controls and its own imbedded tentacle. Some of its eyes looking behind, see a creature appear far down the corridor. A berserk, shambling, growth encrusted thing. An obviously, quite deeply unhappy thing.

Unable to turn, the Coiler calmly watches the unknown beast advance. Whatever the thing is, it's coming, and the only way out of a confrontation would be to snake up one of the stanchions to the communal nest far above. But there is the caught tentacle problem, and it doesn't want to leave Jayderay's body to that fast oncoming creature. The Coiler still has some deep overpowering thoughts of Zthruskaing, and being the Zthruska- er, and watching the Zthruska- ee do the tippy tentacle dance. SO! It will need that fresh body. The advancing damn giant weed must and will be dealt with.

Zthruska! thinks the Coiler, and being smart and practical, it makes the decision it had not wanted to make. From one of the vertical slits about the bulbous body emerges the beak, and promptly snaps the tentacle off at the door, then pulls back inside its pouch.

Freed, the Coiler spins about to face the oncoming threat. It's still some distance away, but the thing is moving fairly fast, despite all the wall bouncing and pounding. The amputation is leaking, but the Coiler isn't overly concerned. Its flesh is much like that of a snake and doesn't bleed much. If the cut limb doesn't seal, perhaps the Ton could cauterize it. She probably would, after all, she has become their *friend,* the friend that wants and needs them for an alliance, for that vague plan of hers. And she doesn't know about this door. This door leading back into her world. Yes, Ton would certainly trade her help for that knowledge.

The Coiler and its nestmates were not totally committed to Ton, undecided if the taking of Deck 19 will be in their best interests. Why fuck with what works? Why should they care about the affairs of the two- leggers? But, inexplicably, many did care about the doings of humans, there seemed to be a certain empathy.

It wasn't really odd for the Coilers to feel a connection with humans. No, not strange at all. They were related.

The Coilers were not extraterrestrial organisms, at least not entirely. They neither knew nor cared, nor spent much time thinking about their origins. After all, there was food gathering, which consumed quite a bit of time, since most of their food tended to be uncooperative about being food. And there was always web repair and expansion, tending to eggs, plus, there was... Zthruskaing. That was an often-overpowering urge. That urge to Zthruska could make them do... stupid things, silly things, things which they later regretted. Yes, the Coilers could be quite human. Very human about some things.

Coiler existence began during the cataclysmic backfiring of an Extender experiment. The disaster that had created the Waydowns; that melting, merging, and altering of several ship decks. And that same scientific circle- jerk had also melted, merged, and altered the creatures within those decks. *All* the creatures, including the human staff. As an added bonus, the screw up also teleported an elevator door. Just the door. That same door that now connects the Waydowns to the Roaton house.

Down the corridor, that mad and marauding Arthur comes. Stopping here and there to smash something left laying long ago. This former man is not discerning, he doesn't have mind enough left for that. He exists to destroy, to kill... to hate. And a Coiler would do quite nicely. Perhaps so, maybe so, Arthur. But even a giant weed can make an error in judgement.

Between the Coiler and the advancing Arthur thing, lies the cold, inert body of Jayderay. The body twitches a thumb, has a brief tremor of leg. Not life, perhaps only the responses of dying muscles no longer receiving the flow of blood. A good and kind woman. A good and kind woman tossed away by her God. Tossed like trash.

———••———

Inside the Roaton house, Frankie lowers the straight razor to the tentacle, taking a deep breath.

Proby has been holding his. He may not remember how to breathe. He stoically looks... away. Looks into the midnight ringlets of Shadow's beautiful hair, he has to look there; that's where he's buried his face. She smells of rose petals, delicate, faded rose petals... and she had told him she loved him. That is enough, that is everything.

Shadow's maimed arms hug her man. Her husband. Her love. Should he be yanked back into those Waydowns, she will follow, she will attack, she will die. She does not fear death, the Waydowns, or its creatures. Loneliness is her fear. For many, many years it was all she has known. And then came Elv-is. She will not live without him. She cannot.

RL stares intently, grimly ready to yank Elvis and the woman back, should the shit hit the fan. He doesn't worry about Frankie. That boy can probably levitate. No doubt giggling.

Princess looks on, whimpering, not understanding, but sensing the human's anguish.

Frankie tenses as he starts to slice into the tentacle.

And the damn thing goes limp, uncoiling, slipping from Proby's ankle, flopping to the floor. The tip wriggles, and then stills.

"What the hell! Did the son of a bitch faint, or—"

Frankie is interrupted by RL shouldering him aside, grabbing both Shadow and Proby, dragging them back several feet. He's not slow about it.

Growling, Princess pads toward the severed tentacle, as everyone looks at it in disbelief. Everyone except RL.

"Let's get in gear damn it," he barks. "Something's happened to it, the monster, it's not caught in the door—the bastard is loose. I'm taking Princess and going in, right now! Shadow, get ready to open the door. Frankie, you go get the guns."

"RL... Sir... I want to come—NO— *I AM* coming with you."

"NO! Elv-is, please not again, I cannot bear—"

"I must, Shadow... I, I just—have to," says a very frightened but determined Proby. *I will be... I am human... I will be a man for her... a MAN!*

CHAPTER 45

INTO THE BREACH

"Boss, it'll take too long for me to get those guns," Frankie says. "By the time I get back, you three will be too far in, I'll never find you."

"Frankie, we've got to have something to fight with, to kill. There's no telling what we may come up against. That octopus thing may not even be gone yet. And that place looked huge, endless. I've got to find her while there's still— at least maybe I can— we can—oh, God damn it, I don't know what the hell we can do!"

"Boss, if you go in now, what the hell are you going to use to kill the monster if it's still there? Spit at it?"

Shadow speaks, "My husb— the man that once owned this house had a machete and a club... and other implements. He used them to... to kill stray dogs and cats that came here." Her facial scar darkens, as she rubs the badly healed arms, remembering the other uses Ezekiel Roaton had found for his tools. "They may still be located in his— in that work shed out back."

"Well, alright RL, that's it! Let's arm ourselves as best we can... and get ready to spit. And I said *spit*... with a 'p'," says Frankie, making a feeble attempt to giggle.

***

In the Waydowns, the Arthur creature's one spastic eye finally sees the Coiler, sees the tentacles writhing and dancing all around it. Artur no longer has enough brain to be afraid, and he's a nightmare himself. Screaming out a saw mill sound, this plant monster heaves forward.

The Coiler watches, studying the plant thing as it comes. The Coiler isn't afraid of it, but recognizes its size and rage; its power, it is definitely a threat to deal with carefully. It prepares; the beak doesn't extend, no need to give the thing any warning, pulling in the tentacles, it curls them close to its body.

Unknown to the preparing Coiler, Arthur doesn't have enough mind left for danger of any kind to register. It just hates, hates anything that moves. As this nearly blind former man surges and shambles toward the Coiler, it never sees anything as small as a limp, unmoving body. It lurches past Jayderay, sounding its buzz saw, wood-grinding scream.

The noise penetrates into the woman, her lashes flutter, eyes opening. Disoriented, concussed, and aching, she turns on her side. Looking up from the corridor floor she sees the mossy, bark-covered back of a huge, towering horror, lurching away from her. Branches grow out from the thing's flesh. Jayderay is beyond screaming.

<hr>

Back in the house, the three men are now armed. Sort of. RL brandishes a rusty machete. Frankie has picked out an ancient hand scythe, plus he has that straight razor tucked in a back pocket. Proby had chosen the club, which turned out to be a blood stained, cracked wooden baseball bat. They had ignored a worn, braided leather quirt; an item Shadow could have told them much about.

They're fairly well outfitted for a street gang, but piss poor for what awaits them on the other side of that door. In the Waydowns. Maybe they can spit.

They gather at the door, Princess straining against the leash, Proby gripping it tightly. All except the dog are badly scared. If the tentacled beast is still on the opposite side of the closet wall, RL will leap, machete swinging; he must, he must DO something. Frankie is Frankie... a badly frightened Frankie, but Frankie. Proby is terrified, his mouth as dry as the Roaton house dust. He does not look at Shadow. He must not look at her, if he does... he will stay.

Shadow stands close by, waiting for the signal to touch that wall, to activate the door, to send them into hell. The violet, star shooting eyes are fixed on Proby, only on Proby. The ebony lips are compressed into a tight black line beneath her scarred nose. Her arms throb.

In the Waydowns, the Coiler glides toward the once-was- a- man thing. Its tentacles are tightly furled into individual rolls, closely held against the wart dotted green body. Most of the eyes look forward, burning brightly orange above the pulsing sack torso. The slashing, ripping beak still remains hidden within the vertical pouch openings. The Coiler slides silently, relentlessly forward. This will be quick. Wonder what it tastes like?

The creature that had been Arthur, continues its stomping, goosestepping charge. Its keening, grinding, chipping scream echoing through the corridor, bouncing on into other hallways. The knotted arms reach out with constantly clutching massive hands. To kill—to murder all that live—to rend all that can move.

Behind the Arthur thing, a terrified Jayderay forces herself erect, using the white wall for support. Slowly and painfully standing, she can see a bit ahead of that moss covered back and the dusky pink roots and branches that stick out from the monster's sides. And beyond, she sees— the Coiler.

Memories flood into her mind like acid. Memories of being caught by tentacles, of fighting, of screaming to God, of being dragged, dragged into what surely must be hell. All she knows for sure, all she can think of, is that she must run, must run anywhere as long as it's away from those two hell spawn monsters. Leaning against the wall, she starts a sliding, limping fast walk. Urging her shaking legs to move faster, she hears the two horrors smash together. Managing a stumbling run, she falls but continues on hand and knees for several feet, before rising again. She runs. She runs. She does not pray.

Seconds before what had been Arthur collides with the Coiler, the tentacles explode outwards in a spray of scaled, unfurling, writhing snakes. The beak thrusts from its pouch, and the Coiler's shrieking squeal fills the area. And the creatures meet. The spread tentacles slap themselves around Arthur, coiling about legs, body, and arms, the beak gouges in.

The grappling monstrosities topple over in a roiling, rolling mass of tentacles, massive tree-like arms and legs, breaking roots, snapping branches, and a rapidly pulsing vomit green body. Both combatants have ceased their war cries, their mouths are full of each other.

———

Inside the house, no one has ever heard a sound from the other side of that closet and its elevator door. And they hear nothing now. The assembled group has no idea what awaits them. What awaits is death.

RL glances over at Shadow, gives a nod, saying, "Do it!"

Shadow touches the wall; the door materializes, immediately opening. The three men freeze up at the sight before them. Even Princess stops pulling against her leash.

A huge ball of flesh, plant and wood all but fill the corridor. The ball surges from wall to wall, bouncing, rolling down the hallway, surging back, throbbing with the intensity of battle, of hate, of murderous rage and death. Bark, moss and bits of tentacles spew out, littering the floor.

Shadow screams, "I see her, I see her! There, running," she points down the hallway, past the battling sphere.

"Where, God damn it?" shouts RL, unable to see past the moving, warring ball of hate, fury, and Coiler.

"There," yells Shadow still pointing, "down past the monst—"

"I can see her," shouts Proby, "I see her!" Barking wildly, Princess pulls him into the corridor. Yelping and straining at the leash, she has Jayderay's scent, she doesn't need to see.

The living, fighting ball surges back toward them, rolling fast, spitting out snapped branches, torn strips of bark, tentacle pieces, and thick pink sap.

As the group piles back through the door, Proby scoops the fearless dog into his arms as he joins the rout back into the basement. With no time to activate the door, Shadow runs to Proby as the throbbing sphere slams into the opening, bulging in like an enormous belly. Tentacles shoot into the room.

Jayderay runs, falls and unable to catch herself, hits the floor hard. Her nose starts bleeding again and her mind reels. She's unconsciously trying to speak words, words that would no longer have meaning for her. "Though I walk through... walk through... I walk through the valley... wall...I walk..." Her mumbling voice fades out as she fights to regain her feet, maimed fingers clawing at the smooth white wall. She stumbles on.

The Coiler thinks that while it might be winning this fight, it's an awfully big fucking might. It also *knows*, it has badly misjudged the strength and madness of the weed beast. Its own ripping, tearing beak has become stuck, imbedded in the plant thing's strangely tough flesh, several tentacles are missing tips, and three of its eyes flop uselessly. This battle is far from over. And it dare not let go. The thing the Coiler is wrapped in combat with evidently feels no pain, nor does it seem to be tiring. What a bastard.

Inside the house, three tentacles thrash about, knocking furniture over, wreaking havoc, mindlessly searching for something living, some part of what the Coiler fights. The scaled, roiling snakes blindly seek Arthur, who... is busy as hell.

To the four humans' credit, none have ran upstairs or out the front door. Were it not for Proby's firm hold on the leash, Princess would have already charged, and been caught and crushed by the Coiler's flailing scaled arms.

Without a word, RL rushes beneath a sweeping tentacle, and sinks the machete deep into it. Frankie, having harsh thoughts about his suicidal boss, runs in, hacking at one with his scythe. Proby pushes the dog's leash into Shadows hand, and readies to swing his bat, which will have about the same effect as swatting an elephant with a switch. But it's all he's got.

On the other side of this desperate group, the Coiler definitely feels their hacking presence. It quickly deduces that fighting a two front war is not the best strategy. It hadn't planned on getting wedged in the door. Damn the weed, this is its fault.

ZTHRUSKA! This shit has got to stop. Pulling out the only tentacle it can free from the ball of fury, it snakes it out into the corridor, and just barely manages to wrap a bleeding tip around a column. Getting a firm grip, the Coiler yanks, pulls and strains, finally popping itself and that stupid weed free from the doorway. Unfortunately that big weed its entwined with comes along. And they start rolling again, as two and a half tentacles slither back from the house.

Proby, having just swung his bat thudding into one of those scaled, writhing Coiler arms, watches in amazement as it sucks back, retreating from the house. *Wow! I, I did that... just like in the movies... I hope Shadow saw me.*

With the room and closet now free from thrashing death, the group rushes to the open door. The fighting monsters, still locked in rolling battle, fight from one wall, bouncing back to the other, blocking their way.

"There!" shouts Shadow, pointing in the direction of the ongoing fight. "I saw her, she turned into a room or passage."

"I'm going in," states RL, gripping that surprisingly effective machete.

"And do what, boss? Sprout fucking wings and fly over that nightmare that's rolling around in front of us."

"When it bounces off a wall, I can dive past it. Shadow said Jayderay turned a corner, I can— I've GOT to get moving, while I can still catch her, before she gets lost in that damn rabbit warren of halls."

"It ain't exactly rabbits I'm worried about, RL. Okay, I'm with you. If you can play dodge ball with a bouncing monster testicle, so can I."

"Yeah, me too! I can't—I *won't* be left behind, RL... sir," states Proby, full of confidence over his successful whacking of the tentacle. The dog's leash is once again clutched in his hand. Shadow stands silently beside them, her hand on his shoulder.

"Right you are, Elvis, my man!" says Frankie, "Right you are! Three men and a dog: into the breach, into the valley of death waltzes a bunch of doomed idiots, into a pile of shi—"

"Shut up, Frankie." RL steps into the Waydowns.

CHAPTER 46

LOVE IN THE WAYDOWNS

Not too far away from that battling ball of monsters, in this tortured, twisted portion of the ship... *bliss* is on the move. It's rapidly moving away from Seevee and moving toward Tanya. She is booting him out. Bliss for one.

"Seevee, you're just way too much of a stud for me; that's enough fun for now," says the naked Ton. Getting up, she starts putting on her lab coat. "And while you're on those blankets in the hall," she says pointedly, "see if you can think of where to find me some clothes that'll fit. There's gotta be some left in lockers somewhere. I'm sick of this damn fucking coat. It stinks."

Seevee sits up; he's kept the khaki shirt on without being told to. She's disgusted by his arms, so now he's ashamed of them too. Love, yes, it's hell.

"No smell bad, Ton always much sweet good smell to Seevee... Seevee much luff Ton."

"Yeah, yeah, I know, I know. You're always *much* telling me. Well... while you're having deep thoughts about *luff*, you can also think and figure out where to get me some clothes. Soon, okay? And don't forget about getting me something to eat beside this damn Crap Cake the ship keeps poking out. I'm sick to death of it. You can start thinking about all that just as soon as you're all snuggled up on the floor." She opens the door and takes several steps back to avoid a parting kiss. Seevee has a long sticky tongue. *Jesus Fucking Christ, I swear, when we take Deck 19, he'll be one of the first to die... even if I have to do it myself.*

Out in the corridor, without a good bye kiss, the Almost stands there for a long while, head down, multi jointed arms hanging. Off in the distance, faint screams and wails echo down the convoluted hallways. He ignores them, such noises are common in the Waydowns. As common as death.

Taking a deep melancholy breath, he settles down on the torn blankets, leaning his back against her door. Drawing up his legs, resting his forehead on the knees, he wraps his awful arms around his awful body. The arms overlap against his back. And Seevee thinks, as he's been told to do. *Where find clothes... must find food... must please Ton. Seevee luff Ton. Luff much.*

Yes, Seevee does love Tanya. The poor, miserable, love bedeviled wretch. Love, a many splendored thing indeed.

Inside her cabin, Tanya is already sound asleep... still in that stinky lab coat and having sweet dreams. Delightful dreams of killing Dr. Lillith Sally Gaust.

As RL steps from the house, the other three join him. All watching the two battling horrors locked in their rolling, ball of combat.

Shadow quickly hugs and kisses Proby on a lavender cheek as he leaves. "You must return to me, Elv-is. I will not bear it if you do not. I cannot. I will come... come for you." Proby nods, not trusting himself to speak. He knows she will die if she steps beyond the house. She stands silently now, the aching, crooked arms hugging herself, the scar across her face dark, violet eyes brimming.

The warring, debris-spitting sphere in front of them, continues smashing back and forth between the corridor walls. Pulsing with moving tentacles, grappling wood fibred limbs and gnarled growths. There is little noise, only the squishing of scaled flesh and the wet snapping of bark, root and branch.

RL makes several attempts to rush between the roiling mess and the walls as the mass ricochets back and forth. And he's rewarded for each effort by very nearly becoming part of that warring, throbbing ball.

Every time. Princess strains against her Proby held leash, barking and whining. Frankie watches, thinking that this whole thing is going exactly as he figured it would. He doesn't giggle.

Somewhere within the battle pulsing sphere, the Coiler is deciding this endeavor is not going as planned. Nope, not exactly. In fact, it decides... that it is getting its green, Zthruskaing ass whipped. The tentacles seem to be accomplishing absolutely nothing but slapping, squeezing, and getting torn. And the ripping, tearing beak is not ripping and tearing anything at all. It's stuffed. It's crammed full of some really, really nasty tasting, pulpy flesh. This crap has just got to cease.

Ol 'Arthur, the Coiler's adversary, certainly no longer thinks at all, he only hates all that moves, and right now... he's got plenty to hate. More than plenty, and if he could feel happy... why, he'd be positively ecstatic, euphoric even.

Watching the furious battle, Frankie says, "Boss, I guess we gotta have those guns—No, wait! I saw a can of kerosine out in the shed; hell, man, let's douse this bouncy bastard and set fire to it. I bet it'll get the fuck out of our way then."

"You're brilliant, Frankie! Go get—"

"NO!" shouts Proby. "If we set fire to it, it might jam itself back in the door and catch the house on fire.

Shadow can't live without that house, she will die. I'll, I'll— I'll club you both if you try." He stands there, gripping the raised bat, his face gone white, the eyes completely black. This is no longer a scared half-breed lizard boy; this is a deadly serious man. A man who means every word he says. They don't get the kerosine.

The Coiler has had enough. It wants to quit. It wants to get the hell out of this Zthruskaing mess. It wants to run, scoot with its tentacles tucked between its tentacles. Hell, let the animated tree stump win, and it can have that woman's body too. If the wood tasting bastard will just let go. Damn this weed. What a prick!

The Coiler figures if it can somehow get the attention of its nestmates, they would settle the sawdust of this insane chunk of wood right quick. It sure as hell can't screech out a call to them; its snappy, rippy beak is full, crammed, jammed full of awful tasting, crazed weed. And that beak is also stuck like glue deep in the pulpy meat of this glorified stick. Maybe if it could get enough rolling momentum built up, it could hit a stanchion hard enough to jar the nestmates to attention. Those lazy fuckers. Something has got to be done. Really soon... like now, while there's still some tentacles left.

Managing to extract two of its scaley, injured arms from the boiling mass it's part of, the Coiler aims all remaining eyes at the nearest long run of a corridor.

Pushing against a wall with all its strength, it shoots off down the hall. Taking that damn weed. And straight at the band of rescuers.

RL and gang dive for the walls like bowling pins hit by a strike. Proby jerking the dog with him. The ball zooms past them, and the closet door, gaining speed.

Scrambling to his feet, shaking a scythe clutching fist, Frankie shouts a farewell.

"Take that, you snaky asshole! And we dare you to come back." Grinning his best chipped tooth, boy scout grin, he looks at the other two. "It must've heard about my idea with the kerosine, I scared it off!"

"Shut up, Frankie," says RL, starting off in the direction Jayderay had ran. Princess immediately yanks Proby along.

Frankie follows, saying "You're just no fun, boss. And where'd all these hedge trimmings come from?"

As Jayderay came to the hall's end, it turned in both directions. Not having the strength to leave the wall supporting her, she slid around the corner, continuing on. She must get away from the creatures fighting behind her. She must.

Slipping to one knee, head resting against the wall, she closes her eyes. *I can't rest, I can't go to sleep, I must go on... Oh, gramma, how I wish I could see your face. I'm so sorry for all them times I sassed you when you were raisin' me... so sorry. And for all of them times I wouldn't listen to you about... about, oh, gramma, about everything... so sorry...*

A little above of Jayderay, a newly grown blot of mold glistens wetly on the wall. Softly bubbling, it extends a yellow tendril toward her. A hungry newborn.

The battered woman sags further to the floor, eyes closing. So tired, so very tired. Minutes pass.

The Gunch oozes out another pod, stretching reaching. Needing to absorb living meat. Getting closer.

Jerking her head up, eyes flying open. *NO! I WILL NOT SLEEP! I got to go on, I got to.* Forcing herself upright, shoulder against the wall, she braces both hands on her knees. And the yellow death drools closer.

Jayderay manages a few awkward steps. She keeps at it, a slow, sliding, step-by-sliding- step, painful advance. Behind her, the mold settles back to the wall.

Craning her neck, looking, squinting, she thinks she can see an elevator ahead. Shaking her head, hair flying, clearing her vision, she looks harder. Yes, it is an elevator. Hard to see, it has been blackened by fire, as have all the walls and floor leading away from it. It may not even be functional, it may be too damaged by heat. And where does it go? It doesn't matter where it might go, she has no choice; if it works, anyplace will be better than this. Don't bet on that, Jayderay, don't bet on it.

Leaving the wall, she staggers toward the blackened area, falling to one knee, but rising. Going on, going on, going on... until she rests her face against the door. The controls are ruined. Of course they are. In desperation, her hand crawls to the melted panel, and she blindly pushes at buttons. Any button, every button, all the buttons.

There are miracles sometimes; the door begins to open. The trouble with miracles is always in the fine print. As in... who sent the miracle? Or what did?

———— ♦ ————

After Ol' Arthur and the Coiler zoom merrily out of the way, the search party heads down the corridor. Almost at a run, Princess tugging and in the lead. Coming to an opening on their left, they look at one another. Stupidly.

"So which way did she go?"

"I don't think Shadow said, but we can't bypass a room she might've gone in."

"But the dog's not interested, she wants to go straight."

"We don't dare not check it, we've at least got to take a quick look."

So ignoring the smartest of the four, the three men

go in. Princess has to be pulled some but follows Proby and the rest. Humans! Huh.

The room is typical of all Waydowns areas. Overturned tables, chairs, and broken glass are strewn across the floor. Whisps of gray vapor float about, as warning lights still flicker dimly as they have through all the terrible years. Computer reads glow and blink redly. A locked door shows evidence of unsuccessful break in attempts. All of it the result of despair, the fruit of abandonment by those in command, the consequence of disease, of twisted, altered minds and bodies—and of madness.

A steel confinement cage is bolted to the floor; its thick wire bulging out on all sides. It still holds its last resident. A lab coat wearing skeleton lays curled at the bottom. Mummified flesh and skin stretch tight against the skull, an earring still clings to a crust like lobe. Someone had taken desperate refuge here, had cowered here. Cowered as former friends, fellow workers, a lover, had chewed at the cage, breaking their teeth pulling on the thick wire mesh. The skeleton has no fingers.

"Christ," says Frankie, staring at the dried skin and bones, shaking his head. "What a godawful way to die." He rakes his shoe across splintered teeth at the base of this final resting place. A cage... where there had been no refuge, no safety, only slow death by starvation.

"Everything about this place is godawful, Frankie," responds RL. "This damn Waydowns place is a nightmare, it's way down all right, way down in hell. And Jayderay is lost in it."

Princess yelps and whines as they search the space, pulling at her leash wanting to return to the hallway. The men finally agree with the smartest, and the dog leads them out. And she promptly find fresh blood smears on the passageway walls.

Behind them, high on a wall, forming a rough circle, several quarter sized yellow spots shine wetly. One stretches out, joining another.

Jayderay jerks her face back as the fire blackened elevator door slides open. It's not empty. Standing there to greet her is a human. All honesty and kindness beaming from a thoughtful, wizened face, wearing a lab coat, and just shining with proper authority.

"Oh, I hope I didn't startle you, my dear. Please, please don't be frightened. I saw you coming as I checked my security cameras and came at once. You look in a terrible, terrible state! What has happened; how can I help?"

Jayderay is beyond being frightened by any mere human, and certainly not by this nice person. After what she's seen and been through, this man looks like an angel. An angel in white.

"Oh, Lord bles— oh, thank you, thank you, thank you! Don't nobody need help like I do! But, but who are you, what is this awful place?"

"Why, I do so apologize, miss, where have I left my manners? I am Dr. Moto, and this is the basement of my private hospital. Please, do come in, and let me get you some cold water. And you certainly do look as if you need some immediate medical attention." *And I am just the person to give you that assistance... you fine strong negroidal. You are absolutely perfect! How fortuitous! The Honored Hydra is about to get her implant volunteer.*

"Oh, Doctor, from all my heart, I—" Jayderay finally succumbs to this ongoing nightmare, falling forward. Moto catches her, lowering her to the floor, not wanting any further damage to the goods.

Dragging Jayderay's limp body further into the elevator, he surveys this gift from the gods. He kneels. *My, my, what exemplary mammary gland development. I will have to keep my baser inclinations at bay... but my examination will be most complete, yes, very, very thorough. The anal cavity... yes...*

Hearing a noise from down the hall, he rises pulling a prod from his coat, thumbing its switch to the kill voltage. This isn't a good time for dealing with Tanya, or any other schlumping residents of the Waydowns.

From around the corner, gallops Princess, yanking Proby along by the leash, the tentacle killing bat bouncing on his shoulder. RL and Frankie are right behind the two. The rescue has arrived. Or not.

Even with the prod set at its deadliest, Moto has no desire to take a chance at battling three men and a dog. It's obvious they're after the woman. He reaches for the door controls.

Seeing Moto move to close the elevator, Proby yells, "Wait! Wait Dr. Moto, it's me, Elvis, it's Proby! I'm bringing some *volunteers*... you know what I mean.

How did that troublesome little shit get down here? Well, no matter, he's bringing two men and a dog! This will be quite an addition, and dog is one of my favorite dishes.

"Well, well, it's Elvis; The King himself! It's really good to see you, and bringing guests too!" exclaims Moto, lowering his hand from the controls. But he doesn't pocket the prod; he thumbs it to stun. It's prudent not to be overly trusting.

Princess tears the leash from Proby's hand, running and whining to Jayderay. Ignoring Moto she starts licking the woman's face. It's dog speak: "Oh, momma, I love you, momma please wake up!"

"Jeepers and gee whiz, Dr. Moto, am I glad to find you," says Proby walking up, smiling. He whacks the good Moto over the head with his bat; the doctor falls, landing like a sack of rice.

"I know this guy," says Proby, talking over his shoulder. "He's a *friend* of mine. This was necessary, guys, very necessary, and everything is cool like a pool," he continues in a calm matter of fact voice. Proby had never been totally taken in by Moto's guise of friendship. Proby had seen too many movies for that. It's best not to be overly trusting.

"Yeah, right... I'm, uh, I'm glad to hear that," says Frankie. "Mmm, Elvis... you and I... we're *real friends*... right?"

RL, already on both knees beside Jayderay, doesn't speak. He can't, not with his heart in his mouth.

CHAPTER 47

GETTING BACK

As RL gently wipes Jayderay's bloody face, Frankie checks her vitals, and her eyes open.

"Oh, RL, RL... you came... I knew—" is all she manages before slipping away again.

"Her pulse is strong, boss, I think we're safe moving her. Hell, we have no choice! How about this lift we're in? Maybe it can take—"

Proby breaks in on this very bad idea. He's extremely adamant and persuasive about them not taking that elevator any place. Things could get much worse. So much worse. He still grips the bat as he talks against taking the lift. The same bat he'd just whopped the living shit out of his *friend* Moto with. They listened.

Jayderay is no feather. Fairly tall, full-figured, and not fully conscious, RL and Frankie manage to get her back into the corridor. Proby slaps the interior door controls, scooting out as it closes. Leaving behind a very silent and very still Dr. Moto; a dead rock couldn't beat his performance.

Some rescue! Yes, they do have Jayderay. What they also have is a long, death-imminent walk ahead before reaching safety. A path through the twisting passages of the Waydowns. Carrying Jayderay. And behind them? Moto will be sending a murderous security squad. Rescue indeed.

RL is being a solicitous pain in the butt, flitting about like a drug-laced fairy, issuing contradictory orders, peppering the semi- conscious Jayderay with ridiculous questions, like: How do you feel? Are you okay? Can you hear me? Do you want a stretcher? A wheelchair? And so on.

With eyes blinking, barely able to raise her head, Jayderay says, "Please, please be quiet, RL. Just... just let me rest."

"No! We have got to get you to the—"

"Shut up, boss, YOU are being her biggest problem. And mine. Give the woman some peace, Jesus!" says Frankie, wishing Frankie were drug- laced.

"Frankie?" says Proby, "I, uh, I did see a stretcher back in that room we searched looking for her. I think. Do you—"

"Well don't just stand there, damn it, man! Go get the son of a bitch," snaps RL, not shutting up.

———

As the stretcher bearing party comes down the corridor, nearing the closet entrance, Proby takes off running. Shadow, standing at the door, starts crying. And she almost makes a fatal dash to meet him.

"ELV-IS!!! Oh, Elv-is, I'm, I'm... Oh... Oh, Elv-is," she breaks down, burying her face in ebony tipped hands, then reaches them out toward him.

Proby all but knocks her down as he flies into the house. The man and woman, this husband and wife, locking together. They stand, silently holding each other. They don't need words, they love each other. Love, it can be, it should be, it is... EVERYTHING.

"Why, yes! We're all fine back here," calls out Frankie. "Thanks for asking."

"Shut up, Frankie," says RL.

———

Quite a way back down the corridor from this joyous home coming, Dr. Moto has managed to first sit up, then crawl to the lift controls. Clawing his way erect, he leans his throbbing forehead against the cold metal surface. Trying to read the swirling, dancing numbers, he also tries to think of exactly what he should do. Events are not happening in a desirous manner.

With a hand hovering over the numbers, he stops and puts both hands to his pulsing, aching head. Blankly staring at nothing, trying to make jarred and jumbled thoughts coherent.

That little treacherous, deceitful, fucking bastard lizard... that lying scaled turd! The Most Honored She Shit will not be pleased.

Quite some time later, back in the Roaton house, a fully conscious Jayderay lays on a bed in a downstairs room. Princess is on the floor as close to her momma as she can get, and a bandaged hand strokes the dog's head. Frankie has competently done all he can, which was considerable. All that boy scout and Navy Medic training had taken over. He hasn't giggled.

RL, doesn't know what to do... period. He futzes, he fiddles, he asks more inane questions, and generally gets in the way. Again.

"We really should take her to a hospital! I can clear out the back of—"

"NO! I'm not going to a hospital. How on God's— how on earth am I gonna explain what's happened to me? How would you? No, RL, they'd put me in some crazy person asylum."

"She's right, boss. No matter what we told the emergency room people, they'd probably call the cops. They'd suspect assault or domestic abuse. And we sure as hell can't tell'em anything even close to the truth. Jayderay is doing fine; I can handle this."

Not telling the truth resonates strongly with RL. To him, the truth is almost always to be avoided... it just causes trouble. Especially with the law.

"Are you sure?" asks the flitting about RL. "Shouldn't she be x-rayed, or—"

"I SAID, I'M NOT GOING, RL! And that's the last time I intend to say it; I don't want to hear no more about this. And if I do... I'm gonna start callin' you by your full name," she finishes with a slight grin.

"Yes'm, Miz Scarlett," RL answers quickly. Very quickly.

"What name?"

"Never you mind, Frankie. That's a little private thing twixt RL and me. Least ways it's private unless there's more hospital talk. Now, there's something I need to ask. That, that purple Elvis thing, it helped rescue me, didn't it?"

"He's a *man*, Jayderay, really he is, and his name actually is Elvis. Without him and his wife, we would never have found you. We would never have even known where you'd been taken," answers RL, contributing something useful for a change.

"His wife? Is that the ghost woman I saw when you carried me in here?"

"She's not a ghost, she's very, very real," answers Frankie, having a bit of private knowledge about just how real that woman is. "Her name is Shadow; she's the only person that could get us into that nightmare place."

"The Roaton house is their home, you don't need to be afraid of them," RL says, adding, "But I told them to stay out of here."

"WHAT! You told the two people responsible for gettin' me out of Hell, you *told* them they can't come into a room, a room in *their* own home!?"

"I, I—I didn't want you scared by them," stammers RL. Frankie keeps quiet.

"Scared?! Scared?! After what took me and what all I seen? I'm Black, in case you forgot, it'd take a lot more than a couple of— *colored people* to scare me! Right now, I don't 'magine I look no prize neither. And you *told* those two, did you, told them in *THEIR* own home, not to come in here. RL! I'm ashamed of you and shamed by you."

"I just thought—"

"NO, RL! You didn't think, you never do. You get

them people in here. NO, you *ask* them in, AND you apologize. You tell them I want to thank them, 'cause I do, I do with all my heart. GO!"

RL went. Frankie kept quiet.

———

A good while after introductions, after heartfelt thanks from Jayderay, after repeated, profuse apologies from RL, Proby clears his throat, turning a deep purple.

"Miss, uh... Jayderay, ma'am... I'm really, truly sorry about that time when we first met," he says, taking a sudden, intensely keen interest in his shoes. Shadow, holding his arm, quickly looks at him, sable eye brows arching quizzically.

"Oh, Elvis!" Jayderay says. "Honey, you don't need to give none of that a thought. You didn't do nothin' wrong. Nothin.' You a man, you just forget all about that. I have."

And being a woman, Jayderay has immediately interpreted Shadow's look. Speaking directly to her: "Your husband first met me when I was havin' a real bad time, Shadow. It was all making me a little snappish, and I'm the one that likely said some wrongs. There ain— there's nothin' he need to apologize for, not a thing. Let's don't even talk about it no more."

Jayderay has just earned Proby's undying gratitude.

He knows from watching all those movies, women can be a little funny about some things. Especially brand-new brides when it concerns *other women*. Most women don't much like other women, and certainly do not trust them. New brides absolutely don't.

Much later, Jayderay has been left alone to get some recovery sleep. But, of course, she can't. She is deeply, profoundly troubled, wrestling with, and tortured by a couple of monumental problems. Problems that have been huge butt-skewering thorns in humanity since forever: God and the soul's salvation.

Oh, Gramma... what did I do wrong? I always try to do right, I always go to church... well, mostly I do. And I always pray and give thanks, always every day. I hardly ever ask for nothin'... Gramma, where was God? Where was God when I really needed him? I needed him bad, awful bad. Is it on account of me chasing after RL? Is he so bad I'm supposed to give up on him? Is it because of me followin' that slick Preacher Dan? I don't... I can't understand... Gramma, I can't ask God... he ain't there.

A light tapping at the door interrupts her soul searching. It's Shadow. And the two women talk for a good while. They talk long about several things.

God works in mysterious ways.

A ROUNDUP

Patty leans the Harley into a curve, with Darren clutching her waist. Tightly clutching. Roaring up behind them are three pickups carrying some decidedly pissed cowboys.

Patty, being Patty, had quite innocently asked them a simple question: Had they gotten those brown teeth by eating their mother's shit? They could have just answered.

Pulling out of the curve onto a long stretch of straight, baking Oklahoma asphalt, she easily increases the gap between the bike and those pursuing trucks. This is fine with Darren. Not so with Patty.

Seeing a wide pull off area ahead, she takes the Harley into a screeching U-Turn. Darren lays his forehead against her back, eyes shutting. *What now?*

Roaring back toward the pissed cowboys, she yanks the pistol from her jeans. With blond hair whipping about and the skull tattoo grinning, she fires gleefully at those oncoming cowboys in their trucks. They quickly lose interest. They are no longer pissed. All three pickups take to the steep ditch beside the highway. Inside, cowboy hats and cowboys bounce like ping-pong balls. The bike roars on.

Quite a few miles later, the bike sits at a rest area. Patty and Darren are at the concrete picnic table, one of them needing a break.

"Well, fuck me, Darren! That son of a bitch shoulda kept his mouth shut. Fuck'em if they can't take a joke. Listen, I been thinkin' about that ol' spooky house. Hell, ain't nobody lives there, we could sorta use it as a, you know, a hide out. A kinda base. It's plenty close to Dallas, and Dallas has every fuckin' thing! We could run back and forth easy. We gots a fuck ton of money, we could even like rent the place or even buy it, be sorta legal."

Darren sits silently, elbows on the concrete table, chin cupped in both hands, his glazed eyes stare catatonically at Patty. He speaks.

"Well... *fuck me*, kiddo, why not."

They laugh, and she reaches out, grabs his face, and kisses him. Pulling back, looking into his eyes silently for a few seconds, she says quietly, almost sadly:

"You and me, we gonna ride this road to the fuckin'

end, ain't we." It's not a question. They both know there is no getting off.

Shanaqueela perches on her bunk, repeatedly pushing her lips in and out. They look like inflating bicycle tires. Not the skinny kind.

"This ain't nothin' but racism," she says to the mixed-race group sharing the holding cell. "I ain't killed that no good Suga' Boo, and I don't know nothin' 'bout them drugs they found at my house. I innocent I tells you, I innocent as shit, and I wouldn't be in here if I was white." A few Blacks nod in agreement, a couple of Whites look resignedly at each other.

Those bike tires inflate dangerously as Shanaqueela continues, "When Black Lives Matta' get hold of this, they gonna be riots in the streets! They'll show those white mutha fuckas. I tell you, this ain't nothin' but racism! Filthy, fuckin' white racism. I innocent, I innocent as shit!"

A gurney, accompanied by a nurse, is wheeled aboard the waiting jet, and flight attendants prepare for transporting the delicate patient. The nurse stands quietly by, being studiously inattentive.

The invalid has been making, and continues to make, sounds from beneath the oxygen mask, wagging the head back and forth. The patient keeps at it, making insistent, unintelligible noises until the nurse finally acknowledges the butthole. Leaning over and stretching away the mask much further than needed, she asks, "And what is it *this* time?"

"I, I go? I, I fucking gone - went?"

"Very soon now, Mr. Conyay, quite soon," replies the nurse, letting the mask snap back into place.

A taxi pulls to the ER entrance, its passenger is arranged oddly in the back seat. The passenger makes a slow and obviously painful entry into the hospital.

After a considerable wait, and interminable questions, the patient is positioned appropriately on an examination table. A very young intern bustles in, reading notes from a pad. She peers into the injured area. She doesn't touch the injured area.

"So, tell me...Hector is it? Tell me how this damage occurred."

Within Deck 19, Dr. Moto stands before the Honored She Shit, aka Dr. Lillith Sally Gaust. He's reporting.

Again. Delivering his report with a bandage turbaned head, and dark bruising that extends from beneath the huge white turban, down to both eyes. Very black, very swollen eyes. He sways slightly. As does the assistant, still standing in its corner, still extremely pregnant.

"That little bastard was in the Waydowns? And he hit you? Hit you with a baseball bat?" Lillith rasps this out. Her shoulder growth is the size of a small melon. Little Igor is doing well and moves slightly beneath the draped towel. Iggy's pulsing is steady and constant. Other than the towel, Dr. Gaust appears to be naked. Moto is exceedingly grateful that she's sitting behind her console. He's in no condition to face that horror.

"Yes, with a baseball bat."

"How remarkable. That's somewhat of an achievement; the first sign of aggression the little shit has shown in all these decades. And he was with two humans and a dog?"

"Yes." Dr. Moto answers, looking at the few wiry, ghastly tufts of hair scattered across her flaking scalp, like dying weeds on poisoned ground. He sees no benefit in mentioning Jayderay. Mustn't cloud the conversation with unimportant details. A soft moan from the corner makes his stunningly blackened eyes dart toward the assistant.

"And you let them all get away, let them flee back into the Waydowns?" She ignores the assistant.

"I was unconscious," says the swaying Moto.

"So you have said, yes, so you have said. Tell me, *Doctor*, what exactly were YOU doing down there?" Her eyes, sunken deeply back into the skull, glow redly like coals. The melon becomes agitated, twitching and pulsing rapidly beneath its towel.

Moto takes note of the eyes and increased lump movement. He must proceed with caution. Clearing his throat, he answers judiciously.

"I was following your orders, Dr. Gaust. I was attempting to locate a suitable implant recipient for you. One not from the rank and file."

"And you thought that among the diseased walking dead of the Waydowns, there would be a likely candidate?" Lillith's eyes burn bright from deep in their caves.

"Yes."

"Be very careful, Moto. You need to be very, very careful. And, *doctor*, since you've failed remarkably in procuring me an implant beneficiary, I've chosen one. Someone you've met before." Pointing to the corner, she says, "Allow me to re- introduce, Gunther Dawson Fly, who is somewhat responsible for my having this growth. After losing his genitalia during volunteer recruitment, Gunther is proving quite adept at pregnancy implantation. We will abort her trial fetus, and *she* will do nicely."

The former male, former attorney, former child molester, moans softly from the corner.

"Do be quiet, Bitch Gunther... you piece of shit," responds Lillith.

Yes, Dr. Gaust is right. Bitch Gunther will do nicely.

Near the pleasant Moto and Gaust meeting, and deep within Proby's cavernous play pen, street lamps flicker, fun machines beep and blink, old movies constantly play... and something grows. In the myriad aisles formed by countless carnival games... inside a long Bowl-a-Rama, a tendril of bright yellow Gunch reaches out from a Spill's severed hand. A hand laying in an opened glass specimen case. The mold has a lot of room to grow. It will.

In town, Manny and Fluffy have made it off the shops floor. Her new tent dress hasn't. She doesn't mind. She never made it shopping or to bingo. She doesn't mind. The cute hearts lip-sticked around her nipples haven't made it either, they've been kissed and nuzzled off. She doesn't mind.

With Fluffy supporting Manny, and Manny supporting Mr. Beam, they *have* made it to the bedroom. She doesn't mind. Neither does Manny, who rattles with the Viagra inside him. Love... it's a thing.

Sparks stayed downstairs. He has a beret to piss on. Again.

In the Waydowns, a happy Seevee is heading to Tanya's cabin, his trimmed feet stepping high. He'd be whistling if he could. The multi jointed arms cradle a load of clothes he has found in a long dead labbie's locker. But the real prize, his ticket to heaven, is perched on the very top. There rides some heavily sealed, U.S. Military rations. No doubt with an expiration date extending beyond the Second Coming. Optimists, that military bunch.

Ton be much happy with Seevee... No crap cake. Seevee much luff Ton... will much show. Make Ton smile. Ton will big smile.

Arriving at Ton's door, he kicks his worn pallet to one side. Wearing his best, hidden teeth smile, Seevee carefully unhinges an arm, not wanting any of those precious ration packets to slide off. About to knock, he hears sounds from inside. *Good! Ton not sleep... Ton much no like Seevee to wake—*

NO!... not good!... Luff sound! No, no, no not be. Much, much not be luff sound!!!

Seevee is about to learn a valuable lesson concerning love. A lesson called heartbreak. Seevee is being cheated on. It's an ancient lesson. It is as old as it is human. And it is always hell. Always.

A tired and thirsty hitchhiker walks down hot U.S 287. He's about half way between the old Rotan house and town, when he spots something laying on the road side. "Finders-Keepers," he chuckles out loud, picking it up.

Gasping in disgust, he drops the thing, unconsciously scooting back. Back into the path of a speeding Buick. The car swerves but clips him enough to send the guy spinning into the high Johnson grass. The car doesn't stop... but the hitchhiker does. As he lays there, waiting for the pain to start, one hand wipes its self constantly back and forth on the ground. Trying to rid its self of feces.

Back at the roads edge, where he had found and then so very quickly dropped them, lay some Nunchucks. They're a deadly thing... count on it.

Waiting for someone to fleece, Frankie leans against that infamous jewelry display case at NEAT STUFF. He's spinning a new toy about on the glass surface. It's a little something that Moto had dropped while having his brain pulverized. It's quite a handy something, with many uses.

After a private consultation with Proby concerning all its functions, Frankie hasn't told anyone else about this nifty new toy. Not even RL. There's no need to worry the boss. He can be prissy.

Frankie once again spins Dr. Moto's prod on the glass case. Below, several newly acquired men's diamond rings glitter gaily. Frankie giggles. He's such a silly bastard.

CHAPTER 49

RL DOESN'T SAY MUCH

RL works at his home desk, but his heart definitely isn't in it. Getting up, he walks to a plastic sack of cow manure, and gingerly pulls out a reproduction metal coke tray. A very good fake, but it's a little too good, just too new, too... mint-y. Such pristine condition of a 1932 advertising piece might cause a buyer to pause, to think things they shouldn't be thinking. And to not buy. Which makes no one happy, particularly RL. Deciding the cow shit hasn't aged the tray enough, he stuffs it back down into the semi- dry doo, sealing the sack.

He talks to George, as he always does, and the cat looks back from his prone position atop the desk. With half lidded golden eyes, he watches his human committing another act of swindling preparation. He wonders why a feline of his infinite excellence stays here in this den of iniquity. As RL chatters on, George closes his eyes. *Oh, the torture of it all.*

Back at the desk, RL picks up one of the hypnosis

books he's been studying: 'HURL YOUR WILL: *Make' em do what you want!*' He has practiced some, and by God he could do it. Well, sort of. It didn't always work, and sometimes it backfired. Disastrously backfired. Like the time he was willing a customer to buy some horrendously overpriced necklace she was holding beneath her chin. Dangling it down low. Extremely low. Unfortunately, she was chesty and wearing a peasant blouse with no bra. He didn't know what his mind had *hurled* at her—but his jaw had ached for weeks. And worse, the damn cow didn't buy.

It's been several days since he and Jayderay came back from their stay at the Roaton house. They have spoken a few times on the phone, but she has not been to visit. And she has absolutely, adamantly, refused to let RL come across the drive to her home. She's said there was no way anyone, but her Tidy Tinas, will lay eyes on her. Not with a face that looks like she's been hit with a sack full of hammers. Women.

Jayderay has been unusually reserved when they've talked. And there has been a remarkable lack of biblical references, or comments about what she sees as RL's innate dishonesty and all around, general, heathenish behavior. This is so unlike her, as to make him miss it. Kind of. He thinks it's from her devastating experience at the Roaton place. Or in that Waydowns, as Elvis

calls it. *I hope to Christ it's not something I've done...
or haven't done... or didn't think about doing... or did
think about doing... or should've thought about doing.
With a woman, there's never any telling.*

This train of thought reminds him of an old joke
about some guy getting a chance to ask God for
anything he wants, anything at all. The man asks the
deity to enable him to understand women. After a very,
very long silence, God finally responds: "You need to
ask for something else." *And ain't that the truth. I don't
think they understand themselves.* RL is not alone in
this thinking. There are millions upon millions of other
suffering wretches to keep him company. And many of
the suffering are not men.

RL truly does hope it isn't something he's done. He
hopes it in every molecule of his throbbing gizzard,
because he hasn't told the woman he loves her... yet.
He's afraid to, he's petrified he will get tongue tied,
strangled, and come across sounding like an asthmatic
Aardvark. So he hasn't told her that little thing yet. But
he's working up to it and figures he can get that done
at the same time he takes care of another small matter.
Another tiny, infinitesimal, microscopic thing.

Yes, he feels he can take care of both those larynx-
freezing small matters without uttering a word. A most
remarkable feat, requiring nothing more than a rock.

Sort of killing two birds with one stone. A really big stone.

He's squirreled away a whopping sized diamond ring, nesting incongruously in his underwear drawer. A spectacular sparkler RL has bought from himself. Himself being one of the precious few he wouldn't rapaciously ream. And he certainly didn't buy it from some greed infused, colon of a jeweler. Those grasping, avaricious swine. Being in love and proposing doesn't mean the afflicted has had a lobotomy. Just almost.

Perhaps amongst a man's underwear is not the most romantic of places, but using himself as a guide, he figures it's the least likely place some thieving bastard would look. Even an RL wouldn't.

"What do you think, George? If you were burglar, would you look in a man's underwear drawer?"

George rolls over onto his back, all four pink toed paws now exposed to the ceiling. He closes his eyes. *What did I ever do to deserve this blathering idiot.*

At this same time, in her home across their two parallel drives, Jayderay is also talking to an animal, Princess. And Princess, being a dog, is a lot more appreciative than George is. George, being a cat, is somewhat of ... a butthole. Just like his human.

Jayderay's one-sided conversation has been going on for a long time. It has been stretched and sprinkled through a lot of makeup applying, and reapplying, and still more reapplying. It has also passed through the sleeves of several blouse changes. At least four. The dog doesn't mind a bit, and is quite enjoying the talk, even thumping her tail during the good parts.

"Sakes, Princess, that talk I had with Shadow has sure changed my mind about lots of things. Things like that Preacher Dan, and the way he run that church. Why, I been goin' there long before that man showed up. His airs and church directin' have got me crossways with the Good Lor—with... higher powers. And that should be the most important thing, but I admit it ain— is not."

Princess follows Jayderay adoringly about the room with her eyes. She doesn't offer any tail thumps at the mention of Preacher Dan. Not even a twitch.

"No, honey, the most important thing to me is... I got to quit bein' silly about RL.

Considerable tail thumping follows the saying of RL's name.

"Yeah, baby, I know you love him. But the problem is... so do I. And I got to quit it... I AM gonna quit it, quit chasin' around after that man. I aim to quit, and I aim to do it today. I know the way I'm foolin' around with all this makeup don't look like it, but the least I can do is be presentable when I tell him."

Jayderay follows this last pronouncement, with a final look in the mirror, a deep breath, and she picks up the phone.

As his landline rings, RL glances at the read out. It's Jayderay... and the sweating starts.

"How you feelin', kid? I've been a little worried about you cooped up all alone over there."

"Oh, I'm pretty good, least ways I think I am, but I'm sure not alone. I got the world's best dog with me," she says, adding softly, "and I owe that to you. Listen, my face gone down quite a bit, my eyes aren't quite as black as they were, and 'cept for this ugly white bandage Frankie keeps puttin' across my nose, I don't think I'll scare any children that might go by. So! Why don't you come on over and we'll have some iced tea and set under the trees before it gets too hot?"

"Couldn't have had a better idea myself! I'm on the way." And then the terror really sets in. *Maybe this is too soon, maybe she'll be horrified when I ask and move away. Maybe I oughta put this off. Maybe I should wait until next Valentine's day... during next Leap Year... Maybe I should... Maybe you should get a grip, RL, you spineless ass. There are no maybes, just do it.*

And then, RL has one of his attacks. An onslaught of the dreaded HUB, as in Head Up Butt. A quite common affliction among men. RL is extremely well acquainted with it. Checking his ironed creases, and then running to the bathroom mirror, raking a comb through his hair, then using his fingers, with both having the same result. Gargling with some throat-searing Listerine, he runs to put his shoes on, and realizes he hasn't spit out the acid, runs back, does, and heads out the back door. And comes back in immediately. Of course he's forgotten the ring. Flinging jockeys out of the way, spilling a couple to the floor, he grabs the velvet box, stuffing it in his jeans pocket. And out the door he goes. Again.

From atop the desk, George languidly ignores all this. It's just standard operating procedure for RL. It's HUB.

And now, this calm, cool, collected man begins his casual stroll, ambling past the Honeysuckle covered fence, and flowing easily across the two drives to Jayderay. Trying hard not to wee in those ironed jeans.

Sitting beneath her big pecan trees, they hold cold sweaty glasses of tea, as the Cicadas serenade away... and Princess lays between them. In absolute heaven. They talk about mostly this, that, and generally nothing.

And they both have hugely important things to say. But don't. People.

And a warthog takes control of RL's brain, and apropos of nothing, he says:

"I prayed for you when you were lost."

She slowly, silently turns and looks at this man, wondering where the real RL is. For this crimson faced person cannot possibly be him.

"You what?" she asks in an oddly inflected, quiet voice.

"I, I prayed when I couldn't find you. I didn't know—I didn't know what else to do." With elbows on his knees, hands clutching the tea tumbler, he stares fixedly at the grass between his shoes. He wants to burrow far, far beneath it.

Jayderay studies him steadily for several agonizing moments. Her eyes don't fill with tears, her lips do not tremble. Nodding slightly, she breathes out a long soft sigh, reaches over, and places a hand on his shoulder.

"I know how much that must have cost you, RL. I really, and truly do. And I thank you for it. But RL... please don't bring this up again. I mean it, okay?"

"I, uh... yes, sure, okay." *Damn it to hell, I've blown it. She thinks I'm lying... well, who wouldn't. Hell, I can't, I don't dare ask or tell her anything now. I am such an idiot.* This is so true.

Taking her hand away, she sits back and begins rolling the glass of tea back and forth between her palms. The condensation drips and the ice rattles. Loudly.

Mortified, RL tries desperately to think of any remotely believable excuse to get back to his house. So he can quietly rip his bleating tongue out. And then send the treacherous, flapping thing down to Blurter's Hell where it belongs... along with its owner. And there he can be persecuted by all the inopportune shit it spews out.

Of course, absolutely nothing comes to their rescue. Their phones don't ring, a plane doesn't drop from the sky, Martians don't land, even the Russians don't invade. So they sit there. The silence is deafening... to both of them.

Turning back to him, she looks at him directly, the brown eyes deathly serious.

"RL, Shadow came to see me that first night at the Roaton place... her home. I like that woman. She been through way, way too much in life. We talked a long time 'bout... important stuff. Things that really matter."

"I figured she'd be fascinating to talk to; I've been thinking about asking her som—"

"Do you know she can't go outside that house; that she will die if she do?"

"Well, yeah, I don't really get it, but I believe it. Why bring that up?"

"'Cause the church gonna sell that property, that's why. What then?

"Look, I can't understand anything about that house, but I do know she has rooms in there that no one but her can find. In some way, they don't exist to other people. Remember, we explored the whole place and never found her or Elvis. So it doesn't matter who buys it, she and Elvis will be fine."

"That's another thing RL, what about Elvis? On account of him helpin' me— SAVING me, he can't go back to that rocket ship thing he come from."

"So what? I sure as hell know love when I see it, and those two belong together. He doesn't want to go back anywhere or be anywhere except where she's at."

"RL... it's a real bad shame you can't always see things that clear." Sighing heavily, wearily, sadly, she continues, "Never mind, it don't matter, don't know why I said that."

And so this man and woman sit silently, looking at their tea, each being tortured by unsaid things. Things that if said would solve a great many problems. And so it goes with men and women the world over, mired in being human.

"RL...RL, this is tearing at my heart. Preacher Dan

done told me his realtor got plans to sell the Roaton house as commercial property. They gonna bulldoze the place flat."

"WHAT?! To hell with that!"

"No, RL, no... it's *GOD DAMN THAT!!!*, and I don't care who hear me say it!"

He's shocked. Jayderay doesn't curse, not really, not ever.

"RL! I *owe* those two people in that house, owe them more than my life, owe them more than I can ever, ever, ever repay."

Still leaning forward, clutching his glass in both hands, elbows on knees, RL doesn't say a word. *Yes, so do I woman, I owe them more than you realize. I owe them for me still having you, but now isn't the time to tell you that. Not the time to pull this damn silly assed ring out either.*

It's HUB again. The man is permeated, riddled with it. This might well be the perfect time, but RL is a man in love, therefore the most stupidest thing there is. So he doesn't say anything. Men. So these two go back to tea contemplations and deep thoughts.

Jayderay sits rigidly, not looking at him, staring straight ahead. She takes a deep breath.

"RL, will you to do somethin' for me? Somethin' real big?"

RL looks over at this woman he loves but won't tell because he can't pull his nerve out of his toenail where it's hiding. He does manage to speak.

"There's nothing I wouldn't do for you, Jayderay. I—I—I— I'll do anything."

"I want you to sell your— I want both of us to sell our homes. I want us to buy the Roaton house. I want us, you and me, to buy it as— as one. Together. I want— I want to come be with you there. In your bed."

RL drops his glass, sloshing tea onto those iron creased jeans. His hands quiver like electrified jelly, blotches of sweat spring through the chambray shirt, his nerve blasts through that toenail.

"I—yes. I—" squeaks RL, and unable to finish, he squeaks no more. Occasionally even a HUB man can almost get something right. More or less.

Jayderay is graven, carved, immobile, still looking straight ahead. Her face getting hot and dark with a spreading blush. *There, Gramma, I did it. It's like you told me, sometime a girl just got to make things happen.* She lets RL be silent; she knows he's thinking. She's wrong.

RL, with those huge, stupid thoughts crammed in his head, that man with the huge diamond ring stuffed in his jeans pocket, that HUB man is not thinking at all.

That man has fainted. Or he's faking. He's like that.

THE END

Want more of this bunch? Then read their other whirlwind adventures: *THE COOL THING* and *THE WAYDOWNS*
Coming soon: *SÉANCE*
   Go where you'll wish you hadn't.

Lush praise, constructive criticism, and constipated complaints can be directed to: rife6000@aol.com
And thanks! Robert Rife
This scribbling reptile lives on an island off the coast of Washington. Under a rock. Only Santa and large women of dubious character are allowed to visit. Santa often skips.